Mike Ashley has been a reader and devotee of fantasy and science fiction for as long as he can remember — which is at least as far as the *Journ*... *Space* serials on the radio, *Quatermass* on television, *Dan D*... bourg and in the *Eagle* and *Superman* ... rning Pictures. He first became act... ence fiction magazines leading, in ... ence Fiction Association and fandon ... tain and America, and in 1974 his fi... *The History of the Science Fiction Ma*... he various sf encyclopedias and m... nd contributor to Brian Ash's *Visua*... s articles and news items will be found in S... *ity, Dark Horizons, Short Stories Magazine, Fantasy New*... and *Rod Serling's Twilight Zone Magazine.* He has also appeared on radio and television.

Other Books by Mike Ashley:

Anthologies and Collections

Best of British SF (4 vols)
The History of the Science Fiction Magazine (4 vols)
Jewels of Wonder
Mrs Gaskell's Tales of Mystery and Horror
SF Choice 77
Souls in Metal
Weird Legacies

Reference
The Complete Index to Astounding/Analog
Fantasy Readers Guide to Ramsey Campbell
Fantasy Readers Guide to the John Spencer Fantasy Publications
The Seven Wonders of the World
Who's Who in Horror and Fantasy Fiction

In Preparation:
The Man Who Was Uncle Paul (a biography of Algernon Blackwood).

THE ILLUSTRATED BOOK OF SCIENCE FICTION LISTS

Mike Ashley

Virgin

Virgin Books

Dedication

To **Reginald Bretnor**
for first having faith in this idea and for being a gentleman

To **All Science Fiction Fans, Writers, Artists & Editors**
for making science fiction such a fascinating, enjoyable, absorbing, bewildering, yet very real world, and for giving us all those futures and alternatives that we will never use.

First published in Great Britain in 1982 by Virgin Books Ltd, 95-99 Ladbroke Grove, London W11 1PG

ISBN 0 907080 45 6

Printed and bound in Great Britain by Richard Clay Ltd (The Chaucer Press), Suffolk

Production services by Book Production Consultants, Cambridge

Design: Cooke Key

Photoset by Portobello Typesetting

Acknowledgements

As with any book the final product is a result of several minds if only one hand. I must thank those contributors who sent me their own personal lists of preferences, and those record-holders who gave me much inside information to help me assemble the lists more accurately. I must also thank Harlan Ellison and Forrest J Ackerman who responded spontaneously to requests for help, and I am grateful to Stephen Holland, Philip Harbottle, George Hay, Michael Parry, Ron Goulart, Richard Dalby, and others who supplied facts and figures with no knowledge of whether they would feature in the end results. (There are plenty more lists where these came from!) Finally my thanks to Mervyn Warner for helping with the illustrations by way of his photographic expertise, and to his wife Iris whose invaluable knowledge of foreign languages helped me resolve further matters. To all, and others I have unintentionally overlooked, my most grateful thanks.

SECTION A
WHAT IS THIS THING...?

SECTION B
EXPERT OPINION

SECTION C
THE RECORDHOLDERS

SECTION D
ODDITIES AND ENTITIES

FOR THOSE WHO READ INTRODUCTIONS

I've always been a nut for making lists. I think I was only six or seven when I started copying out lists of kings and queens of various nations, or of the elements, the planets, stars and constellations, countries and their capitals, longest rivers, highest waterfalls and on and on. I always tried to expand on the usual lists by filling in gaps, checking out the information in other books, and sorting out the discrepancies. For discrepancies there were. It never ceased to amaze me how often one standard reference work would contradict information given in another standard work. Which did you believe?

What it was that started me off compiling lists, I don't know, but I do know that the urge to fill in gaps in those lists and to satisfy myself over which facts are correct and which are false, has driven me on ever since.

When I discovered the world of science fiction and fantasy it was a natural for lists. Very early on I was listing all sf books and stories in chronological order, in author order, in all kinds of orders, and I still am. My mind seems to naturally collect facts and figures that relate and form automatically into lists, and for the last nineteen years I have been pigeonholing all this data. Now, at last, thanks to Virgin Books, I have had an opportunity to off-load my over-loaded mind and filing system and to share all these lists with whomsoever is interested.

The record-breakers side of the list I find the most fascinating, especially prolific writers, who never cease to bedazzle me. This part of the book began in 1969 when I compiled a list of the most ubiquitous of magazine editors as part of an article destined for a fanzine. Somehow or other my article never reached that fanzine, and then the fanzine folded anyway. The article circuitously found its way to an Australian fanzine editor who was interested in the article but asked me to update it (it was now nearly two years since I had written it). Once again the gremlins intervened and my article vanished or, at least, I heard no more about it. My plans to publish any of *The Illustrated Book of Science Fiction Lists* as it had now become, over the next few years were dogged by such fate. As recently as 1979 there were plans to incorporate some of these records, in a different format to that presented here, in a book being assembled by Reginald Bretnor but again, at the last moment, this all fell through. So at last, I hope, these records will see the light of day. But remember, if you never read these words, you'll never know what happened. I wonder how many other such things there are that we never knew had happened? Perhaps I'll make a list of them . . .

Mike Ashley, Walderslade, December 1981.

SECTION A
WHAT IS THIS THING...?

In which we learn what people think science fiction is, and discover who are the leading authors, novels, stories, themes, magazines and artists.

10 DEFINITIONS OF SCIENCE FICTION

A1

If you asked 50 sf enthusiasts for a definition of sf you'd probably get a hundred different answers and none would be in agreement. Science fiction has been called a literature of ideas, of possibilities and of alternatives and because it is ever changing it defies definition. Nevertheless, here are ten attempts at defining the indefinable.

1 By 'scientifiction' I mean the Jules Verne, H.G. Wells and Edgar Allan Poe type of story — a charming romance intermingled with scientific fact and prophetic vision. — Hugo Gernsback *Amazing Stories,* April 1926. It was Gernsback who to all intents invented the term 'science fiction' after a few years of calling it 'scientifiction', so he ought to know what he meant by it. The problem was he was trying to put a label on something that could no longer be labelled.

2 Science fiction is a branch of fantasy identifiable by the fact that it eases the 'willing suspension of disbelief' on the part of its readers by utilizing an atmosphere of scientific credibility for its imaginative speculations in physical science, space, time, social science, and philosophy. — Sam Moskowitz *Explorers of the Infinite,* 1963

3 We might try to define science fiction in this broader sense as fiction based upon scientific or pseudo-scientific assumptions (space-travel, robots, telepathy, earthly immortality, and so forth) or laid in any patently unreal though non-supernatural setting (the future, or another world, and so forth). — L. Sprague de Camp *Science-Fiction Handbook,* 1953

4 A science fiction story is a story built around human beings, with a human problem, and a human solution, which would not have happened at all without its speculative scientific content. — Theodore Sturgeon as amended by Damon Knight *A Century of Science Fiction,* 1962

Hugo Gernsback

5 Science fiction is that branch of literature which is concerned with the impact of scientific advance upon human beings. — Isaac Asimov *Modern Science Fiction* edited by Reginald Bretnor, 1953. Twenty-five years later Asimov thought that definition still held good though he made a slight change:

5a Science fiction is that branch of literature that deals with human responses to changes in the level of science and technology. *Isaac Asimov's Science Fiction Magazine,* (March-April 1978)

6 Science fiction is that class of prose narrative treating of a situation that could not arise in the world we know, but which is hypothesised on the basis of some innovation in science or technology, or pseudo-science or pseudo-technology, whether human or extra-terrestrial in origin. — Kingsley Amis *New Maps of Hell,* 1961

7 Science fiction is the search for a definition of man and his status in the universe which will stand in our advanced but confused state of knowledge (science), and is characteristically cast in the Gothic or post-Gothic mould.
— Brian W. Aldiss *Billion Year Spree,* 1973

8 A literary genre developed principally in the 20th Century, dealing with scientific discovery of development that, whether set in the future, in the fictitious present, or in the putative past, is superior to or simply other than that known to exist.
— Fred Saberhagen *Encyclopedia Britannica* 15th edn, 1979

9 That branch of fiction that deals with the possible effects of an altered technology or social system on mankind in an imagined future, an altered present, or an alternative past.
— Barry N. Malzberg *Collier's Encyclopedia,* 1981

10 Science fiction deals with improbable possibilities, fantasy with plausible impossibilities.
— Miriam Allen deFord *Elsewhere, Elsewhen, Elsehow,* 1971

THE 20 ALL-TIME BEST AUTHORS

A2

In 1976 *Locus,* the newspaper of the science fiction field, asked its readers to nominate their favourite author. 164 authors were nominated but after the first twenty the number of votes cast for individual authors became too small to be meaningful. *Locus* had previously taken the same poll in 1973 when 130 authors had been nominated. Going back further in time in 1966, P. Schuyler Miller, the book reviewer for *Analog,* the leading science fiction magazine, asked readers to vote on their top ten favourite writers. 414 readers responded and the full list appeared in the November 1966 issue. A similar poll was conducted in 1971 with a different system of voting.

Below is the 1976 poll in full with an indication of the position held by those writers in the earlier counts.

1976	Author	Votes	1973	1971	1966
1	**Robert A. Heinlein**	297	1	1	2
2	**Isaac Asimov**	238	2	2	1
3	**Arthur C. Clarke**	198	3	3	3
4	**Ursula K. LeGuin**	170	16	—	—
5	**Robert Silverberg**	140	4	—	—
6	**Larry Niven**	131	13	—	—
7	**Harlan Ellison**	124	7	8	—
8	**Roger Zelazny**	109	8	12	—
9	**Fritz Leiber**	94	22	—	—
10	**Philip K. Dick**	86	12	—	—
11	**Theodore Sturgeon**	81	6	6	8
12	**Poul Anderson**	79	5	4	5
13	**Jack Vance**	73	—	—	—
14	**Ray Bradbury**	57	11	9	9
15	**Alfred Bester**	56	—	—	—
16	**Samuel R. Delany**	45	10	—	—
17	**Philip José Farmer**	41	14	—	—
17	**Cordwainer Smith**	41	14	—	—
19	**Frank Herbert**	40	—	—	—
20	**J.R.R. Tolkien**	38	—	—	—

Robert A. Heinlein *Isaac Asimov* *Arthur C. Clarke*

Those who have fallen highest from grace are A.E. van Vogt who ranked fourth in 1966 and by 1976 was not even in the top twenty-five; Clifford D. Simak who was seventh in 1966, thirteenth in 1971, eighth in 1973 and twenty-second in 1976; H.G. Wells who was sixth in 1966 but twenty-third by 1976. The top three, however, remain indisputable.

THE 20 BEST ALL-TIME BOOKS

A3

In 1966, the readers of *Analog* voted on their favourite all time sf book (which could include novel, story collection or anthology). An earlier poll in 1956 had supplied interesting, if now rather dated, results. Where a book listed below had also appeared in the 1956 list, its position is noted in brackets. Surprisingly no such poll has been conducted since, and we must turn to the Award Winning Novels for further examples.

1	**The Foundation Trilogy** Isaac Asimov (*Foundation* alone)	19)
2	**Seven Famous Novels of H.G. Wells**	(10)
3	**Slan** A.E. van Vogt	(6)
4	**The Rest of the Robots** Isaac Asimov	(–)
5	**The Demolished Man** Alfred Bester	(5)
6	**Childhood's End** Arthur C. Clarke	(–)
7	**The City and the Stars** Arthur C. Clarke	(16)
8	**The Martian Chronicles** Ray Bradbury	(11)
9	**City** Clifford D. Simak	(2)
10	**A Canticle For Leibowitz** Walter M. Miller	(–)
11	**Starship Troopers** Robert A. Heinlein	(–)
12	**I, Robot** Isaac Asimov	(–)
13	**To the End of Time** Olaf Stapledon	(20)
14	**The Man Who Sold the Moon** Robert A. Heinlein	(4)
15	**Mission of Gravity** Hal Clement	(26)
16	**The Stars My Destination** Alfred Bester	(–)
17	**Stranger in a Strange Land** Robert A. Heinlein	(–)
18	**World of Null-A** A.E. van Vogt	(8)
19	**More Than Human** Theodore Sturgeon	(12)
20	**Adventures in Time and Space** Raymond J. Healy and Francis J. McComas	(1)

THE 26 ALL-TIME BEST NOVELS

A4

This poll was conducted by the news magazine *Locus* and published in the issue for April 15th 1975. There were 351 novels nominated.

		Votes
1	**Dune** Frank Herbert	104
2	**Childhood's End** Arthur C. Clarke	97
3	**The Left Hand of Darkness** Ursula K. LeGuin	90
4	**Stranger in a Strange Land** Robert A.Heinlein	63
5	**A Canticle for Leibowitz** Walter M. Miller	57
6	**The Foundation Trilogy** Isaac Asimov	53
7	**The Stars My Destination** Alfred Bester	50
8	**The Moon is a Harsh Mistress** Robert A. Heinlein	41
9	**More Than Human** Theodore Sturgeon	40
10	**Lord of Light** Roger Zelazny	35
11	**Stand on Zanzibar** John Brunner	34
12	**Ringworld** Larry Niven	32
13	**The Dispossessed** Ursula K. LeGuin	31
14	**The Demolished Man** Alfred Bester	30
15	**Lord of the Rings** J.R.R. Tolkien	29
16	**Mission of Gravity** Hal Clement	25

17 The City and the Stars
Arthur C. Clarke 23
To Your Scattered Bodies Go
Philip Jose Farmer 23
19 Dying Inside
Robert Silverberg 22
20 Rendezvous with Rama
Arthur C. Clarke 20
The Time Machine
H.G. Wells 20
22 The Man in the High Castle
Philip K. Dick 17
Starship Troopers
Robert A. Heinlein 17
24 The Space Merchants
Frederik Pohl and
Cyril M. Kornbluth 16
War of the Worlds
H.G. Wells 16
The Martian Chronicles
Ray Bradbury 16

THE 57 AWARD WINNING SF NOVELS SINCE 1951

A5

These novels received one or more of the recognised international science fiction awards. Awards limited to books published in one nation are excluded. For instance the Ditmar Award is given to the Best Australian novel. However, there is also a Ditmar Award for the Best International Novel and this is included. Similarly the British Science Fiction Award, originally limited to a British paperback, is excluded. In 1981, however, the Award was made international and is included for that year. The Awards covered, therefore, are the International Fantasy Award (denoted as IFA below), the Hugo, the Nebula, the Locus Award, the John W. Campbell Award (JWC below), the Jupiter, the Ditmar International (Ditmar below) and, from 1981, the British Science Fiction Award (BSFA).

1951 Earth Abides
George R. Stewart (IFA)
1953 City
Clifford D. Simak (IFA)
The Demolished Man
Alfred Bester (Hugo)
1954 More Than Human
Theodore Sturgeon (IFA)
1955 A Mirror For Observers
Edgar Pangborn (IFA)
They'd Rather Be Right
Mark Clifton & Frank Riley (Hugo)
1956 Double Star
Robert A. Heinlein (Hugo)
1957 The Lord of the Rings
J.R.R. Tolkien (IFA)
1958 The Big Time
Fritz Leiber (Hugo)

1959 **A Case Of Conscience**
James Blish (Hugo)

1960 **Starship Troopers**
Robert A. Heinlein (Hugo)

1961 **A Canticle for Leibowitz**
Walter M. Miller (Hugo)

1962 **Stranger in a Strange Land**
Robert A. Heinlein (Hugo)

1963 **The Man in the High Castle**
Philip K. Dick (Hugo)

1964 **Here Gather The Stars**
Clifford D. Simak (Hugo) — later retitled **Way Station**

1965 **The Wanderer**
Fritz Leiber (Hugo)

1966 **Dune**
Frank Herbert (Hugo & Nebula)

...And Call Me Conrad
Roger Zelazny (joint Hugo)

1967 **Babel-17**
Samuel R. Delany (joint Nebula)

Flowers For Algernon
Daniel Keyes (joint Nebula)

The Moon is a Harsh Mistress
Robert A. Heinlein (Hugo)

1968 **Lord of Light**
Roger Zelazny (Hugo)

The Einstein Intersection
Samuel R. Delany (Nebula)

1969 **Stand on Zanzibar**
John Brunner (Hugo)

Rite of Passage
Alexei Panshin (Nebula)

Camp Concentration
Thomas M. Disch (Ditmar)

1970 **The Left Hand of Darkness**
Ursula K. LeGuin (Hugo & Nebula)

Cosmicomics
Italo Calvino (Ditmar)

1971 **Ringworld**
Larry Niven (Hugo, Nebula, Ditmar, Locus)

1972 **To Your Scattered Bodies Go**
Philip Jose Farmer (Hugo)

A Time of Changes
Robert Silverberg (Nebula)

The Lathe of Heaven
Ursula K. LeGuin (Locus)

1973 **The Gods Themselves**
Isaac Asimov (Hugo, Nebula, Ditmar, Locus)

Beyond Apollo
Barry N. Malzberg (JWC)

1974 **Rendezvous with Rama**
Arthur C. Clarke (Hugo, Nebula, Jupiter, Locus, joint JWC)

Malevil
Robert Merle (joint JWC)

1975 **The Dispossessed**
Ursula K. LeGuin (Hugo, Nebula, Jupiter, Locus)

Flow My Tears, The Policeman Said
Philip K. Dick (JWC)

Protector
Larry Niven (Ditmar)

1976 **The Forever War**
Joe Haldeman (Hugo, Nebula, Locus, Ditmar)

The Year of the Quiet Sun
Wilson Tucker (JWC retrospective)

1977 **Where Late the Sweet Birds Sang**
Kate Wilhelm (Hugo, Jupiter, Locus)

Man Plus
Frederik Pohl (Nebula)

The Alteration
Kingsley Amis (JWC)

The Space Machine
Christopher Priest (Ditmar)

1978 **Gateway**
Frederik Pohl (Hugo, Nebula, Locus, JWC)

The Silmarillion
J.R.R. Tolkien (Ditmar)

A Heritage of Stars
Clifford D. Simak (Jupiter)

1979 **Dreamsnake**
Vonda McIntyre (Hugo, Nebula, Locus)
The White Dragon
Anne McCaffrey (Ditmar)
Gloriana
Michael Moorcock (JWC)

1980 **The Fountains of Paradise**
Arthur C. Clarke (Hugo, Nebula)
Titan
John Varley (Locus)
On Wings of Song
Thomas M. Disch (JWC)
The Hitchhiker's Guide to the Galaxy
Douglas Adams (Ditmar)

1981 **Timescape**
Gregory Benford (Nebula, JWC, BSFA)
The Snow Queen
Joan D. Vinge (Hugo, Locus)

THE BEST SHORT FICTION

This is a general heading for the next few lists because things become a little complicated here. Short Fiction is divided into several categories by reason of wordage. In 1968 the Nebula Committee of the Science Fiction Writers of America decided to set the following limits. Anything over 40,000 words was a novel. 17,500 to 40,000 words constituted a novella, 7,500 to 17,500 words was a novelette, and under 7,500 words was a short story. This arbitrary division hasn't always been recognised but for the purposes of the following lists, regardless of how the story was designated at the time, I've applied those limits.

THE 16 BEST SF SHORT STORIES PUBLISHED PRE-1965

A6

In 1969 the Science Fiction Writers of America voted to select those stories they felt warranted a retrospective Nebula Award. The results formed Volume 1 of the triple-decker anthology *The Science Fiction Hall of Fame* edited by Robert Silverberg. Only the first 16 stories had recordable voting results.

1 **Nightfall**
Isaac Asimov
2 **Martian Odyssey**
Stanley G. Weinbaum
3 **Flowers for Algernon**
Daniel Keyes
4 **Microcosmic God**
Theodore Sturgeon
First Contact
Murray Leinster
6 **A Rose for Ecclesiastes**
Roger Zelazny
7 **The Roads Must Roll**
Robert A. Heinlein
Mimsy Were the Borogoves
Lewis Padgett (Henry Kuttner)
Coming Attraction
Fritz Leiber
The Cold Equations
Tom Godwin
11 **The Nine Billion Names of God** Arthur C. Clarke
12 **Surface Tension**
James Blish
13 **Twilight**
John W. Campbell, Jr
The Weapon Shop
A.E. van Vogt
15 **The Star**
Arthur C. Clarke
16 **Arena**
Fredric Brown

THE 24 BEST SF NOVELLAS PUBLISHED PRIOR TO 1965

A7

As with the previous list, these appeared in Volumes 2 and 3 of the triple-decker *The Science Fiction Hall of Fame* edited this time be Ben Bova. The lists were not presented in order of popularity so are presented here in chronological order of first publication.

1 **The Time Machine**
H.G. Wells (1895)
2 **The Machine Stops**
E.M. Forster (1909)
3 **Who Goes There?**
John W. Campbell, Jr. (1938)
4 **Universe**
Robert A. Heinlein (1941)
5 **Nerves**
Lester del Rey (1942
6 **Vintage Season**
Henry Kuttner & C.L. Moore (1946)
7 **E for Effort**
T.L. Sherred (1947)
8 **With Folded Hands...**
Jack Williamson (1947)
9 **In Hiding**
Wilmar H. Shiras (1948)
10 **The Witches of Karres**
James H. Schmitz (1949)

11 **The Fireman**
Ray Bradbury (1951 — original version of *Fahrenheit 451*)

12 **The Marching Morons**
Cyril M. Kornbluth (1951)

13 **And Then There Were None**
Eric Frank Russell (1951)

14 **The Specter General**
Theodore R. Cogswell (1952)

15 **Baby is Three**
Theodore Sturgeon (1952)

16 **The Martian Way**
Isaac Asimov (1952)

17 **Earthman, Come Home**
James Blish (1953)

18 **The Midas Plague**
Frederik Pohl (1954)

19 **A Canticle for Leibowitz**
Walter M. Miller (1955)

20 **Call Me Joe**
Poul Anderson (1957)

21 **The Big Front Yard**
Clifford D. Simak (1958)

22 **Rogue Moon**
Algis Budrys (1960)

23 **The Moon Moth**
Jack Vance (1961)

24 **The Ballad of Lost C'Mell**
Cordwainer Smith (1962)

THE 20 BEST ALL-TIME SF SHORT FICTION

A8

In 1971 Michael Shoemaker of the Washington Science Fiction Association through the auspices of *The Reference Library* in *Analog* asked readers to vote on what they considered were the best sf short stories of all time. Only 108 readers responded but P. Schuyler Miller, who reprinted and analysed the results in the October 1971 issue, believed that 'on the whole it is a good list'.

		Votes
1	**Nightfall** Isaac Asimov	49
2	**The Star** Arthur C. Clarke	42
	The Green Hills of Earth Robert A. Heinlein	42
	Flowers For Algernon Daniel Keyes	42
5	**A Rose for Ecclesiastes** Roger Zelazny	36
6	**Light of Other Days** Bob Shaw	29
7	**The Nine Billion Names of God** Arthur C. Clarke	27
	'Repent Harlequin,' Said the Ticktockman Harlan Ellison	27
9	**Rescue Party** Arthur C. Clarke	26
	The Cold Equations Tom Godwin	26
	First Contact Murray Leinster	26
	By His Bootstraps Robert A. Heinlein	26
13	**Microcosmic God** Theodore Sturgeon	23
	The Little Black Bag Cyril M. Kornbluth	23

15	**The Last Question** Isaac Asimov	22
	I Have No Mouth and I Must Scream Harlan Ellison	22
17	**The Big Front Yard** Clifford D. Simak	21
	The Sentinel Arthur C. Clarke	21
	Surface Tension James Blish	21
20	**It's a Good Life** Jerome Bixby	20

THE 24 BEST SHORT STORIES PUBLISHED PRIOR TO 1940

A9

Michael Shoemaker's poll also called for a special vote on the best oldies with a cut-off date at 1940. Although only thirty-eight readers responded there were still 318 different stories nominated.

		Votes
1	**Who Goes There?** John W. Campbell, Jr.	25
	Twilight John W. Campbell, Jr.	25
3	**A Martian Odyssey** Stanley G. Weinbaum	20
4	**Helen O'Loy** Lester del Rey	19
5	**Night** John W. Campbell, Jr.	17
6	**Forgetfulness** John W. Campbell, Jr.	14
7	**Black Destroyer** A.E. van Vogt	13
	The Lost Machine John Beynon (Wyndham) Harris	13
9	**Marooned Off Vesta** Isaac Asimov	12
10	**Sands of Time** P. Schuyler Miller	11
	The Machine Stops E.M. Forster	11
12	**Proxima Centauri** A.E. van Vogt	10
	The Colour Out of Space H.P. Lovecraft	10
14	**Life-Line** Robert A. Heinlein	9
	Armageddon 2410 A.D. Philip Francis Nowlan	9
16	**Robot's Return** Robert Moore Williams	8
	The Adaptive Ultimate Stanley G. Weinbaum	8
	I Robot Eando Binder	8
19	**The New Accelerator** H.G. Wells	7
	The Country of the Blind H.G. Wells	7
	He Who Shrank Henry Hasse	7
	Politics Murray Leinster	7
	The Blue Giraffe L. Sprague de Camp	7
	The Faithful Lester del Rey	7

THE 39 SF AWARD-WINNING NOVELLAS

A10

Remember, these are all the stories between 17,500 and 40,000 words that have won one or more of the science fiction awards (even though some of them are fantasy and have also won one or more fantasy awards).

1955 **The Darfstellar**
Walter M. Miller (Hugo)

1959 **The Big Front Yard**
Clifford D. Simak (Hugo)

1963 **The Dragon Masters**
Jack Vance (Hugo)

'Galaxy' August 1962

1964 **No Truce with Kings**
Poul Anderson (Hugo)

1965 **Soldier, Ask Not**
Gordon R. Dickson (Hugo)

1966 **He Who Shapes**
Roger Zelazny (joint Nebula)
The Saliva Tree
Brian W. Aldiss (joint Nebula)

1967 **The Last Castle**
Jack Vance (Hugo & Nebula)

1968 **Behold the Man**
Michael Moorcock (Nebula)
Weyr Search
Anne McCaffrey (joint Hugo)
Riders of the Purple Wage
Philip Jose Farmer (joint Hugo)

1969 **Dragonrider**
Anne McCaffrey (Nebula)
Nightwings
Robert Silverberg (Hugo)

1970 **A Boy and his Dog**
Harlan Ellison (Nebula)
Ship of Shadows
Fritz Leiber (Hugo)

1971 **Ill Met in Lankhmar**
Fritz Leiber (Hugo & Nebula)
The Region Between
Harlan Ellison (Locus)

1972 **The Missing Man**
Katherine MacLean (Nebula)

1973 **A Meeting with Medusa**
Arthur C. Clarke (Nebula)
The Word for World is Forest
Ursula K. LeGuin (Hugo)
The Gold at the Starbow's End
Frederik Pohl (Locus)

1974 **The Death of Dr Island**
Gene Wolfe (Nebula, Locus)
The Girl Who Was Plugged In
James Tiptree, Jr. (Hugo)
The Feast of St Dionysius
Robert Silverberg (Jupiter)

1975 **Born With The Dead**
Robert Silverberg (Nebula, Locus)
A Song for Lya
George R.R. Martin (Hugo)
Riding the Torch
Norman Spinrad (Jupiter)

1976 **Home is the Hangman**
Roger Zelazny (Hugo, Nebula)
The Storms of Windhaven
George R.R. Martin & Lisa Tuttle (Locus)

1977 **Houston, Houston, Do You Read?**
James Tiptree, Jr. (Hugo, Nebula, Jupiter)
By Any Other Name
Spider Robinson (joint Hugo)
The Samurai and the Willow
Michael Bishop (Locus)

1978 **Stardance**
Spider & Jeanne Robinson
(Hugo, Nebula, Locus)
In the Hall of the Martian Kings
John Varley (Jupiter)
1979 **The Persistence of Vision**
John Varley (Nebula, Hugo, Locus)
1980 **Enemy Mine**
Barry B. Longyear (Nebula, Hugo, Locus)
1981 **Unicorn Tapestry**
Suzy McKee Charnas (Nebula)
Lost Dorsai
Gordon R. Dickson (Hugo)
Nightflyers
George R.R. Martin (Locus)

'Analog' May 1975

THE 32 SF AWARD-WINNING NOVELETTES

A11

The stories between 7,500 and 17,500 words.

1956 **Exploration Team**
Murray Leinster (Hugo)
1960 **Flowers For Algernon**
Daniel Keyes (Hugo)
1961 **The Longest Voyage**
Poul Anderson (Hugo)
1966 **The Doors of His Face, the Lamps of His Mouth**
Roger Zelazny (Nebula)
1967 **Call Me Lord**
Gordon R. Dickson (Nebula)
1968 **Gonna Roll the Bones**
Fritz Leiber (Hugo & Nebula)
1969 **Mother to the World**
Richard Wilson (Nebula)
The Sharing of the Flesh
Poul Anderson (Hugo)
1970 **Time Considered as a Helix of Semi-Precious Stones**
Samuel R. Delany
(Nebula & Hugo)
1971 **Slow Sculpture**
Theodore Sturgeon
(Nebula & Hugo)
1972 **The Queen of Air and Darkness**
Poul Anderson
(Hugo, Nebula, Locus)
1973 **Goat Song**
Poul Anderson
(Nebula & Hugo)
1974 **Of Mist, and Grass, and Sand**
Vonda McIntyre (Nebula)
The Deathbird
Harlan Ellison
(Hugo, Jupiter, Locus)
1975 **If the Stars are Gods**
Greg Benford (Nebula)
Adrift Just Off the Islets of Langerhans...
Harlan Ellison
(Hugo & Locus)
The Seventeen Virgins
Jack Vance (Jupiter)
1976 **San Diego Lightfoot Sue**
Tom Reamy (Nebula)
The Borderland of Sol
Larry Niven (Hugo)
The New Atlantis
Ursula K. LeGuin (Locus)

1977 The Bicentennial Man
Isaac Asimov (Hugo, Nebula, Locus)
The Diary of the Rose
Ursula K. LeGuin (Jupiter)
1978 The Screwfly Solution
Raccoona Sheldon (Nebula)
Eyes of Amber
Joan D. Vinge
Time Storm
Gordon R. Dickson (Jupiter)
1979 A Glow of Candles, A Unicorn's Eye
Charles L. Grant (Nebula)
Hunter's Moon
Poul Anderson
The Barbie Murders
John Varley (Locus)
1980 Sandkings
George R.R. Martin (Nebula, Hugo, Locus)
1981 The Ugly Chickens
Howard Waldrop (Nebula)
The Cloak and the Staff
Gordon R. Dickson (Hugo)
The Brave Little Toaster
Thomas M. Disch (Locus, BSFA)

THE 35 SF AWARD-WINNING SHORT STORIES

A12

The stories of less than 7,500 words.

1955 Allamagoosa
Eric Frank Russell (Hugo)
1956 The Star
Arthur C. Clarke (Hugo)
1958 Or All the Seas With Oysters
Avram Davidson (Hugo)
1959 That Hell-Bound Train
Robert Bloch (Hugo)
1966 'Repent, Harlequin!' said the Ticktockman
Harlan Ellison (Hugo & Nebula)
1967 The Secret Place
Richard McKenna (Nebula)
Neutron Star
Larry Niven (Hugo)
1968 Aye, and Gomorrah
Samuel R. Delany (Nebula)
I Have No Mouth and I Must Scream
Harlan Ellison (Hugo)
1969 The Planners
Kate Wilhelm (Nebula)
The Beast That Shouted Love at the Heart of the World
Harlan Ellison (Hugo)
1970 Passengers
(Nebula)
1972 Good News From The Vatican
Robert Silverberg (Nebula)
Inconstant Moon
Larry Niven (Hugo)
1973 When It Changed
Joanna Russ (Nebula)
Eurema's Dam
R.A. Lafferty (joint Hugo)

'F & SF' July 1977.
(Special Harlan Ellison issue.)

The Meeting
Frederik Pohl & Cyril M. Kornbluth (joint Hugo)
Basilisk
Harlan Ellison (Locus)

1974 **Love is the Plan, the Plan is Death**
James Tiptree, Jr (Nebula)
The Ones Who Walk Away From Omelas
Ursula K. LeGuin (Hugo)
A Suppliant in Space
Robert Sheckley (Jupiter)

1975 **The Day Before the Revolution**
Ursula K. LeGuin (Nebula, Jupiter, Locus)
The Hole Man
Larry Niven (Hugo)

1976 **Catch That Zeppelin!**
Fritz Leiber (Hugo & Nebula)
Croatoan
Harlan Ellison (Locus)

1977 **A Crowd of Shadow**
Charles L. Grant (Nebula)
Tricentennial
Joe Haldeman (Hugo & Locus)
I See You
Damon Knight (Jupiter)

1978 **Jeffty Is Five**
Harlan Ellison (Nebula, Hugo, Jupiter, Locus)

1979 **Stone**
Edward Bryant (Nebula)
Cassandra
C.J. Cherryh (Hugo)
Count The Clock That Tells the Time
Harlan Ellison (Locus)

1980 **The Way of Cross and Dragon**
George R.R. Martin (Hugo & Locus)
giANTS
Edward Bryant (Nebula)

1981 **Grotto of the Dancing Deer**
Clifford D. Simak (Hugo, Nebula, Locus)

THE 25 AWARD-WINNING FANTASY NOVELS

A13

The Fantasy Awards, as distinct from those in the sf fraternity, are the World Fantasy Award (WFA below), known affectionately as the Howard after *H(oward)* P. Lovecraft and Robert E. *Howard,* the Balrog, named after the denizen of the deep that fought Gandalf to the bitter end in *Lord of the Rings,* and the British Fantasy Award (the novel award is named after August Derleth). In addition *Locus* has instituted a separate entry for Fantasy Novel in its annual poll, and for just two years a Gandalf Award was presented for Best Fantasy Novel by Lin Carter at the Hugo ceremony. A few fantasy novels, as you'll have seen, also received sf awards.

1972 **The Knight of the Swords**
Michael Moorcock (ADFA)

1973 **The King of the Swords**
Michael Moorcock (ADFA)
The Fallible Fiend
L. Sprague de Camp (this received the ADFA for Short Fiction although it is of novel length)

1974 **Hrolf Kraki's Saga**
Poul Anderson (ADFA)

1975 **The Forgotten Beasts of Eld**
Patricia McKillip (WFA)
The Sword and the Stallion
Michael Moorcock (ADFA)

1976 **Bid Time Return**
Richard Matheson (WFA)
The Hollow Lands
Michael Moorcock (ADFA)

1977 **Dr Rat**
William Kotzwinkle (WFA)
The Dragon and the George
Gordon R. Dickson (ADFA)

1978 **Our Lady of Darkness**
Fritz Leiber (WFA)
A Spell for Chameleon
Piers Anthony (ADFA)
The Silmarillion
J.R.R. Tolkien (Gandalf, Locus)

1979 **Gloriana**
Michael Moorcock (WFA)
The Chronicles of Thomas Covenant
Stephen Donaldson (ADFA)
Blind Voices
Tom Reamy (Balrog)
The White Dragon
Anne McCaffrey (Gandalf)

1980 **Watchtower**
Elizabeth Lynn (WFA)

Death's Master
Tanith Lee (ADFA)
Dragondrums
Anne McCaffrey (Balrog)
Harpist in the Wind
Patricia McKillip (Locus)

1981 **Shadow of the Torturer**
Gene Wolf (WFA)
To Wake the Dead
Ramsey Campbell (ADFA)
The Wounded Land
Stephen Donaldson (Balrog)
Lord Valentine's Castle
Robert Silverberg (Locus)

THE 18 FANTASY AWARD-WINNING SHORT STORIES

A14

The August Derleth Fantasy Award (ADFA) originally presented by the British Fantasy Society for both novels and short fiction was later reserved for novels alone and the short story received the British Fantasy Award (BFA). The other awards are the same as for the novel.

1974 **The Jade Man's Eyes**
Michael Moorcock (ADFA)

1975 **Pages From a Young Girl's Diary**
Robert Aickman (WFA)
Sticks
Karl Edward Wagner (ADFA)

1976 **Belsen Express**
Fritz Leiber (WFA)
(The BFA was given to a collection *The Second Book of Fritz Leiber* rather than a specific story.)

1977 **There's a Long, Long Trail A'Winding**
Russell Kirk (WFA)
Two Suns Setting
Karl Edward Wagner (BFA)

1978 **The Chimney**
Ramsey Campbell (WFA)
In the Bag
Ramsey Campbell (BFA)

1979 **Naples**
Avram Davidson (WFA)
Jeffty is Five
Harlan Ellison (BFA)
Death From Exposure
Pat Cadigan (Balrog)

1980 **The Woman Who Loved The Moon**
Elizabeth Lynn (co-WFA)
Macintosh Willy
Ramsey Campbell (co-WFA)
The Button Moulder
Fritz Leiber (BFA)
The Last Defender of Camelot
Roger Zelazny (Balrog)

1981 **The Ugly Chicken**
Howard Waldrop (WFA)
The Stains
Robert Aickman (BFA)
The Web of the Magi
Richard Cowper (Balrog)

THE 10 BEST FANTASY NOVELS PUBLISHED PRIOR TO 1971

A15

In 1979 members of the British Fantasy Society were asked to vote on which they felt were the best horror and fantasy stories in the categories Novel, Novelette and Short Story in the years prior to 1971 when the first of the British Fantasy Society Awards were presented. There were forty responses in a two-part ballot and the results were as follows, presented here in full for the first time.

		Votes
1	**The Lord of the Rings** J.R.R. Tolkien	65
2	**The Broken Sword** Poul Anderson	36
3	**Stormbringer** Michael Moorcock	32
4	**The Hobbit** J.R.R. Tolkien	31
5	**Titus Groan** Mervyn Peake	30
6	**Gormenghast** Mervyn Peake	25
7	**The Night Land** William Hope Hodgson	22
8	**Jurgen** James Branch Cabell	21
	The King of Elfland's Daughter Lord Dunsany	21
10	**Eyes of the Overworld** Jack Vance	18

THE 10 BEST HORROR NOVELS PUBLISHED PRIOR TO 1971

A16

		Votes
1	**The House on the Borderland** William Hope Hodgson	61
2	**The Case of Charles Dexter Ward** H.P. Lovecraft	53
3	**Something Wicked This Way Comes** Ray Bradbury	42
4	**The Lurker at the Threshhold** August Derleth & H.P. Lovecraft	40
5	**Dracula** Bram Stoker	37
6	**I Am Legend** Richard Matheson	36
7	**Conjure Wife** Fritz Leiber	30
8	**Frankenstein** Mary W. Shelley	23
9	**The Ghost Pirates** William Hope Hodgson	14
10	**The Boats of the Glen Carrig** William Hope Hodgson	13

THE 10 BEST FANTASY NOVELETTES PUBLISHED PRIOR TO 1971

A17

'Fantastic' August 1963

1	**Worms of the Earth** Robert .E. Howard	42
2	**Bazaar of the Bizarre** Fritz Leiber	41
3	**The Dream-Quest of Unknown Kadath** H. P. Lovecraft	40
4	**Doomed Lord's Passing** Michael Moorcock	34
5	**The Time Machine** H. G. Wells	30
	Adept's Gambit Fritz Leiber	30
7	**Behold The Man** Michael Moorcock	29
8	**The Last Castle** Jack Vance	26
9	**Guyal of Sfere** Jack Vance	24
10	**Ill Met in Lankhmar** Fritz Leiber	21

THE 10 BEST HORROR NOVELETTES PUBLISHED PRIOR TO 1971

A18

1 **The Dunwich Horror**
H. P. Lovecraft 39

2 **It**
Theodore Sturgeon 37

3 **At The Mountains of Madness**
H. P. Lovecraft 28

Skull-face
Robert E. Howard 28

4 **The Shadow Over Innsmouth**
H. P. Lovecraft

The Colour Out of Space
H. P. Lovecraft 24

7 **Shambleau**
C. L. Moore 22

8 **A Bit of the Dark World**
Fritz Leiber 21

9 **The White People**
Arthur Machen 17

The Strange Case of Dr Jekyll & Mr Hyde
Robert Louis Stevenson 17

THE 10 BEST FANTASY SHORT STORIES PUBLISHED PRE-1971

A19

1 **Liane The Wayfarer**
Jack Vance 44

2 **Valley of the Worm**
Robert E. Howard 42

3 **Black God's Kiss**
C. L. Moore 37

4 **The Quest of Iranon**
H. P. Lovecraft 26

5 **Dark Eidolon**
Clark Ashton Smith 25

6 **Idle Days on the Yann**
Lord Dunsany 24

7 **The Dragon**
Ray Bradbury 21

8 **Yesterday Was Monday**
Theodore Sturgeon

City of the Singing Flame
Clark Ashton Smith 20

10 **Tlon, Uqbar, Orbis Tertius**
Jorge Luis Borges 16

THE 10 BEST HORROR SHORT STORIES PUBLISHED PRE-1971

A20

		Votes
1	**I Have No Mouth and I Must Scream** Harlan Ellison	55
2	**Oh, Whistle, and I'll Come to You, My Lad** M.R. James	44
3	**Rats in the Walls** H.P. Lovecraft	35
4	**The Fall of the House of Usher** Edgar Allan Poe	26
5	**The Cellars** Ramsey Campbell	24
6	**The Voice in the Night** William Hope Hodgson	22
7	**The Outsider** H.P. Lovecraft	21
8	**Midnight in the Mirror World** Fritz Leiber	15
	Pickman's Model H.P. Lovecraft	15
10	**The Stalls of Barchester Cathedral** M.R. James	13

It's interesting to note just how many of the above, whether classified as fantasy or horror, equally classify as science fiction.

Illustration From 'Ghosts & Scholars' For 'Oh Whistle, And I'll Come To You'

10 WORKS THAT COULD EACH BE THE FIRST WORKS OF SF

A21

Since the first of our lists showed that no one has a clear cut definition of science fiction, by the same token no one can really say which was the first work of science fiction. However, by using a fairly liberal definition, each of the following could claim that honour for one reason or another.

1 **The Epic of Gilgamesh** A Sumerian mythography first set down in print in about 2100 BC, but of considerably more ancient verbal tradition. *The Encyclopedia of Science Fiction* (page 209) calls it 'the oldest of all works ever claimed as ancestral to sf.' It qualifies under the category of 'fantastic voyage'.

2 **The Odyssey** of Homer. Although no one is actually sure who wrote this epic poem it is generally attributed to the blind poet Homer who lived *c*750 BC. Peter Nicholls in his *Encyclopedia of Science Fiction* (page 292) says: 'While it would be absurd to claim the *Odyssey* as sf *per se*, it is clearly ancestral to sf, especially in its openness to wonder, allied to a hard-headed scepticism.'

3 **The Birds** by Aristophanes. 414 BC. N.R. Teitel of New York University called this play 'unique among Aristophanic comedy. Its purpose is sheer entertainment.' It tells of the birth of a new city, a paradise, constructed by the birds between Heaven and Earth and called Nephelococcygia or, as we know it better, Cloud-Cuckoo-Land. This was the first work of fabricated fantasy which was original in itself rather than merely retelling or embellishing myths and legends.

4 **Timaios** and **Kritias**; the dialogues of Plato. *c*350 BC. L. Sprague de Camp has called this 'Plato's most important contribution to science fiction' as it is from these works that the whole legend of lost Atlantis arose. Plato had other science fictional devices in works like *The Republic* – 'the grandfather of utopias' and *Phaidon* which refers to islands floating in the sky and hollows of various sizes inside the Earth.

5 **Heliopolis** by Iamboulos. *c* 260 BC. Another account of a fictional utopia inspired, L. Sprague de Camp suggests, by garbled accounts of Ceylon. Its people have flexible bones and forked tongues enabling them to carry on two conversations at once.

6 **The Argonautica** by Apollonios the Rhodian. *c* 250 BC. Another fantastic voyage, this relates the legendary quest of Jason and the Argonauts for the Golden Fleece. At one point the intrepid travellers sail close to the Moon, though they don't land, and Orpheus espies golden cities on the lunar surface.

7 **Somnium Scipianus (Scipio's Dream)** by Marcus Cicero. 45 BC. A brief essay in which Scipio has a vision of the planets in a dream. The tract, which appears in *De Republica,* is rather more philosophical than fanciful although in the light of the knowledge of the day it was equally scientific.

8 **Facies in Orbe Lunare (Of the Face Which Appears on the Orb of the Moon)** Plutarch *c*100 AD. Included in his collection *Symposiaca* this work takes the form of a dialogue between eight friends including a mathematician, a literary man, a philosopher and an astronomer. Plutarch discusses all the known opinions of the Moon and at one point one of the group, Sextius Sylla, is asked to relate his story *The Myth of the Moon,* itself another fantastic voyage which talks about after-life on the Moon.

9 **Of Marvels Beyond Thule** by Antonius Diogenes. *c*100 AD. One of the great mystery books of the Roman era, all trace of the work is lost save a brief outline given in one of the earliest ever bibliographies by Photius. Nothing

is known about Diogenes and it is possible the book had been written as much as three centuries earlier. It tells of a party of travellers who venture beyond Thule — the remotest land in the far North — and come at last to the Moon. This is believed to be the first fanciful visit to the Moon in fiction.

10 **Alethes Historia (True History)** by Lucian of Samosata. *c*170 AD. The *True History* was a spoof of all fantastic voyage epics and a biting satire, Lucian having one of the most wicked wits in the Roman Empire. Lucian and 50 colleagues travel by ship beyond the Pillars of Herakles and are thence sucked up by a huge waterspout and deposited on the Moon, in the midst of a war between the Moon and the Sun. The *True History* has been described as the first interplanetary romance and the first true work of science fiction, and when it was translated into English by Francis Hicks in 1634 and subsequently into French, it started the first wave of interplanetary satires thus forming the link between the old world dialogues and the new world of fantastic adventures. Lucian's influence may be found in the works of Rabelais, Cyrano de Bergerac and even Jonathan Swift.

13 SF STORIES BY THE FIRST REGULAR SF WRITERS

A22

The first regular writer of science fiction was undoubtedly Edgar Allen Poe. Indeed, although the epithet 'The Father of Science Fiction' has been bestowed upon Jules Verne, H.G. Wells and even Hugo Gernsback, it rightly belongs to Poe. It is a mark of his genius that he is equally the founding father of horror fiction and of detective fiction. The following are 13 of his most significant sf stories listed in order of their first publication.

Sketch Of Edgar Allan Poe By Ben Damman

1 **Ms. Found in a Bottle,** *The Baltimore Saturday Visitor* October 19th 1833. An encounter with a ghostly ship drawn inexorably along the ocean currents towards the South Pole and the entrance to the centre of the Earth.

2 **Hans Phaall — A Tale,** *Southern Literary Messenger* June 1835. A balloon flight to the Moon.

3 **The Narrative of Arthur Gordon Pym of Nantucket,** *Southern Literary Messenger* January-February 1837. Poe's longest story, a sea adventure amongst lost races at the South Pole. It was left unfinished at much the same point as **Ms. Found in a Bottle.**

4 **William Wilson,** *Gentleman's Magazine* October 1839. A study of split personalities.

5 **The Conversation of Eiros and Charmion,** *Gentleman's Magazine* December 1839. All life on Earth is destroyed after a comet

passes through the atmosphere.

6 **A Descent Into the Maelstrom,** *Graham's Magazine* May 1841. An early story unpublished for a decade it tells of two fishermen trapped in an enormous whirlpool.

7 **A Tale of the Ragged Mountains,** *Godey's Lady's Book* April 1844. Time travel into the past induced by morphine.

8 **The Balloon Hoax,** *The New York Sun* April 13th 1844. The first trans-Atlantic balloon flight.

9 **The Thousand-and-Second Tale of Scheherazade,** *Godey's Lady's Book* February 1845. A catalogue of wonders of the present and future.

10 **Some Words With a Mummy,** *The American Review* April 1845. An Egyptian Mummy is brought back to life to compare the achievements of the modern world with ancient Egypt.

11 **The Facts in the Case of M. Valdemar,** *The American Review* December 1845. A man's brain is kept alive by mesmerism after his body dies.

12 **Mellonta Tauta,** *Godey's Lady's Book* February 1849. Set a thousand years in the future (2848) and detailing the society and wonders in America.

13 **Von Kempelen and his Discovery,** *Flag of Our Union* March 17th 1849. The transmutation of lead into gold.

15 OF THE FIRST FICTIONAL SPACE VOYAGES

A23

After Lucian's *True History* and before Jules Verne's *From the Earth to the Moon* (1865) there were hundreds of stories of interplanetary travel both by physical or spiritual (astral) means. Many were poor excuses for philosophical discussions or satirical comparisons with Earth but a few are important for their originality and inventiveness. Indeed Verne's own novel is rather poor in comparison with some of the following.

1 **Beyond the Moon — 1692** *A Voyage to the World of Cartesius* by Gabriel Daniel. After a spirit voyage to the Moon inhabited by the spirits of Earth's dead, the narrator then explores a cosmos based on the theory of rotating vortices as put forward by Rene Descartes 50 years earlier.

2 **A Tour of the Solar System — 1757** *The History of Israel Jobson* by Miles Wilson (died 1776). This may be a later version of a long-lost pamphlet *The Man in the Moon* written by the curate of Halton Gill in Littondale, one of the remotest parts of Yorkshire. The hero, a cobbler, ascends to the Moon by ladder from the top of Mount Pen-y-Ghent and after adventures on the Moon has a conducted tour of the solar system and beyond in a form of Elijah's chariot. Today Pen-y-Ghent is a centre for hang-gliding, so perhaps Wilson was a visionary after all.

3 **Uranus — 1784** *A Journey Lately Performed Through the Air, in an Aerostatic Globe, to the Newly Discovered Planet, Georgium Sidus* by 'Vivenair'. Until 1781 the solar system was believed to contain only the planets Mercury, Venus, Mars, Jupiter, Saturn and, of course, the Earth. In 1781, however, William Herschel discovered a seventh which he called Georgium Sidus (George's Star) in honour of King George III, but which was later renamed Uranus. Three years later the pseudonymous Vivenair used the planet as a vehicle to satirize the government and monarchy of England. The journey was accomplished by balloon just a year after the Montgolfier brother's first flight.

4 **Imaginary Planets — 1816** *Armata* by Thomas Erskine. Showing more ingenuity than scientific sense Erskine conceives of an inhabited planet attached to the South pole and which is reached by ship.

5 **Alien Life Forms — 1838** *A World of Wonders* by Joel R. Peabody. Hitherto all the inhabitants of other worlds were recognisably human in some form, albeit giants, macrocephalic or bird-like. In this mental tour of the solar system by a clairvoyant a number of truly alien life forms are encountered.

6 **Rocket Propulsion — 1852** *Gulliver Joi* by Elbert Perce. Although Cyrano de Bergerac is usually credited with the idea of introducing rocket propulsion into fiction, in his *Voyage to the Moon* (1650), firework-rockets are attached to the hero's machine with less than successful results. In Perce's book, cited in George Locke's *Voyages in Space,* a rocket-propelled space-ship is used to convey Gulliver Joi to the newly discovered planet of Kailoo.

7 **Matter Transmission — 1855** *Helionde* by Sidney Whiting. 'The protagonist, undergoing hydropathic treatment, falls asleep in the sun. He dreams that he dissolves into vapour and is transmitted to an inhabited, civilised sun'. (*Voyages In Space,* George Locke). A slightly more technical approach to matter transmission was used by Fred T. Jane in *To Venus in Five Seconds* (1897).

8 **Earth Satellites — 1869** *The Brick Moon* by Edward Everett Hale — the first story to deal with the concept of an artifical satellite.

9 **Vulcan — 1882** *A Thousand Years Hence* by 'Nunsowe Green'. Vulcan was a planet that was believed to orbit the Sun within the orbit of Mercury. Its existence was put forward by Leverrier in 1845 to explain away irregularities in the orbit of Mercury. Its first appearance in fiction appears to be in this future history which includes a tour of the solar system.

10 **Terraforming and Faster-Than-Light travel — 1886** *Man Abroad* Anonymous. In this remarkable novel planetary colonisation is taken for granted with conditions suitable for human habitation having been specially created. The hero roams the spaceways in a faster-than-light spaceship. George Locke cites this as the 'earliest example of conflict between different planets — i.e. the space opera — so far located'.

11 **Neptune — 1889** *Earth-Born!* by 'Spirito Gentil'. Neptune had been discovered by Galle in 1846, its existence having been predicted by Leverrier and Adams, but it does not appear to have been used as a fictional milieu until this pseudonymous work where it is depicted as a glacial but inhabited planet.

12 **Counter-Earth — 1896** *From World to World* by D.L. Stump. John Norman's notorious *Gor* series uses as its locale a planet in the same orbit as Earth but diametrically opposite and thus hidden by the Sun. Its first use appears to be in this novel which was subsequently revised as *The Love of Meltha Laone* in 1913.

13 **Mentally-Created Planet — 1898** *Ariel* by Mary Platt Parmele. 'The power of the authorial mind has created an artificial satellite 400 miles across and 400,000 miles distant... It is peopled by products of the author's imagination, including Frankenstein's monster'. (George Locke, *Voyages In Space)*

14 **Interstellar Conflict — 1900** *The Struggle For Empire* by Robert W. Cole. Set in the year 2236 the Anglo-Saxon Federation has now colonised the solar system and is on the brink of war with an advanced race from the planet Kailoo (see 6 above) in orbit around Sirius.

15 **Pluto — 1912** *Their Winged Destiny* by Donald W. Horner. Although Pluto was not discovered until 1930 by Clyde Tombaugh its existence had been accepted by Percival Lowell as early as the 1890s. Horner's novel deals with a spaceflight to Alpha Centauri but as they leave the solar system they pass an outer planet beyond the orbit of Neptune. The discovery of Pluto was immediately incorporated into sf with *In Plutonian Depths* (1931) by Stanton Coblentz.

5 OF THE FIRST FICTIONAL VOYAGES THROUGH TIME

A24

1 **From the Present to the Future.** *Anno 7603* published in 1781 by the Norwegian dramatist Johan Hermann Wessel. 'In this comedy, a friendly fairy transports the young couple Leander and Julia into a future where the men occupy the roles of women and vice versa.' (Jon Bing and Tor Age Bringsvaerd *Science Fiction Studies* March 1976)

2 **From the Present to the Past.** *Missing One's Coach* an anonymous tale from the *Dublin Literary Magazine* in 1838 and resurrected by August Derleth in his anthology *Far Boundaries* (1951). The narrator strays through a 'fault in the strata of time' and finds himself back a thousand years in the time of the Venerable Bede.

3 **From the Future to the Present.** *An Uncommon Sort of Spectre* by Edward Page Mitchell, first published in 1879, tells of an old baron who is visited by the ghost of his son from forty years in the future. Along the same spectral lines it is arguable that the Ghost of Christmas Yet to Come who takes Scrooge on his last and most terrifying journey in Charles Dickens's *A Christmas Carol* (1843) is also a visitor from the future.

4 **From the Past to the Present.** *The Hour Glass* by Robert Barr first published in *The Strand Magazine* for December 1898 it tells of a man from the past who comes to lay claim to a recently purchased and now antique hour glass.

5 **A Time Machine.** *The Clock That Went Backward* by Edward Page Mitchell, first published in the New York *Sun* for September 18th 1881 is the earliest story yet traced that employs a mechanical device to travel through time. It anticipated H.G. Wells's *The Time Machine* in its earliest form by seven years. This story was saved from obscurity by Sam Moskowitz who included it in a volume of Mitchell's stories *The Crystal Man* (1973). It was also one of the first stories to suggest time paradoxes and alternate realities.

20 OTHER MAJOR SF THEMES AND THEIR ORIGINS

1 **Aliens on Earth** The first aliens to visit Earth in fiction were two giants, one from Saturn and one from Sirius who make a number of satirical observations in *Micromegas* (1750) by Voltaire, the French philosopher and historian. The first story in which Earth is invaded by hostile aliens is probably, according to Peter Nicholls in his *Encyclopedia of Science Fiction, The Germ Growers* by the Australian clergyman Robert Potter. First published in 1892 it preceded H.G. Wells's considerably more influential *The War of the Worlds* by six years.

2 **Alternate Worlds** These are worlds which have a common history with our own time-line until one moment where events happen otherwise, e.g. William of Normandy was defeated at Hastings, or the South won the American Civil War. Probably the earliest use of this theme was by Edmund Lawrence in *It May Happen Yet* (1899) which conjectured on Napoleon's invasion of Britain.

3 **Anti-Gravity** The germ of the idea of anti-gravity is present in Cyrano de Bergerac's *A Voyage to the Moon* (1650) wherein the never-to-be-outdone adventurer builds an iron frame and then casts a lodestone high into the air. The iron frame rises to meet the lodestone which is then cast higher and so on up-and-up by his bootstraps. Of greater importance is *A Voyage to the Moon* by George Tucker published in New York in 1827 under the pen name Joseph Atterley. Here the spacecraft is coated with an anti-gravity substance which anticipates H.G. Wells's use of Cavorite in *The First Men in the Moon* (1901) by nearly 75 years.

4 **Cities of the Future** *Memoirs of the Year Two Thousand Five Hundred* (1771) — originally *L'An 2440* — by the French playwright Louis-Sebastien Mercier is the seminal work depicting a beautiful and technologically utopian Paris over 700 years hence.

5 **Computer Intelligences** In *The Ablest Man in the World* (1879) by Edward Page Mitchell, a calculating machine is transplanted into the brain of an idiot thus making him a genius. Mitchell also wrote *The Tachypomp* (1874) about a super-calculator, but the first major computer story was undoubtedly *The Machine Stops* (1909) by E.M. Forster.

6 **The End of the World** As regards the end of the human race and the destruction of civilisation the first true apocalyptic novel was *The Last Man* (1805) by the French renegade priest Cousin de Grainville. As regards the literal end of the world this theme was handled masterfully for the first time by the French astronomer and populariser of science Camille Flammarion in *Omega: The Last Days of the World* (1893-4).

7 **Extra-Sensory Perception** Its first appearance in fiction was probably in *The Bohemian* by Fitz-James O'Brien where a girl reveals ultra-perceptive powers under hypnosis. Obviously written before O'Brien's death in 1862 the story was not published until 1885. By then the first telepathic aliens had appeared in print in *Fifteen Months in the Moon* (1880) by G.H. Ryan.

8 **The Fourth Dimension** In 1884 the British pseudo-scientist C. Howard Hinton produced a pamphlet asking *What Is The Fourth Dimension?* The following year the San Francisco writer Robert Duncan Milne wrote *A Mysterious Twilight* wherein three people in a room adjacent to one where an experimental electrical apparatus is functioning are witnesses to a bizarre overlapping of time streams. Science fiction's foremost historian, Sam Moskowitz, who unearthed the story, has suggested that: 'If Hinton were the seminal source of the 'modern' fourth dimension theme, then Milne may very well

The Struldbrugs from 'Gulliver's Travels'

Illustration From 'The Worlds Of The Imperium' A32

have been the first writer to incorporate it into fiction'. It was used again by J.-H. Rosny *aîné* in *Another World* (1895) and by H.G. Wells in several stories including *The Plattner Story* (1896)

9 **Immortality** The quest for the elixir of life is a time honoured theme in literature as well as science. Immortals first appear in early sf in Book III of Jonathan Swift's *Gulliver's Travels* (1726) where he encounters the Struldbrugs on the island of Luggnagg who are born with a red spot over the left eye which is a mark meaning that they shall never die. The main influence on immortality in sf is the legend of the Wandering Jew which thrived during the early 1800s within such Gothic novels as *Melmoth the Wanderer* (1820) by Charles Maturin. However, an earlier gothic novel introduced artificial immortality via an elixir of life in *St Leon* (1791) by William Godwin. Godwin was the father of Mary Shelley (the author of *Frankenstein)* who also wrote a story of immortality in *The Mortal Immortal* (1834).

10 **Invisibility** The tireless delvings of Sam Moskowitz have discovered that possibly the earliest story where a human is rendered invisible is *The Crystal Man* (1881) by Edward Page Mitchell. Other early examples are *Stella* (1895) by C. Howard Hinton and *The Invisible Man* (1897) by H.G. Wells. The theme has earlier origins, however, in the form of naturally invisible creatures originating with *What Was It?* (1859) by Fitz-James O'Brien.

11 **Lost Races** All the time there were large expanses of 'terra incognita' it was easy for writers to choose a location on the Earth's surface to establish an isolated community such as in Thomas More's *Utopia* (1516) or Jonathan Swift's *Gulliver's Travels* (1726) Much earlier had existed exotic travel books such as *The Travels of Sir John Mandeville* (1366) which has much in common with tales in the *Arabian Nights.* The real lost race theme came into its own when the full extent of the Earth's surface was known leaving only isolated pockets wherein to place survivors from Atlantis, Mu, Lemuria or some other early culture. Although it was H. Rider Haggard who was responsible for the popular revival of the lost race novel with the success of *King Solomon's Mines* in 1885, the man who had helped prime the market was Ignatius Donnelly with his non-fiction work *Atlantis, the Antediluvian World* (1882) Although lost worlds continued to turn up in Africa, South America, central Australia, central Asia, the Arctic and the Antarctic — and not to forget isolated Pacific islands — there was an increased trend to place such societies inside the Earth or under the sea. (See 16 and 19 below)

12 **Matter Transmission** *The Man Without a Body* by Edward Page Mitchell first published in the New York *Sun* for March 25, 1877 is described by sf historian Sam Moskowitz as 'the first fictional exposition yet discovered of breaking matter down into energy scientifically and transmitting it to a receiver where it may be re-formed.'

13 **Mutations** Throughout history there have been recorded details about freaks of nature — children born with two heads or no legs — or circus freaks such as bearded ladies. Science fiction adopted the theme readily, especially once the work of Gregor Mendel, Charles Darwin and Hugo DeVries pointed towards scientific rationales for mutations and evolution. Hitherto the freak was confined to the genre of horror fiction, such as the werewolf, and the first scientific version of the werewolf transformation brought about through mental derangement occurs in Robert Louis Stevenson's *The Strange Case of Dr Jekyll and Mr Hyde* (1886)

14 **Nuclear Power** The energy potential of the atom had first been realised with certain experiments conducted by Pierre Curie in 1901, and when Albert Einstein's famous equation $E = MC^2$ showed the relationship between energy and mass it gave the science fiction writer all the information he needed. Garrett P. Serviss employed an atomic-powered space-ship to take his adventurers

to Venus in *A Columbus in Space* (1909) whilst in *The World Set Free* (1914) H.G. Wells envisions atomic warfare.

15 **Robots** The word robot came into the English language from the Czech *robota* (labour) in Karel Capek's play *R.U.R.* (1921) and was rapidly adopted by the science fiction fraternity. Capek's robots, however, were organic and such constructs were termed as androids in sf. Mechanical (as opposed to clockwork) men may trace their origin in fiction to Herman Melville's *The Bell-Tower* (1885) though of more significance is the robot fiancée in Villers de L'isle Adam's *The Future Eve* (1886), the 'muglugs' in William Wallace Cook's *A Round Trip to the Year 2000)* (1903) and the automaton chess-player in Ambrose Bierce's *Moxon's Master* (1909)

16 **Subterranean Worlds** Long before Alice went down the rabbit-hole in Lewis Carroll's famous story there were novels set in subterranean worlds. The first important work was by the Danish writer Ludvig Holberg *Nicolai Klimii iter Subterraneum (Niels Klim's Underground Journey* 1741) whilst Britain's first contribution to the theme was the very popular *The Life and Adventures of Peter Wilkins* (1751) published anonymously by Robert Paltock set in an immense cavern beneath the South Pole.

17 **Supermen** Although H.G. Wells created superbeings in *The Food of the Gods* (1904) Upton Sinclair had an isolated man develop super powers in *The Overman* (1906) and J.D. Beresford chronicled the development of a super-child in *The Hampdenshire Wonder* (1911). The one true superman novel, and indeed the book that inspired the Superman comic-strip was *Gladiator* (1930) by Philip Wylie.

18 **Suspended Animation** In its simplest form suspended animation first appeared in fiction with the protagonist merely falling asleep for several hundred years as happened in Louis-Sebastien Mercier's *L'An 2440* (1771) which pre-dates even Washington Irving's *Rip Van Winkle* (1819). More recently suspended animation has been put on a more scientific basis with the new science of Cryonics — the preservation of the body by super-cooling — a theme anticipated in fiction as early as 1887 with W. Clark Russell's *The Frozen Pirate.*

19 **Under the Sea** It is a common misconception that Jules Verne conceived of the submarine in his famous *Twenty Thousand Leagues Under the Sea* (1870), even though submarines actually existed long before this. Robert Fulton's most famous submarine, built in 1801, was actually called the *Nautilus.* Theophile Gautier incorporated a submarine in his story *Les Deux Etoiles* (1848). Submarine societies were not so common in early fiction but once established in Andre Laurie's *The Crystal City Under the Sea* (1895) and David M. Parry's *The Scarlet Empire* .(1906) there was little else to say on the subject for many years.

20 **Weather Control** Something close to our heart in Britain today was equally close to the heart of the father of the Dictionary, Samuel Johnson, who in *Rasselas* (1759) includes a deranged scientist who claims to have power over the weather and the seasons. Weather control was a part of everyday life in Jane Webb's *The Mummy!* (1827) set in the year 2130 AD.

The next 17 lists go back over these themes and single out what I think are the most significant novels in each category. Having seen how the themes originated, these now show how each theme developed and the two lists together can serve as a basic reading list.

5 IMPORTANT NOVELS ABOUT ALIENS ON EARTH

A26

1 **The War of the Worlds**
H.G. Wells (1898)
2 **The Puppet Masters**
Robert A. Heinlein (1951)
3 **The Day of the Triffids**
John Wyndham (1951)
4 **Childhood's End**
Arthur C. Clarke (1953)
5 **Nightwings**
Robert Silverberg (1969)

'Childhood's End' by Arthur C. Clarke

5 IMPORTANT NOVELS ABOUT ALTERNATE WORLDS

A27

1 **The Sound of His Horn**
'Sarban' (1952) – Germany won World War II.
2 **Bring the Jubilee**
Ward Moore (1953) – the South won the American Civil War.
3 **The Man in the High Castle**
Philip K. Dick (1962) – Japan and Germany successfully invade America after World War II.
4 **Pavane**
Keith Roberts (1966) – the Spanish Armada was successful and Queen Elizabeth I was assassinated.
5 **The Alteration**
Kingsley Amis (1976) – the Spanish Armada was successful and the Reformation did not take place.

5 MEMORABLE NOVELS ABOUT FUTURE CITIES

A28

1 **When the Sleeper Wakes**
H.G. Wells (1899)
2 **The Caves of Steel**
Isaac Asimov (1954)
3 **The City and the Stars**
Arthur C. Clarke (1956)
4 **Cities in Flight**
James Blish (1970)
5 **The World Inside**
Robert Silverberg (1971)

'Analog' September 1962

5 INTERESTING NOVELS ABOUT COMPUTERS

A29

1 **They'd Rather Be Right**
Mark Clifton & Frank Riley (1957)
2 **The Moon Is A Harsh Mistress**
Robert A. Heinlein (1966)
3 **The Tale of the Big Computer**
Olof Johannesson (1966)
4 **Colossus**
D.F. Jones (1966)
5 **When Harlie Was One**
David Gerrold (1972)

5 DEVASTATING NOVELS ABOUT THE END OF THE WORLD

A30

1 **The Purple Cloud**
M.P. Shiel (1901)

2 **Last and First Men**
Olaf Stapledon (1930)

3 **When Worlds Collide**
Philip Wylie & Edwin Balmer (1933)

4 **Death of a World**
J.J. Farjeon (1948)

5 **After Doomsday**
Poul Anderson (1962)

5 MIND-BENDING NOVELS ABOUT ESP

A31

1 **Slan**
A.E. van Vogt (1940)

2 **The Demolished Man**
Alfred Bester (1952)

3 **More Than Human**
Theodore Sturgeon (1953)

4 **Dying Inside**
Robert Silverberg (1972)

5 **The Dead Zone**
Stephen King (1979)

5 NOVELS ABOUT OTHER DIMENSIONS

A32

1 **The Worlds of the Imperium**
Keith Laumer (1962)

2 **All Flesh is Grass**
Clifford D. Simak (1965)

3 **October the First Is Too Late**
Fred Hoyle (1966)

4 **Nine Princes in Amber**
(1970) and sequels Roger Zelazny

5 **The Gods Themselves** Isaac Asimov (1972)

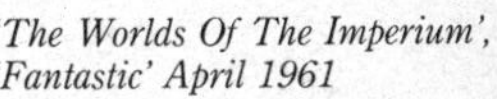
'The Worlds Of The Imperium', 'Fantastic' April 1961

5 IMMORTAL NOVELS ABOUT IMMORTALITY

A33

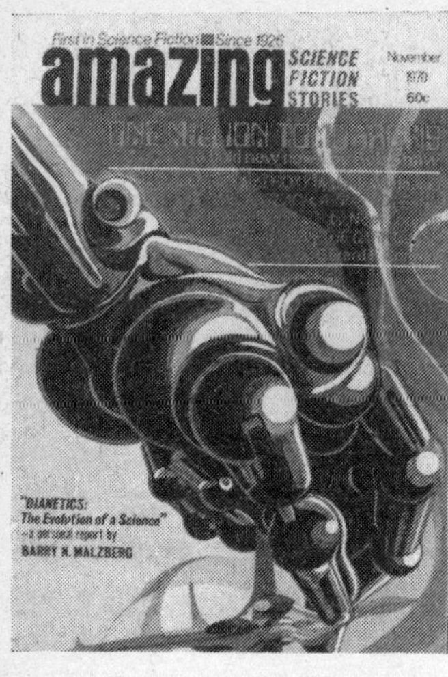

1 **To Live Forever**
Jack Vance (1956)

2 **The Immortals**
James E. Gunn (1962)

3 **Joyleg**
Avram Davidson & Ward Moore (1962)

4 **Way Station**
Clifford D. Simak (1963)

5 **One Million Tomorrows**
Bob Shaw (1970)

'Amazing Stories' November 1970

5 NOT-TO-BE-LOST NOVELS ABOUT LOST WORLDS

A34

1 **The Lost World**
Arthur Conan Doyle (1912)

2 **Polaris of the Snows**
(1915-16) and sequels by Charles B. Stilson

3 **The Land That Time Forgot**
Edgar Rice Burroughs (1918)

4 **Lost Horizon**
James Hilton (1933)

5 **The Man Who Missed The War**
Dennis Wheatley (1945)

5 NOVELS INVOLVING MATTER TRANSMISSION

A35

1 **Rogue Moon**
Algis Budrys (1960)
2 **Way Station**
Clifford D. Simak (1963)
3 **Echo Round His Bones**
Thomas M. Disch (1969)
4 **Web of Everywhere**
John Brunner (1974)
5 **Who Goes Here?**
Bob Shaw (1977)

5 NOVELS ABOUT MUTATIONS

A36

1 **The Island of Dr Moreau**
H.G. Wells (1896)
2 **The Island of Captain Sparrow**
S. Fowler Wright (1928)
3 **The Chrysalids**
John Wyndham (1955)
4 **The Star of Life**
Edmond Hamilton (1959)
5 **The Eleventh Commandment**
Lester del Rey (1962)

Illustration From 'The Island Of Captain Sparrow', 'Famous Fantastic Mysteries' April 1946

5 NOVELS SET AFTER A NUCLEAR WAR

A37

1 **Shadow of the Hearth**
Judith Merril (1950)

2 **On the Beach**
Nevil Shute (1957)

3 **The Long Loud Silence**
Wilson Tucker (1962)

4 **Sos the Rope**
(1968) and sequels Piers Anthony

5 **The Company of Glory**
Edgar Pangborn (1975)

5 NOVELS ABOUT ROBOTS

A38

1 **The Humanoids**
Jack Williamson (1949)

2 **The Naked Sun**
Isaac Asimov (1957)

3 **Do Androids Dream of Electric Sheep?**
Philip K. Dick (1968)

4 **A Choice of Gods**
Clifford D. Simak (1972)

5 **The Soul of the Robot**
Barrington J. Bayley (1974)

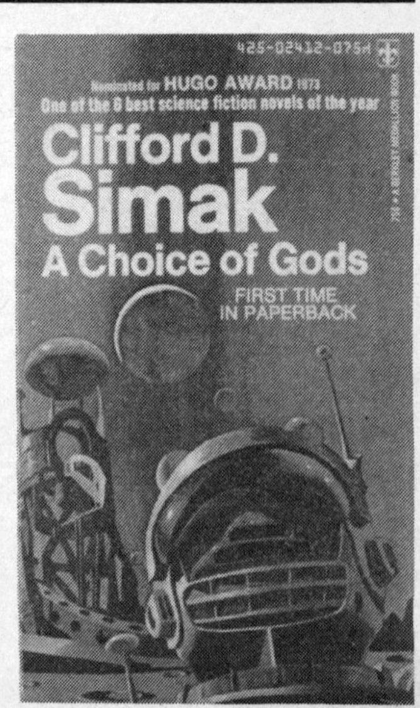

5 WAY-OUT NOVELS ABOUT SPACE EXPLORATION

A39

1 **The Moon is Hell**
John W. Campbell (1950)

2 **The Martian Chronicles**
Ray Bradbury (1951)

3 **All Judgement Fled**
James White (1967)

4 **Macroscope**
Piers Anthony (1969)

5 **The Far Call**
Gordon R. Dickson (1978)

5 DOWN-TO-EARTH NOVELS ABOUT SUBTERRANEAN WORLDS

A40

1 **At The Earth's Core**
(1914) and sequels by Edgar Rice Burroughs

2 **The Secret People**
John Wyndham (1935)

3 **Land Under England**
Joseph O'Neill (1935)

4 **In Caverns Below**
Stanton Coblentz (1935; also published as *Hidden World*)

5 **The Hero of Downways**
Michael G. Coney (1973)

5 NOVELS ABOUT SUPERMEN

A41

1 **The End of Eternity**
Isaac Asimov (1955)
2 **Past Master**
R.A. Lafferty (1968)
3 **Up the Line**
Robert Silverberg (1969)
4 **Our Children's Children**
Clifford D. Simak (1973)
5 **The Man Who Folded Himself**
David Gerrold (1973)

5 NOVELS ABOUT TIME TRAVEL

A42

1 **Seeds of Life**
John Taine (1931)
2 **The Intelligence Gigantic**
John Russell Fearn (1933)
3 **The New Adam**
Stanley G. Weinbaum (1939)
4 **Brain Wave**
Poul Anderson (1954)
5 **Extro**
Alfred Bester (1974; also published as *The Computer Connection)*

THE MOST POPULAR SF & FANTASY ARTISTS

A43

Each year the news magazine *Locus* asks its readers to vote on who they feel is the Best Artist. The following is the 1981 listing complete together with the positions for earlier years. There was no published listing for 1978.

1981	Artist	1980	1979	1977	1976
1	**Michael Whelan**	1	2	11	—
2	**Don Maitz**	6	—	—	—
3	**Boris Vallejo**	3	1	10	—
4	**Vincent DiFate**	4	4	4	5
5	**Stephen Fabian**	2	3	2	2
6	**Rowena Morrill**	13	—	—	—
7	**Kelly Freas**	5	5	3	3
8	**Paul Lehr**	8	—	—	—
9	**Alicia Austin**	10	12	—	—
10	**Tim Kirk**	11	9	6	4
11	**Alexis Gilliland**	12	18	—	—
12	**Rick Sternbach**	17	6	1	1
13	**Frank Frazetta**	—	8	7	9
14	**Carl Lundgren**	17	—	—	—
14	**Leo & Diane Dillon**	—	—	15	12
16	**Darrell Sweet**	9	11	12	10
17	**Ron Walotsky**	24	—	—	—
17	**H.R. Giger**	7	—	—	—
19	**George Barr**	15	7	5	6
20	**John Schoenherr**	—	—	9	7

Plus a few who have fallen from grace:

—	**Jack Gaughan**	21	17	8	8
—	**The Brothers Hildebrandt**	19	15	16	—
24	**David Hardy**	20	10	—	—

Michael Whelan

THE 20 HUGO AWARD-WINNING ARTISTS

A44

The first of the Hugo Awards presented in 1953 included two categories for Cover Artist and Interior Illustrator. Subsequent presentations were to Professional Artist with an additional category for Fan Artist started in 1967. In that year Jack Gaughan became the only artist to win both a fan and professional artist award. The following list, instead of logging the results year by year, has combined the awards and listed them in the order of the artists who have won the most awards.

1	**Frank Kelly Freas**	10	1955; 1956; 1958; 1959; 1970; 1972; 1973; 1974; 1975; 1976
2	**Tim Kirk (fan)**	5	1970; 1972; 1973; 1974; 1976
3	**Ed Emshwiller**	5	1953; 1960; 1961; 1962; 1964
4	**Jack Gaughan**	4	1967 (pro & fan); 1968; 1969
5	**Rick Sternbach**	2	1977; 1978
6	**Phil Foglio (fan)**	2	1977;1978
7	**William Rotsler (fan**	2	1975; 1979
8	**Michael Whelan**	2	1980; 1981
9	**Hannes Bok**	1	1953 (tie)
10	**Virgil Finlay (interior)**	1	1953
11	**Roy Krenkel**	1	1963
12	**John Schoenherr**	1	1965
13	**Frank Frazetta**	1	1966
14	**George Barr (fan)**	1	1968
15	**Vaughn Bode (fan)**	1	1969
16	**Leo & Diane Dillon**	1	1971
17	**Alicia Austin (fan)**	1	1971
18	**Vincent DiFate**	1	1979
19	**Alexis Gilliland (fan)**	1	1980
20	**Victoria Poyser (fan)**	1	1981

THE 10 MOST CONSISTENTLY POPULAR ARTISTS

A45

The following list takes into account not only the winners of the Hugo Award for Best Artist but those nominated for the Award. Where a first-second-and-third place vote is known I have allocated points to show both popularity and consistency.

	Artist	Nominations	Points
1	**Frank Kelly Freas**	18	45
2	**Jack Gaughan**	13	23
3	**John Schoenherr**	11	19
4	**Vincent DiFate**	9	18
5	**Ed Emshwiller**	8	16
6	**Stephen Fabian**	9	15
7	**Michael Whelan**	4	14
8	**Rick Sternbach**	4	11
9	**Virgil Finlay**	7	10
	Leo & Diane Dillon	3	10

THE MOST POPULAR SF & FANTASY MAGAZINES

Each year the news magazine *Locus* asks its readers to vote on a number of categories including Best Magazine. Edward Ferman's *Magazine of Fantasy and Science Fiction* wins every year but it's worth noting the positions of the other magazines. The list includes non-professional and fan magazines, and the position of *Locus* itself is inevitable. The following reprints the 1981 listing complete, together with the positions of those magazines in the voting for the last five years.

1981	Magazine	1980	1979	1978	1977	1976
1	**Magazine of Fantasy & SF**	1	1	1	1	1
2	**Locus**	2	2	2	—	2
3	**Analog**	3	3	3	2	3
4	**Omni**	5	5	—	—	—
5	**Asimov's SF Magazine**	4	4	4	—	—
6	**Science Fiction Review**	6	6	6	—	5
7	**Fantasy Newsletter**	10	—	—	—	—
8	**Destinies**	7	9	—	—	—
9	**Starship (Algol)**	9	7	8	—	6
10	**Amazing/Fantastic (combined)**	—	—	11	4	7
	(earlier years **Fantastic**)	—	—	13	5	8
11	**Thrust**	12	—	—	—	—
12	**Science Fiction Chronicle**	—	—	—	—	—
13	**Starlog**	14	10	10	—	—
14	**Future Life**	—	14	—	—	—
15	**Questar**	—	—	—	—	—
16	**Janus**	15	—	—	—	—
17	**File 770**	—	—	—	—	—
18	**Cinefantastique**	—	—	17	—	—

Below are some of the leaders in earlier years no longer present in the popularity polls.

1981	Magazine	1980	1979	1978	1977	1976
—	**Galaxy**	—	12	5	3	4
—	**Whispers**	13	14	15	—	13
—	**Unearth**	—	11	12	—	—
—	**Galileo**	8	8	9	7	14
—	**Asimov's SF Adventure Mag.**	11	13	—	—	—

Kelly Freas

THE HUGO AWARD-WINNING MAGAZINES

From 1953 to 1972 one of the Hugo Award categories was for Best Professional Magazine. In 1954 there was no Award, and in 1957, when the World SF Convention was held in England, the category was split into American and British magazines. From 1973 onwards the category was dropped in favour of Best Professional Editor. The following list combines details for magazines and editors for all thirty awards.

Year	Magazine	Editor
1953 (tie)	**Astounding & Galaxy**	John W. Campbell, Jr. & Horace L. Gold
1955	**Astounding**	John W. Campbell, Jr.
1956	**Astounding**	John W. Campbell, Jr.
1957	**Astounding (US)**	John W. Campbell, Jr.
	New Worlds (UK)	John Carnell
1958	**F & SF**	Anthony Boucher
1959	**F & SF**	Robert P. Mills
1960	**F & SF**	Robert P. Mills
1961	**Astounding/ Analog**	John W. Campbell, Jr.
1962	**Analog**	John W. Campbell, Jr.
1963	**F & SF**	Avram Davidson
1964	**Analog**	John W. Campbell, Jr.
1965	**Analog**	John W. Campbell, Jr.
1966	**If**	Frederik Pohl
1967	**If**	Frederik Pohl
1968	**If**	Frederik Pohl
1969	**F & SF**	Edward L. Ferman
1970	**F & SF**	Edward L. Ferman
1971	**F & SF**	Edward L. Ferman
1972	**F & SF**	Edward L. Ferman
1973	**Analog**	Ben Bova
1974	**Analog**	Ben Bova
1975	**Analog**	Ben Bova
1976	**Analog**	Ben Bova
1977	**Analog**	Ben Bova
1978	**Isaac Asimov's SF Magazine**	George Scithers
1979	**Analog**	Ben Bova
1980	**Isaac Asimov's SF Magazine**	George Scithers
1981	**F & SF**	Edward L. Ferman

In summary, it produces the following:

Magazine	No.Awards	Editor	No. Awards
Astounding/ Analog	14	**John W. Campbell**	8
F & SF	9	**Ben Bova**	6
If	2	**Edward L. Ferman**	5
Asimov's SF Mag.	2	**Frederik Pohl**	3
Galaxy	1	**Robert P. Mills**	2
		George Scithers	2

THE MAGAZINE OF
Fantasy AND
Science Fiction
FEBRUARY 75c • UK 30p.
Isaac Asimov
THE ASYMMETRY OF LIFE
TWO GREAT NEW NOVELETS
GOAT SONG
by Poul Anderson
PAINWISE
by James Tiptree, Jr.

'F & SF' A46

New Worlds	1	**Horace L. Gold**	1
		John Carnell	1
		Anthony Boucher	1
		Avram Davidson	1

THE 12 MOST CONSISTENTLY POPULAR SF MAGAZINES

A48

The following list takes into account the nominations for the Best Magazine Hugo Award rather than just the winner. However, I have allotted a points system so that runners-up receive more points than those who failed to make the top three.

	Magazine	Nominations	Points
1	**Astounding/Analog**	18	37
2	**Magazine of F & SF**	15	33
3	**Galaxy**	15	21
4	**Amazing Stories**	8	13
5	**If**	5	8
6	**New Worlds**	6	7
7	**Science Fantasy**	3	4
8	**Fantastic**	2	2
	Infinity	2	2
10	**Nebula**	1	1
	Fantastic Universe	1	1
	Vision of Tomorrow	1	1

10 IMPORTANT EARLY SF ARTISTS

A common thread throughout the history of art is the surreal fantasy evident in the early work of Hieronymous Bosch in the fifteenth century down to artists like Salvador Dali and M.C. Escher in the twentieth. The following list, however, concentrates on those artists whose work depicted either technological progress or cosmological wonder, the basic premises of science fiction.

1 **Giovanni Batista Piranesi** 1720-1778. Piranesi produced a number of etchings both forbidding and foreboding such as *The Cellar of Invention* which portrays a blend of some Chamber of the Inquisition with the growth of factory slavery in the Industrial Revolution.

2 **John Martin** 1789-1854. Although starting out in life as an heraldic and enamel painter Martin found fame when in 1812 he exhibited at the Royal Academy. His work was described as displaying 'immeasurable space, innumerable multitudes, and gorgeous prodigies of architecture and landscape'. Martin's engravings include the *Fall of Babylon* (1819) and *The Deluge* (1826).

3 **Isidore Grandville** 1803-1847. Real name Jean Ignace Isidore Gérard, this French caricaturist and illustrator has been called the first of the true science fiction artists, a reputation that rests chiefly on his book *Un Autre Monde,* published in 1844. Grandville not only illustrated the volume but wrote the accompanying story under another alias, Taxile Delord. The work is particularly rich in the creation of weird creatures called 'doublivores'. Grandville suffered from depression and ended his days in a Paris lunatic asylum.

4 **Gustave Doré** 1833-1883. Perhaps the most famous and accomplished of the apocalyptic painters, Dore's illustrations for *The Bible* remain unequalled. He also illustrated such works as Rabelais' *Pantagruel* and *Gargantua,* Dante's *Inferno,* the *Contes* of Perrault, *The Wandering Jew, Paradise Lost,* la Fontaine's *Fables* (which had earlier been illustrated by Grandville) and Raspe's *Munchhausen.* Doré was probably the most influential of the nineteenth century visionaries.

5 **Hildibrand** France was without a doubt the home of the sf artist in the nineteenth century. With the success of the works of Jules Verne a number of artists were employed to illustrate his work. Hildibrand provided some of the best known pictures to adorn *From the Earth to the Moon* (1865).

6 **Albert Robida** 1848-1926. The real father of sf illustration, Robida not only illustrated works by others but, more importantly, produced volumes of his own work. These were originally produced in homage to Jules Verne but so spectacular were Robida's own visions of the future that he can claim to be Verne's equal if not superior in terms of technological predictions. His major works were *Voyages très extraordinaires* (1879/80), *Le Vingtième Siècle* (1882) and *La vie electrique* (1883).

7 **Paul Hardy** The boom in popular magazines at the end of the last century and the parallel rise in science fiction by people like Conan Doyle and H.G. Wells brought about a rash of sf illustrators. Hardy, and the three that follow, were amongst the most ubiquitous. Hardy illustrated the quaint *Letters From the Planets* by the Reverend W.S. Lach-Szyrma which appeared sporadically in *Cassell's Family Magazine* from 1887 to 1893.

8 **Warwick Goble** Probably the best known of this group of artists, Goble was regularly employed in illustrating the work of H.G. Wells and provided the illustrations to *The War of the Worlds* (1898).

9 **Stanley L. Wood** Wood provided some particularly worthy illustrations to George Griffith's *Stories of Other Worlds* serialised in *Pearson's Magazine* during 1900 and later published as *A Honeymoon in Space* (1901).

10 **Fred T. Jane** 1865-1916. The noted originator of *Jane's Fighting Ships,* Jane produced many illustrations showing air and sea ships of the future, and depicted many scenes of future warfare.

Illustration by Stanley L. Wood to Griffith's Story

THE 10 FIRST SIGNIFICANT SF FILMS

A50

Science fiction films are as old as cinematography itself, for as soon as the film-makers discovered how to produce trick photography they began a series of trick films most of only a minute or two duration. If I restricted this list solely to the ten first 'trick' films, they would all be about sausage machines, so I have been rather more selective in my choice.

1 **The Sausage Machine** (Biograph, 1897) See what I mean? Lasting just sixty seconds this film showed how in one continuous operation bowler-hatted butchers could load dogs into one end of a machine and produce strings of sausages at the other.

2 **The Laboratory of Mephistopheles** (Robert-Houdin, 1897) Produced by the movie magician himself, George Méliès (1861-1938), this short-short starred Méliès himself as Mephistopheles working a variety of magical and technological wonders.

3 **The X-Ray Fiend** (GAS, 1897) Produced by British film-maker George A. Smith, who had also made his own 'sausage' film, this has a machine which reveals the embracing skeletons of two lovers.

4 **Gugusse and the Automaton** (Robert-Houdin, 1897) Also known as *The Clown and the Automaton* this is another of Méliès' productions and has also been cited as 'the one that may be the first true sf film'. The film is now lost but it is believed to have portrayed the screen's first robot.

5 **A Novice at X-Rays** (Robert-Houdin, 1898) Méliès again. In this the character's skeleton walks right out of his body which collapses as a heap on the floor.

6 **The Astronomer's Dream** (Robert-Houdin, 1898) In which the Moon comes down to the Earth. Méliès again.

7 **Coppelia** (Robert-Houdin, 1900) Would you believe Méliès again, with another robot film fashioned on Delibes' ballet of the same name.

8 **The Flying Machine** (Pathe, 1901) Produced by Ferdinand Zecca this was the first film to portray a solo aviator peddling his contraption above the town of Belleville.

9 **A Trip to the Moon** (Star, 1902) Often cited as the first true sf film, this was Méliès first real masterwork, blending elements of Verne's and Wells's novels to take his heroes to the Moon. The film promptly spawned hoards of imitations and the sf film genre can be said to have been christened.

10 **Whirling the Worlds** (Star, 1904) Another Méliès classic, this film, originally entitled *Voyage a Travers l'Impossible* cost the equivalent of £2,000 to produce and lasted twenty-four minutes. In a machine which combines every known means of locomotion – the Automabouloff – our fourteen heroes set off to explore the world and the solar system. Douglas Menville and Robert Reginald in their book *Things to Come* (1977), said that in this film 'Méliès brought to fruition all his abilities as showman, storyteller, artist, caricaturist and camera wizard'.

Still From 'A Trip To The Moon'

SECTION B
EXPERT OPINION

In which we learn the special likes and dislikes of the professionals.

FORREST J ACKERMAN'S 21 FAVOURITE SF & FANTASY AUTHORS

B1

Forrie Ackerman is, without a doubt, science fiction's Number One Fan and Number One Personality. You'll find his name mentioned throughout this book either as a record-holder in his own right or having assisted in providing some obscure items of information. An agent, editor, lecturer, archivist, researcher, esperantist and anthologist (as his letterhead declares) there is no one more closely at the core of science fiction than Ackerman. It was he who coined the term 'sci-fi' for science fiction. His Ackermansion holds the Fantasy Foundation and the Ackerman Archives, the world's largest single repository of books, films and sf associated paraphernalia. I therefore have no qualms in offering not just one, but four preference lists from Mr Ackerman. First, the favourite authors, in no particular order —

1 **H.G. Wells**
2 **A.E. van Vogt**
3 **Ray Bradbury**
4 **Robert A. Heinlein**
5 **Henry Kuttner**
6 **David H. Keller**
7 **C.L. Moore**
8 **Theodore Sturgeon**
9 **Edgar Rice Burroughs**
10 **Olaf Stapledon**
11 **Arthur C. Clarke**
12 **Stanley G. Weinbaum**
13 **William F. Temple**
14 **L. Ron Hubbard**
15 **Ray Cummings**
16 **Stanton A. Coblentz**
17 **Robert Bloch**
18 **John Taine**
19 **Edmond Hamilton**
20 **Nat Schachner**
21 **E.E. Smith**

©1982 Forrest J Ackerman Exclusive for the Illustrated Book of Science Fiction Lists

FORREST J ACKERMAN'S 14 FAVOURITE ARTISTS

B2

1 **Frank R. Paul**
2 **Virgil Finlay**
3 **Hannes Bok**
4 **Elliot Dold**
5 **Lawrence Sterne Stevens**
6 **Leydenfrost**
7 **Hans Wessolowski**
8 **Margaret Brundage**
9 **Frank Frazetta**
10 **Kelly Freas**
11 **Karel Thole**
12 **Josh Kirby**
13 **Edd Cartier**
14 **J. Allen St. John**

FORREST J ACKERMAN'S 24 FAVOURITE SF & FANTASY BOOKS

1 **The World Below**
S. Fowler Wright

2 **Childhood's End**
Arthur C. Clarke

3 **Slan**
A.E. van Vogt

4 **The Four-sided Triangle**
William F. Temple

5 **The Mastermind of Mars**
Edgar Rice Burroughs

6 **Tarzan of the Apes**
Edgar Rice Burroughs

7 **The Forever War**
Joe Haldeman

8 **Gray Lensman**
E.E. Smith

9 **The Martian Chronicles**
Ray Bradbury

10 **The New Adam**
Stanley G. Weinbaum

11 **The Man Who Mastered Time**
Ray Cummings

12 **Fear**
L. Ron Hubbard

13 **Northwest Smith**
C.L. Moore

14 **Ralph 124C41 +**
Hugo Gernsback

15 **The War of the Worlds**
H.G. Wells

16 **The Sunken World**
Stanton A Coblentz

17 **Quayle's Invention**
John Taine

18 **The Vicarion**
Gardner Hunting

19 **At the Earth's Core**
Edgar Rice Burroughs

20 **Deliver Me From Eva**
Paul Bailey

21 **Final Blackout**
L. Ron Hubbard

22 **The Legion of Space**
Jack Williamson

23 **Rendezvous with Rama**
Arthur C. Clarke

24 **Sinister Barrier**
Eric Frank Russell

Frank R. Paul

FORREST J ACKERMAN'S 27 FAVOURITE IMAGI-MOVIES

1 **Metropolis**
2 **Things to Come**
3 **Frankenstein** (1931, Karloff)
4 **Dracula** (1931, Lugosi)
5 **King Kong** (1933 version)
6 **The Invisible Man**
7 **Bride of Frankenstein**
8 **Star Wars**
9 **The Empire Strikes Back**
10 **CE3K**
11 **Invasion of the Body Snatchers** (1956)
12 **The Lost World** (1925)
13 **The Thief of Bagdad** (1926 version)
14 **Siegfried**
15 **Rosemary's Baby**
16 **Alien**
17 **The Exorcist**
18 **Village of the Damned**
19 **The Creeping Unknown** (US title for *The Quatermass Xperiment*)
20 **High Treason** (second British talking film)
21 **The Phantom of the Opera** (1925, Chaney)
22 **The Day the Earth Stood Still**
23 **The War of the Worlds**
24 **The Seventh Voyage of Sinbad**
25 **J'accuse**
26 **The Thing**
27 **The Mummy** (1932 version)

Still From 'Metropolis'

THE 10 MOST IMPORTANT BRITISH SF NOVELS ACCORDING TO BRIAN W ALDISS

B5

Brian Aldiss is in the front rank of world sf writers. There isn't much within the field that he hasn't done since his first stories in 1954. He won a Hugo Award in 1962 for his series of stories published as *Hothouse,* and won a Nebula in 1966 for his novella *The Saliva Tree.* He has written a history of science fiction, *Billion Year Spree,* a score or more novels, edited several anthologies and most recently was one of the Judging Panel for the 1981 Booker Prize. The following list, which Aldiss will not have prepared lightly, is in chronological order of publication.

1 **Frankenstein**
Mary Shelley (1818)

2 **The Time Machine**
H.G. Wells (1895)

3 **The War of the Worlds**
H.G. Wells (1898)

4 **Last and First Men**
Olaf Stapledon (1930)

5 **Star-Maker**
Olaf Stapledon (1937)

6 **Land Under England**
Joseph O'Neill (1935)

7 **The Terminal Beach**
J.G. Ballard (1964) (Yes, I know it's not a novel)

8 **Gloriana**
Michael Moorcock (1978)

9 **Russian Hide and Seek**
Kingsley Amis (1980)

10 **The Sirian Experiments**
Doris Lessing (1981)

Brian Aldiss

POUL ANDERSON'S 10 OR 11 MOST INFLUENTIAL SF PEOPLE

B6

Poul Anderson is one of the most popular and prolific writers in both science fiction and fantasy. He has won a whole sideboard full of awards both in and out of the sf field. Over to Mr Anderson:
In my opinion, the most influential people in science fiction — not all of them among the best writers or editors, but the most influential — have been:

1 **Jules Verne**
2 **H.G. Wells**
3 **Hugo Gernsback**
4 **Stanley G. Weinbaum**
5 **John W. Campbell**
6 **H.L. Gold**

7 **Anthony Boucher**
8 **Robert A. Heinlein**
9 **Isaac Asimov**
10 **Ursula K. LeGuin**
or **David G. Hartwell:**
Mrs LeGuin because she, by her excellence, probably had the most to do with the large-scale entry of women into the field; or Mr Hartwell because he now heads the publishing programme which is economically most significant in this generally bad time, and maintains a high standard.

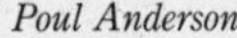
Poul Anderson

POUL ANDERSON'S 10 WRITERS OR BOOKS THAT MOST INFLUENCED HIS CAREER

B7

The order is roughly chronological, not necessarily in order of importance:

1 **Homer**
2 **The Bible**
3 **The Icelandic Eddas and sagas**
4 **Shakespeare**
5 **H.G. Wells**
6 **John W. Campbell**
7 **Robert A. Heinlein**
8 **Johannes V. Jensen**
9 **Hal Clement**
10 **Rudyard Kipling**

ISAAC ASIMOV'S 5 FAVOURITE OF HIS OWN SF STORIES

B8

1 **The Last Question**
(because of the concept)
2 **The Bicentennial Man**
(because it moved me)
3 **The Ugly Little Boy**
(because it moved me)
4 **The Gods Themselves**
(because of the extraterrestrials)
5 **The Caves of Steel**
(because of the sf/mystery combination)

'Isaac Asimov's Science Fiction Magazine'

... AND HIS 5 LEAST FAVOURITE

B9

1 **The Portable Star**
2 **Black Friar of the Flames**
3 **Magnificent Possession**
4 **The Secret Sense**
5 **The Weapon Too Dreadful To Use**
— These were all early stories and just didn't gel.

ROBERT BLOCH'S 11 FAVOURITE STORIES BY H.P. LOVECRAFT

B10

Robert Bloch, famed as the author of *Psycho,* was one of the last disciples of H.P. Lovecraft, corresponding with and being encouraged by the man himself in his final years. Although Bloch has achieved the pinnacle of fame as a writer he has never forgotten his origins, and one of his most recent novels, *Strange Eons,* returned to Lovecraft's Cthulhu Mythos. The following list is derived from an interview given by Bloch and published in *Robert Bloch: A Bio-Bibliography.*

1 **Pickman's Model**
2 **The Whisperer In Darkness**
3 **The Shadow Over Innsmouth**
4 **The Dunwich Horror**
5 **The Call of Cthulhu**
6 **The Silver Key**
7 **The Picture in the House**
8 **The Outsider**
9 **The Thing on the Doorstep**
10 **The Colour Out of Space**

Robert Bloch

JOHN BRUNNER'S 10 SF NOVELS EVERY POLITICIAN SHOULD READ

B11

John Brunner

1 **1984** George Orwell. For its portrait of a totally efficient tyranny.

2 **Earth Abides** George R. Stewart. For reminding us about how fragile our society is.

3 **No One Will Escape (Keiner Kommt Davon)** Hans Hellmut Kirst. For its picture of Europe declining into nuclear war.

4 **After All, This is England** Robert Muller. For its hideously convincing depiction of how fascism might come to us in the guise of patriotism.

5 **The Other Man** Giles Cooper. For its protagonist, a British officer dutifully serving the all-conquering Nazis.

6 **The Man Who Held the Queen to Ransom and Sent Parliament Packing** Peter van Greenaway. For the hope it offers us that someone might break through the deadlock we are trapped in.

7 **Make Room! Make Room!** Harry Harrison. For showing us what it would be like if we had to live as millions do in overcrowded poverty-stricken nations.

8 **The Devil's Alternative** Frederick Forsyth. For the only credible scenario I know that suggests why Russia might want to invade the West.

9 **The Time Machine** H.G. Wells. For the way it enables us to view out petty modern concerns *sub specie aeternitatis.*

10 **The Shockwave Rider** John Brunner. In all diffidence because Alvin Toffler and others regard it as a reasonable projection of a computerised society.

ALGIS BUDRYS' 10 MOST PROMISING NEW SCIENCE FICTION & FANTASY WRITERS

B12

Budrys is one of science fiction's most respected writers and critics, the author of such books as *Who?* and *Rogue Moon.* In compiling the following he added: 'New' means people to whom John Varley is a Grand Old Man, which means that most of these names won't mean much in Britain yet, but I would advise any reader to keep an eye open for stories by all the following. They won't be disappointed.

Algis Budrys

1 **Paul Preuss**
2 **Parke Godwin**
3 **Arsen Darnay**
(technically, not as 'new' as some of the others, three of whom have no prose in print as yet under their sf bylines but have made sales)
4 **Michael Swanwick**
5 **Somtow Sucharitkul**
6 **Victor Besaw**
7 **Lucius Shepard**
8 **Madeleine Robins**
9 **Robert L. Forward**
10 **Robert Frazier**
It'll be interesting to look back on that list in, say 10 years time. Budrys adds: 'Besaw is a retired schoolteacher who has just begun to have his science-fantasy novels published. The rest are, in the main, young and upcoming'.

HAL CLEMENT'S 10 SF NOVELS HE HAS MOST RE-READ

B13

Clement is noted in the sf field for his hard-science novels like *Mission of Gravity* and *Close to Critical,* so the following list may come as something of a surprise.

1 **Who Goes There?** John W Campbell — In my firm opinion the best sf story ever written is not novel length. I like it because it combines, better than any other story I have ever seen, tension and action with an essentially scientific problem and an essential scientific solution which the reader had a fair chance to foresee.

2 **Too Many Magicians** Randall Garrett — I like this because Garrett has made a science out of magic — that is, he has extrapolated from science, and provided a frame where, again, the reader has a fair chance to pull ahead of the author. Also, the Lord

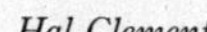
Hal Clement

D'Arcy stories are excellent take-offs on old detective stories; it's fun to spot the connections.

3 **Witches of Karres** James H. Schmitz — I don't know why I like this — someone can try a psychoanalysis if they like. I don't believe in psionics or klatha, but I like Schmitz's Telzey Amberdon stories, too.

4 **Retief's War** Keith Laumer

5 **A Bicycle Built For Brew** Poul Anderson — These two are simply funny.

6 **The High Crusade** Poul Anderson

7 **Spacehounds of the I.P.C.** E.E. Smith

8 **Drums of Tapajos** and **Troyana** S.P. Meek

9 **The Land That Time Forgot** Edgar Rice Burroughs

10 **Under Pressure (or Dragon In the Sea)** Frank Herbert — There's an obvious predominance of space opera here; I don't apologise.

L. SPRAGUE DE CAMP'S 8 FAVOURITE HEROIC FANTASY NOVELS

B14

Although a first class writer of science fiction, de Camp is probably better known for his associations with fantasy fiction, most notably his work in resurrecting the Conan stories of Robert E. Howard, and adding those by himself and others to the series.Over to Mr de Camp: For favourite heroic-fantasy novels I could list (aside from any of my own):

1 **Conan the Conqueror** Robert E. Howard

2 **The Well of the Unicorn** Fletcher Pratt

3 **The Lord of the Rings** J.R.R. Tolkien

4 **The Worm Ouroboros** E.R. Eddison

5 **The King of Elfland's Daughter** Lord Dunsany

6 **Witch World** Andre Norton

7 **Three Hearts and Three Lions** Poul Anderson

8 **Silverlock** John Myers Myers

...and then there are a lot of others that I have enjoyed but which I find hard to rank.

L. SPRAGUE DE CAMP'S 10 FAVOURITE SF & FANTASY AUTHORS

B15

1 **H.G. Wells**

2 **Thorne Smith**

3 **Robert A Heinlein**

4 **Poul Anderson**

5 **Avram Davidson**

6 **Andre Norton**

7 **Fritz Leiber**

8 **Robert E. Howard**

9 **Jack Vance**

10 **A. Merritt**

L. SPRAGUE DE CAMP'S 9 FAVOURITE SF & FANTASY CHARACTERS

B16

1 **Robert E. Howard's** *Conan*
2 **Poul Anderson's** *Cappen Varra*
3 **T.H. White's** *Merlin*
4 **Lord Dunsany's** *Marano*
5 **Jane Gaskell's** *Cija*
6 & **Fritz Leiber's** *Fafhrd*
7 and the *Gray Mouser*
8 **Jack Vance's** *Magnus Ridolph*
9 **C.L. Moore's** *Jirel*

L. Sprague De Camp

VINCENT DI FATE'S 10 FAVOURITE MAGAZINE COVERS

B17

Vincent Di Fate is one of the bright new artists in science fiction. His paintings have adorned most of the magazines, in particular *Analog,* and he has been nominated nine times for the Hugo Award for Best Artist, winning it in 1979. Over to Mr Di Fate: 'Frankly, I'm a bit disdainful of the magazine art which has appeared since the mid-1950s and was hard pressed to come up with the ten items, listed in chronological order'.

1 **Astounding Stories**
December 1934
— Howard V. Brown
2 **Astounding SF**
October 1939 — Hubert Rogers
3 **Startling Stories**
November 1939
— Howard V. Brown
4 **Astounding SF**
May 1951 — Hubert Rogers
5 **Space SF** September 1952
— Earle K. Bergey

'Space SF' September 1952

6 **Astounding SF**
October 1953 — Kelly Freas

7 **Analog**
September 1962 — Solonovich

8 **Analog**
May 1966 — John Schoenherr

9 **Analog**
December 1967
— John Schoenherr

10 **Analog**
July 1975 — John Schoenherr

VINCENT DI FATE'S 8 FAVOURITE SF ARTISTS

B18

1 **Earle K. Bergey**
2 **John C. Berkey**
3 **Robert Foster**
4 **Paul Lehr**
5 **Stanley Meltzoff**
6 **Fred Pfeiffer**
7 **Hubert Rogers**
8 **John Schoenherr**

STEPHEN R. DONALDSON'S 10 FAVOURITE FANTASY NOVELS OF ALL TIME

B19

Stephen R. Donaldson is the author of the block-busting *Chronicles of Thomas Covenant* trilogy which shot into the best-selling lists in Britain in 1978. He is working at present on the second trilogy of which the first volume, *The Wounded Land* appeared in 1980 and promptly topped the best-selling list. The second volume, *The One Tree,* had appeared in the States at the time of publication and should shortly be available in Britain.

In compiling this list Stephen Donaldson commented that there were many books which he regretted omitting, but still managed to squeeze 22 volumes in a list of 10!

1 **Lord of the Rings**
J.R.R. Tolkien

2 **The Once and Future King**
T.H. White

3 **The Chronicles of Narnia**
C.S. Lewis

4 **The Riddle-Master Trilogy**
Patricia McKillip

5 **The Book of the Dun Cow**
Walter Wangerin, Jr

6 **The Spellcoats**
Diana Wynne Jones

7 **The Gormenghast Trilogy**
Mervyn Peake

8 **Salem's Lot**
Stephen King

9 **The Wind in the Willows**
Kenneth Grahame

10 **The Children of Ilyr**
Evangeline Walton

JAMES GUNN'S 10 MOST INFLUENTIAL SF PEOPLE

B20

1 **H.G. Wells** Author — for demonstrating the literary potential of speculative materials — and its popularity.

2 **Jules Verne** Author — for demonstrating the popularity of technological adventure, and capturing the imaginations of succeeding generations of readers.

3 **Hugo Gernsback** Publisher, founder of *Amazing Stories* in 1926 — for the enthusiasm and entrepreneurial skills that created the science-fiction magazine and provided a place where it could build a genre.

4 **John W. Campbell, Jr** Editor of *Astounding/Analog,* 1937-71 — for recognising the potential of science fiction to deal with the problems of his times and for persuading a generation of writers to follow him into the golden age.

5 **Horace L. Gold** Editor of *Galaxy* 1950-59 — for redirecting science fiction writers towards narrative excitement and restoring Wellsian irony and wit to the genre.

6 **Robert A. Heinlein** Author — for developing new narrative techniques in order to describe background, particularly social background, for marrying story and theme, and for pioneering new media.

7 **Anthony Boucher** Editor of *F & SF* 1949-58 — for his gentle insistence in his magazine that science fiction could be and ought to be literature, and for nudging his writers into doing it that way.

8 **Edgar Rice Burroughs** Author — for turning millions of youthful readers toward the fantastic by the colour and vigour of his imagination.

9 **Isaac Asimov** Author — for exemplifying the narrative power of the rational mind at work, and for so clearly delighting in the writing process.

10 **Stanley Kubrick & George Lucas** Film makers — for demonstrating the potential of the science fiction and fantasy film.

H.G. Wells

JAMES GUNN'S IMPORTANT SF FILMS

James Gunn is noted as both a science fiction writer and academic. His books include *The Joy Makers* (1961) and *The Immortals* (1962) as well as an illustrated history of science fiction *Alternate Worlds* (1975) and a three-volume anthology reprinting examples of sf from its long history *The Road to Science Fiction* (1977/79). More recently he turned his attention to the sf cinema and has produced his own list of milestones. It first appeared in the February 1980 issue of *Isaac Asimov's Science Fiction Magazine.*

Still From 'The ? Motorist'

1898 **An Astronomer's Dream**
1899 **She**
1902 **A Trip to the Moon**
1906 **The ? Motorist**
1909 **A Trip to Jupiter**
1910 **A Trip to Mars**
1919 **The First Men in the Moon**
1924 **Aeleta**
1925 **The Lost World**
1926 **Metropolis**
1930 **Just Imagine**
1931 **Frankenstein**
1932 **The Island of Lost Souls**
1933 **King Kong**
The Invisible Man
Deluge
1934 **Transatlantic Tunnel**
1936 **Things to Come**
1936/40 **Flash Gordon & Buck Rogers serials**
1937 **Lost Horizon**
1950 **Destination Moon**
The Thing From Another World
The Day The Earth Stood Still
The Man in the White Suit

1951 When Worlds Collide
1953 The War of the Worlds
1954 1984
1955 20,000 Leagues Under the Sea
1956 Forbidden Planet
The Invasion of the Body Snatchers
1957 The Incredible Shrinking Man
1958 The Wonderful Invention
1960 The Time Machine
Village of the Damned
1963 The Day of the Triffids
1964 From the Earth to the Moon
Dr Strangelove
1965 The Tenth Victim
Alphaville
1966 Fahrenheit 451
Fantastic Voyage
1967 Barbarella
1968 2001: A Space Odyssey
Planet of the Apes
Charly
1970 Colossus: The Forbin Project
1971 A Clockwork Orange
The Andromeda Strain
THX 1138
1972 Silent Running
1973 West World
Soylent Green
1974 Young Frankenstein
Zardoz
1975 A Boy and His Dog
The Land That Time Forgot
Rollerball
The Stepford Wives
1976 The Food of the Gods
Futureworld
King Kong
Logan's Run
The Man Who Fell to Earth
1977 Close Encounters of the Third Kind
Demon Seed
The Island of Dr Moreau
The People That Time Forgot
Star Wars
Wizards
1978 The Invasion of the Bodysnatchers
Lord of the Rings
Superman
Watership Down
1979 Alien

ROBERT LOWNDES' 18 MOST IMPORTANT 'WONDER' STORIES

B22

Robert A.W. Lowndes became a professional sf editor in 1940 and remained in the field for the next thirty years. He was amongst the most popular editors of the 1950s with his magazines *Science Fiction Stories* and *Future SF* where he worked wonders on a miniscule budget. Lowndes is one of the few fans who has not only read, but oft re-read, all of the stories published in the pulp magazines during that all-important impressionable period of infancy, 1926-1937, after which John Campbell took sf by the scruff of the neck and shook it into maturity. I have called this pre-Campbell era the 'Wonder' period, because the stories are those that most evoke that 'sense of wonder', and because one of the most important publications at that time was *Wonder Stories.* Over to Mr Lowndes:

Most of the new writers in the sf magazines of the late 1930s and the 40s had been avid readers of the magazines in the late 1920s and early 30s. Many of them developed or worked variations of themes in stories they'd read in those earlier issues. Some of the themes noted in this list may have appeared in stories published in various magazines before March 1926, when the April *Amazing Stories* started the game; but it is their appearance for the first time in all-sf publications that was most effective. And not a few of these themes re-echo in today's science fiction.

1 **Beyond The Pole** A. Hyatt Verrill, *Amazing Stories* October-November 1926. First detailed exploration of a highly technological, non-humanoid civilization. (These were super-evolved, land-living lobsters here on Earth).

2 **The Machine-Man of Ardathia** Francis Flagg, *Amazing Stories* November 1927. Super-evolved humanity entirely dependent upon technological artifacts, etc. The 'machine man' cannot survive outside his mechanical cocoon.

3 **The Skylark of Space** Edward Elmer Smith, Ph.D., *Amazing Stories* August-October 1928. Interatomic energy, faster-than-light travel, intergalactic cruises uncovering human civilizations.

4 **Armageddon 2419 A.D.** Philip Francis Nowlan, *Amazing Stories* August 1928. One cannot deny the importance and influence of the story that sparked the radio show and comic strip, *Buck Rogers in the 25th Century.*

5 **The Shot Into Infinity** Otto Willi Gail, *Science Wonder Quarterly* Fall 1929. From then on, rocket propulsion became *the* means of interplanetary travel; gravity-screens, etc, faded away.

Illustration From 'The Skylark Of Space'

6 **The City of the Living Dead** Laurence Manning and Fletcher Pratt, *Science Wonder Stories* May 1930. Introducing the dream machine and the ultimate in turning on and dropping out.

7 **Paradise and Iron** Miles J. Breuer, MD., *Amazing Stories Quarterly* Summer 1930. A mechanical civilization in which the non-humanoid machines have taken over — but not a direct 'revolt' of the machines.

8 **The Revolt of the Machines** Nathan Schachner and Arthur Leo Zagat, *Astounding Stories* July 1931. Here the non-humanoid 'master machine' decides to elimate humanity.

9 **The Exile of Time** Ray Cummings, *Astounding Stories* April-July 1931. Conflict through various periods in time, plus a revolt of humanoid machines (robots).

10 **The Jameson Satellite** Neil R. Jones, *Amazing Stories* July 1931. A Man becomes immortal through having his brain put into a mechanical 'body'.

11 **A Conquest of Two Worlds** Edmond Hamilton, *Wonder Stories* February 1932. The first portrayal of ugly Earthmen destroying harmless alien cultures on other planets, out of greed.

12 **Ancestral Voices** Nathan Schachner, *Astounding Stories* December 1933. The first use of science fiction to deal directly with a current social problem (theories of racial 'purity' and superiority); the 'timely' story. (A good thing?).

13 **A Martian Odyssey** Stanley G. Weinbaum, *Wonder Stories* July 1934. The first alien creature equal to humans in intelligence, but largely incomprehensible; it 'thinks' like a man — but 'thinks' differently.

14 **Old Faithful** Raymond Z. Gallun, *Astounding Stories* December 1934. Empathic relations and successful co-operation between an alien non-humanoid being on another planet and humans here on Earth.

15 **Proxima Centauri** Murray Leinster, *Astounding Stories* March

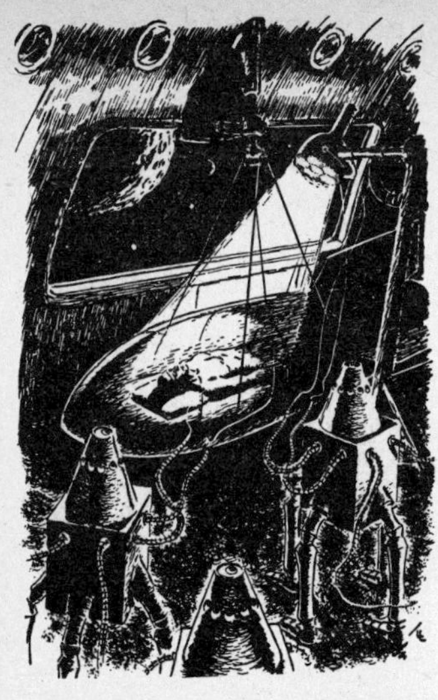

1935. The first generation spaceship en route to a star.

16 **The Escape** Don A. Stuart (John W. Campbell) *Astounding Stories* May 1935. Lovers in revolt against 'scientifically selected' mates, are psychologically reconditioned to accept and enjoy the situation. The author defies you to prove that it *isn't* a happy ending.

17 **The Phantom Dictator** Wallace West, *Astounding Stories* August 1935. Control of people through subliminal suggestions on a cartoon film, anticipating *The Hidden Persuaders* by nearly twenty years.

18 **Galactic Patrol** Edward E. Smith, Ph.D., *Astounding Stories* September 1937-February 1938. Inertialess drives make galactic civilizations and empires possible.

Illustration From 'The Jameson Satellite'

ANNE McCAFFREY'S 10 WRITERS WHO MOST INFLUENCED HER DEVELOPMENT AS A WRITER

B23

Anne McCaffrey is known to millions as the writer of the Dragon books including *Dragonflight* and *Dragonquest. The White Dragon* has already sold in excess of a million copies, and the whole series (with number seven in progress at this moment) is destined to become one of the great works of this (and any other) century. The following list is not in any order of preference. You could say, for different reasons, they are all firsts.

1 **Rudyard Kipling**
— the first influence in my life.
2 **Austin Tappan Wright**
— the keener influence.
3 **James Blish**
4 **Robert Silverberg**
5 **Randall Garrett**
6 **Keith Laumer**
7 **James H. Schmitz**
8 **Harlan Ellison**
9 **Gordon R. Dickson**
10 **Poul Anderson**

(As a postscript to those who do not know Austin Tappan Wright (1883-1931), he wrote a mammoth work, creating a whole society with its fables, family genealogies, the lot, in the years before Tolkien. The book was *Islandia* published in 1942).

PATRICK MOORE'S 10 FAVOURITE SF NOVELS

B24

Although renowned as an astronomer and television personality, it might not be realised that Patrick Moore has a keen interest in science fiction, having written several books for young readers such as *The Frozen Plant* (1954) and *Caverns of the Moon* (1964), and a survey of science fiction called *Science and Fiction* (1957).

1 **Last and First Men**
Olaf Stapledon
2 **Star Maker**
Olaf Stapledon
3 **Journey to the Centre of the Earth**
Jules Verne
4 **From the Earth to the Moon and Round It**
Jules Verne
5 **The Time Machine**
H.G. Wells
6 **The First Men in the Moon**
Jules Verne
7 **The Sands of Mars**
Arthur C. Clarke
8 **I, Robot**
Isaac Asimov
9 **The Chrysalids**
John Wyndham
10 **A Son of the Stars**
Fenton Ash (I read this when I was ten, and I still think it's a superb boys' yarn!)

(Note about Fenton Ash. This was a pseudonym used by both father and son Francis Atkins Sr. and Jr. It has never been satisfactorily concluded who wrote what, and as Patrick Moore read this story after the death of both writers it was thus probably a reprint. F. Atkins, Sr. (1847-1927) started writing in 1895 as Frank Aubrey with *The Devil Tree of El Dorado*; F. Atkins, Jr. wrote with his father as Fenton Ash, and wrote on his own as F. St. Mars. Jr. died in 1921 aged only 38.)

From 'The First Men In The Moon'

LARRY NIVEN'S 9 SF IDEAS WHICH ARE NOW IMPOSSIBLE

B25

Every planet in the solar system has suffered the depredations of the probes:

1 Mercury isn't a one-face world.
2 Venus isn't a swamp.
3 The Moon doesn't have an atmosphere on the back side.
4 Mars has almost no atmosphere and no canals.
5 Jupiter's radiation belt makes it damn difficult to get close.
6 Every description of Saturn's rings is now obsolete or incomplete.
Never mind. Every batch of new information generates new stories:

Larry Niven

Clarke's *A Meeting With Medusa,* or anything by John Varley. Remember Saturn's braided ring? Watch for *Footfall* from me and Jerry Pournelle, around September 1983. Most of these obsolete ideas are subject of fiddling. Obsolete solar planets may still circle other stars — see Poul Anderson's *The Day of Their Return* for his version of what Barsoom should have looked like.

7 You can't have invisibility, but you can have mobile spy-cameras the size of a housefly.

8 You can't have tractor beams or antigravity, but you can have gravity generators and gravity-wave beams that will do most of what you thought you wanted.

9 Under normal circumstances you can't have people floating through interplanetary space in bikinis; but see my novel *The Smoke Ring* in a couple of years.

MICHAEL PARRY'S 16 SF & FANTASY FILM DIRECTORS AND THEIR BEST FILMS

B26

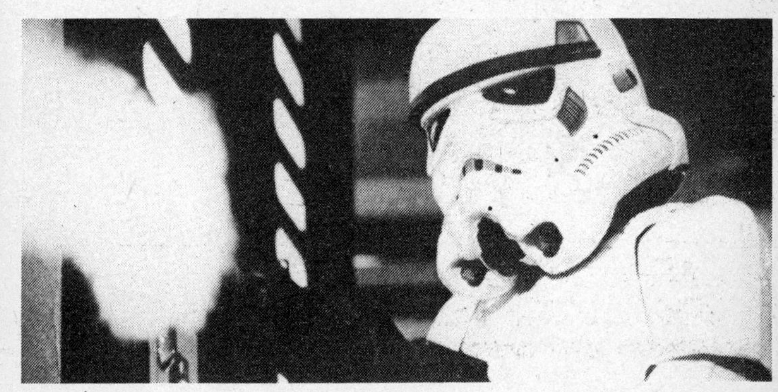

Still From 'Star Wars'

Michel Parry is one of Britain's most prolific anthologists of horror stories and a budding screenwriter. It was, in fact, his knowledge of the film industry — which was reflected in his anthologies *The Rivals of Dracula, The Rivals of King Kong* and so on — that prompted the following four categories. First, the film directors and their films. None of these lists, by the way, is in any special order.

1 **The Incredible Shrinking Man**
Jack Arnold
2 **Raiders of the Lost Ark**
Steven Spielberg
3 **Tom Thumb**
George Pal
4 **The Tomb of Ligeia**
Roger Corman
5 **Night of the Living Dead**
George Romero
6 **Metropolis**
Fritz Lang
7 **Star Wars**
George Lucas
8 **The Thief of Bagdad**
Michael Powell (co-director)
9 **Escape from New York**
John Carpenter
10 **The Time Bandits**
Terry Gilliam
11 **The Inauguration of the Pleasure Dome**
Kenneth Anger
12 **Eraserhead**
David Lynch
13 **Scanners**
David Cronenberg
14 **Carrie**
Brian Da Palma
15 **The Mysterians**
Ishoshiro Honda
16 **Suspiria**
Dario Argento

MICHEL PARRY'S 10 FAVOURITE SF & FANTASY FILMS

B27

1 **The Thief of Baghdad**
(1940 version)
2 **The Wizard of Oz**
3 **Performance**
4 **Eraserhead**
5 **The Forbidden Planet**
6 **Star Wars**
7 **Raiders of the Lost Ark**
8 **King Kong**
9 **Suspiria**
10 **Things to Come**

MICHEL PARRY'S 15 WORST SF & FANTASY FILMS

B28

1 **Cat Women of the Moon**
2 **The Astro-Zombies**
3 **Moon Zero Two**
4 **The Dead One**
5 **Slithis**
6 **Dracula versus Frankenstein**
7 **The Cape Canaveral Monsters**
6 **Dracula versus Frankenstein**
7 **The Cape Canaveral Monsters**
8 **The Final Programme**
9 **Who?**
10 **Frankenstein's Daughter**
11 **Prey**
12 **The Body Stealers**
13 **The Clones of Bruce Lee**
14 **The Terrornauts**
15 **Outer Touch** (aka *S.E.C.K.S.*)

Still From 'Moon Zero Two'

MICHEL PARRY'S 10 ENJOYABLY BAD SF & FANTASY FILMS

B29

1 Plan Nine from Outer Space
2 Robot Monster
3 Night of the Blood Beast
4 Attack of the Crab Monsters
5 Star Crash
6 Matango, Fungus of Terror
7 Bride of the Monster
8 The Humanoid
9 Queen of Outer Space
10 Invasion of the Saucer People

THE 10 LAST LINES GEORGE SCITHERS HOPES HE'S SEEN THE LAST OF

B30

George Scithers was the editor of *Isaac Asimov's Science Fiction Magazine* and, like every editor worth his salt, can tell instantly from the first and last lines of a story whether it has any potential or whether it's another pot of cliches. In the February 16th 1981 issue of *Asimov's,* George produced a list of last lines that he hoped he'd never see again.

1 '...but it was all a dream!'
2 '...and then the Sun went nova!'
3 '...for the horrible monsters were really from Earth!'
4 '...and so, Eve, we'll have to populate this empty planet.'
5 '...I'm calling this planet I created in school, Earth!'
6 '...for the time-traveller had *caused* what he had travelled through time to prevent!'
7 '...but — but you mean I'm already dead?'
8 '...for the invaders' spaceship was too small to notice!'
9 '...they were really unborn babies!' (ants, frogs, robots or giant lobsters)
10 '...for it was the evil extraterrestrials that had made them all go made.' (or wage war, or invent science fiction, or develop rocketry!)

ROBERT SILVERBERG'S 10 FAVOURITE OF HIS OWN BOOKS

B31

Since Silverberg ranks as one of the most prolific sf writers in the world, and has been nominated for more Awards than any other writer, it seemed a good idea to see which of his many, many books, he liked the best. The following list could thus serve as a neophyte's introduction to Silverberg. Over to Mr Silverberg:

My ten favourites? All right, I'll try — in no particular order —

1 **Dying Inside**
2 **Book of Skulls**
3 **Born With the Dead**
4 **The World Inside**
5 **Son of Man**
6 **Tower of Glass**
7 **Capricorn Games** (short story)
8 **Sundance**
9 **Nightwings**
10 **Downward to the Earth**

That's today. I might have a slightly different list next week.

JACK WILLIAMSON'S 10 FAVOURITE WORKS OF H.G. WELLS

B32

Not only is Jack Williamson one of sf's pioneers and foremost writers, but he is an expert on the works of H.G. Wells. His Ph.D thesis was later expanded and published as *H.G. Wells: Critic of Progress* (1973).

1 **The Time Machine**
2 **The War of the Worlds**
3 **First Men in the Moon**
4 **The Island of Dr Moreau**
5 **The Invisible Man**
6 **When the Sleeper Wakes**
7 **The Country of the Blind**
8 **The Man Who Could Work Miracles**
9 **Experiment In Autobiography**
10 **Discovery of the Future**

Jack Williamson adds: 'I regard Wells as the principal founder of modern science fiction. He had two things going for him: a genius for the creation of great fiction, that he tended to neglect and even to disown through the latter part of his career, and a knowledge of Darwinian evolution, gained during the year that he was a student of T.H. Huxley, which gave him a rationale for thinking about the future of man as an evolving species, that was new to literature.'

JACK WILLIAMSON'S 10 MOST OPTIMISTIC FUTURES

B33

When I used to teach science fiction, I liked to select class readings that could be discussed as briefs, pro and con, on the benefits of technology, the shape of man's future, the stature of man himself, as master of his destiny or victim of misguided cleverness. Most of these titles would go on my utopian list — as opposed to the dystopias, which are often more popular and more powerful as drama. (Bad news is more dramatic than good news.)

1 Plato's **Republic**
2 Thomas More's **Utopia**
3 Edward Bellamy's **Looking Backward**
4 Olaf Stapledon's **First and Last Men**
5 Arthur C. Clarke's **The City and the Stars**
6 Robert A. Heinlein's **Have Spacesuit — Will Travel**
7 Isaac Asimov's **I, Robot**
8 Clifford D. Simak's **City**
9 Gene Wolfe's **The Shadow of the Torturer**
10 Jack Williamson's **The Equalizer**

THE 10 STORIES FREDERIK POHL IS MOST PLEASED TO HAVE BOUGHT AS AN EDITOR

B34

Frederik Pohl, as you will see elsewhere in this book, has been associated with editing, either of magazines and anthologies or as a consultant editor to a publishing house, from his late teens until very recently. He won the Hugo Award for three successive years on behalf of *If* in the mid-1960s when he was editor. Of the following he commented that they aren't necessarily the best, but just the ones that he is most glad to have bought — for varying reasons.

1 **Skylark DuQuesne** by E.E. Smith, Ph.D. (serialised in *If* June-October 1965)
2 **Dhalgren** by Samuel R. Delany (Bantam Books, New York, 1974)
3 **Let There Be Light** by Robert A. Heinlein (*Super Science Stories* May 1940, under the alias Lyle Monroe)
4 **The Moon is a Harsh Mistress** by Robert A. Heinlein (serialised in *If* December 1965-April 1966)
5 **The Dragon Masters** by Jack Vance (*Galaxy* August 1962)
6 **Into the Darkness** by Ross Rocklynne (*Astonishing Stories* June 1940)

Fred Pohl

7 **Genus Homo** by L. Sprague de Camp and P. Schuyler Miller (*Super Science Novels Magazine* March 1941)
8 **The Ballad of Lost C'Mell** by Cordwainer Smith (*Galaxy* October 1962)
9 **Country Doctor** by William Morrison (*Star SF Stories*, Ballantine Books, New York, 1953)
10 **For I Am a Jealous People** by Lester del Rey (*Star Short Novels*, Ballantine Books, New York, 1954)

BAIRD SEARLES' 20 BEST SF AND FANTASY FILMS EVER MADE

B35

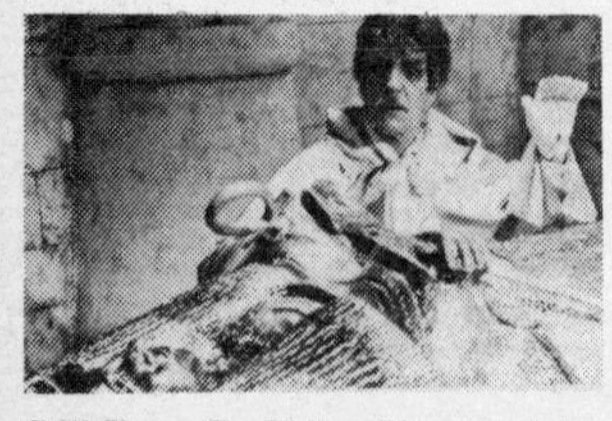
Still From 'Dr Phibes Rises Again'

Science Fiction

1 **2001: A Space Odyssey**
2 **Star Wars**
3 **Star Trek — The Motion Picture**
4 **THX — 1138**
5 **The Empire Strikes Back**
6 **Zardoz**
7 **The Thing**
8 **Things to Come**
9 **Frankenstein**
10 **On the Beach**

Fantasy

1 **Beauty and the Beast** (Cocteau)
2 **Fantasia**
3 **Tales of Hoffman**
4 **Orpheus** (Cocteau)
5 **The Emperor's Nightingale** (Trnka)
6 **Stairway to Heaven**
7 **Dr Phibes Rises Again**
8 **Carnival of Souls**
9 **The Innocents**
10 **The Picture of Dorian Gray**

Other authors nominated their favourite films, including:

Brian W. Aldiss: **Solaris**
John Brunner: **La Voie Lactee** (Bunuel)
Larry Niven: sf **Dark Star** and **Star Wars**;
fantasy **Time Bandits** and **Carrie**

BAIRD SEARLES' 12 MOST MEMORABLE LINES FROM SF FILMS

B36

Apart from being one of the proprietors of The Science Fiction Shop in New York, Baird Searles reviews films regularly for *The Magazine of Fantasy & Science Fiction* and books for *Isaac Asimov's SF Magazine*.

1 'For me, it started last Thursday.' (Kevin McCarthy in *Invasion of the Body Snatchers)*
2 'There's a herd of killer rabbits on the way here.' (Stuart Whitman in *Night of the Lepus)*
3 'Easy enough to talk of soul, spirit, and essential worth, but not when you're three feet tall.' (Grant Williams in *The Incredible Shrinking Man)*
4 'All the universe — nothingness — Which shall it be, Passworthy?' (Raymond Massey in *Things to Come)*
5 'The city is infested with killer cockroaches!' (Paul Winfield in *Damnation Alley)*
6 'It's alive! It's alive!' (Colin Clive in *Frankenstein)*
7 'Let the dead stay dead.' (Boris Karloff in *Bride of Frankenstein)*
8 'I know I've made some mistakes lately.' (Douglas Rain (Hal) in *2001: A Space Odyssey)*
9 'Star sapphires take a week to crystallize. Will diamonds or emeralds do?' (Robbie the Robot in *Forbidden Planet)*
10 'I hate dat qveen!' (Zsa-Zsa Gabor in *Queen of Outer Space)*
11 'Man see, man do.' (Maurice Evans in *Planet of the Apes)*
12 'They're coming to get you, Barbara!' (Keith Wayne (?) in *Night of the Living Dead)*

Robbie The Robot In 'Forbidden Planet'

A few others nominated their favourite lines from films:

Brian W Aldiss: 'An intellectual carrot? The mind boggles.' (the reporter in *It Came From Outer Space*)
John Brunner: 'No, the use of nuclear weapons is out of the question in *any* built-up area!' (the brigadier on the phone to HQ in *Gorgo*)
Larry Niven: 'Any good quantum mechanic could fix that.' (from *Forbidden Planet*)

MARY ELIZABETH COUNSELMAN'S 10 FAVOURITE WEIRD TALES

B37

Mary Elizabeth Counselman was the queen of *Weird Tales* with thirty stories appearing in its pages including *The Three Marked Pennies* (1934), voted as one of the most popular stories the magazine ever published. Some of her stories have been collected in *Half in Shadow*.

1 **Rats in the Wall** by H.P. Lovecraft (March 1924) This was my introduction to *Weird Tales* read aloud at a lake cottage by an early-early fan club in Tallahassee, where my Dad was superintendent of schools.

2 **The Watcher in the Green Room** by Hugh B. Cave (September 1933) I never clear out a bureau now without a shudder.

3 **The Return of Andrew Bentley** by August Derleth and Mark Schorer(September 1933) This one for a descriptive adjective — 'flaffing' — that set me off 'creating' expressive words where Roget offered none.

4 **Shambleau** by C.L. Moore (November 1933) I didn't really like spacies until I fell in love with C.L.'s Northwest Smith and later wrote a few of my own for *Planet*.

5 **The Beast of Averoigne** by Clark Ashton Smith (May 1933) This is the original 'atomic beast', so dear to the bombed Japanese. C.A.S. wrote many more that I loved, besides this.

6 **Wings in the Night** by Robert E. Howard (July 1932) Bob and I both seemed to dig pterodactyls, but I beat him to it with a third grade 'first bird' tome that horrified my bird-watching teacher!

7 **The Hand of Glory** by Seabury Quinn (July 1933) I loved all of Sea's de Grandin (his mother's maiden name) stories, but this legend intrigued me most.

8 **Revelations in Black** by Carl Jacobi (April 1933) Carl's vampire story hit me so hard, I later bound a tear-out of it from his paperback, exactly as his vampire's evil book was described in the yarn.

9 **Mrs Lorriquer** by Henry S. Whitehead (April 1932) I think Henry invented the 'zombie cocktail' with his jumbee tales. But this yarn leaves a worse hangover!!

10 **Slime** by Joseph Payne Brennan (March 1953) Joe's eerie descriptions in all his tales and poems 'send me', but this one tops all of them for sheer 'grue'!

ROBERT A HEINLEIN'S 5 RULES FOR SUCCESS IN WRITING

B38

Robert A. Heinlein is the most popular and probably the most successful of all science fiction writers. Back in 1947 he contributed an article *On the Writing of Speculative Fiction* to a symposium edited by Lloyd A. Eshbach entitled *Of Worlds Beyond*, and he included these five rules as part of that article. In 1973 Heinlein delivered the James Forrestal Memorial Lecture to the Brigade of Midshipman at his *alma mater*, the U.S. Naval Academy at Annapolis. Entitled *Channel Markers* his talk included these same five rules, unaltered. Clearly Heinlein felt the rules had stood the test of over twenty-five years and are as relevant now as ever. Here they are:

1. You must **write.**
2. You must **finish** what you write.
3. You must refrain from rewriting except to editorial order.
4. You must put it on the market.
5. You must keep it on the market until sold.

'That's all,' Heinlein adds. 'That's a sure-fire formula for getting anything — anything at all! — published. But so seldom does anyone follow all five rules that the profession of writing is a soft touch for those who do — even though most professional writers are not too bright, not too wise, not too creative.'

If you want to read the whole of Heinlein's speech — the speech that inspired John Varley to write and was directly responsible for his appearance — it was reprinted in the January 1974 *Analog.*

* *1947, 1973 for Robert A. Heinlein.*

THE 10 BOOKS MARION ZIMMER BRADLEY WOULD MOST LIKE TO HAVE WRITTEN HERSELF

B39

Although Marion Zimmer Bradley has long been a much respected and popular writer in the United States she has only recently begun to establish herself in Britain with her long-running series of novels set on the Planet Darkover.

1. **Quicksand**
   John Brunner
2. **The Mask of Circe**
   C.L. Moore
3. **The Starmen of Llyrdis**
   Leigh Brackett
4. **The King Must Die**
   Mary Renault
5. **Dracula**
   Bram Stoker
6. **The Hound of the Baskervilles**
   Conan Doyle
7. **Jane Eyre**
   Charlotte Bronte
8. **Don't Bite The Sun**
   Tanith Lee
9. **The Sea Priestess**
   Dion Fortune
10. **The Dispossessed**
    Ursula K. LeGuin

...AND THE 10 BOOKS THAT HAVE INFLUENCED MARION ZIMMER BRADLEY

B40

1. **The King in Yellow**
   Robert W. Chambers
2. **More Than Human**
   Theodore Sturgeon
3. **She, Ayesha, Wisdom's Daughter** (trilogy)
   H. Rider Haggard
4. **The Devil's Guard**
   Talbot Mundy
5. **Dracula**
   Bram Stoker
6. **Islandia**
   Austin Tappan Wright
7. **The Lovers**
   Philip Jose Farmer
8. **Odd John**
   Olaf Stapledon

9 **The Dwellers In The Mirage**
and all works by A. Merritt

10 **The Dark World**
C.L. Moore (yes, I know the name it was published under was Henry Kuttner, but Catherine wrote it.)

RICHARD A. LUPOFF'S ALTERNATIVE HEROES

B41

Dick Lupoff has his fingers in so many pies that it's a wonder he has any left with which to type. An innovative author (take a look at *One Million Centuries, Sacred Locomotive Flies* and *Sword of the Demon),* a stalwart critic and reviewer, a keen researcher (try *Edgar Rice Burroughs: Master of Adventure)* and an anthologist. It is the latter finger-in-pie that concerns us here. Lupoff has so far assembled four volumes in his anthology series *What If?* which contains those stories which he felt should have won the Hugo Award during the years 1952 and 1978. I asked Dick if he would extend the list back in time and imagine what stories would have won the Hugo Award if one had existed from the year of the first science fiction magazine — *Amazing Stories* — in 1926. By combining the two lists we now have a complete run down on the alternative Hugos.

1926 'Through the Vortex'
Donald E. Keyhoe
(Weird Tales)

1927 'Evolution Island'
Edmond Hamilton
(Weird Tales)

1928 'The Miracle of the Lily'
Clare Winger Harris
(Amazing Stories)

1929 'The Dunwich Horror'
H.P. Lovecraft *(Weird Tales)*

1930 'A Visitor From Egypt'
Frank Belknap Long
(Weird Tales)

1931 'Through the Purple Cloud'
Jack Williamson
(Wonder Stories)

1932 'The Space Coffin'
A. Rowley Hilliard
(Wonder Stories)

1933 'Shambleau'
C.L. Moore *(Weird Tales)*

1934 'The Literary Corkscrew'
David H. Keller, MD.
(Wonder Stories)

1935 'Star Ship Invincible'
Frank K. Kelly
(Astounding Stories)

1936 'A Rival From The Grave'
Seabury Quinn *(Weird Tales)*

1937 'The Resurrection of Jimber Jaw'
Edgar Rice Burroughs *(Argosy)*

1938 'Exiles From the Universe'
Stanton A. Coblentz *(Amazing)*

1939 'None But Lucifer'
H.L. Gold & L. Sprague de Camp *(Unknown)*

1940 'Farewell to the Master'
Harry Bates *(Astounding)*

1941 'The Vortex Blaster'
E.E. Smith, Ph.D.
(Cosmic Stories)

1942 'Via Jupiter'
Gordon A. Giles (Otto Binder)
(Thrilling Wonder)

1943 'Frontier Planet'
Manly Wade Wellman
(Thrilling Wonder)

1944 'And the Gods Laughed'
Fredric Brown *(Planet Stories)*

1945 'First Contact'
Murray Leinster
(Astounding SF)

1946 'The Chronokinesis of Jonathan Hull'
Anthony Boucher *(Astounding)*

1947 'The Fires Within'
Arthur C. Clarke *(Fantasy)*

1948 'Mars is Heaven'
Ray Bradbury *(Planet Stories)*

1949 **'Gulf'**
Robert A. Heinlein *(Astounding SF)*

1950 **'Bindlestiff'**
James Blish *(Astounding SF)*

1951 **'Common Denominator'**
John D. MacDonald *(Galaxy)*

1952 **'Firewater'**
William Tenn *(Astounding SF)*

1953 **'Four In One'**
Damon Knight *(Galaxy)*

1954 **'The Golden Helix'**
Theodore Sturgeon *(Thrilling Wonder)*

1955 **'One Ordinary Day, With Peanuts'**
Shirley Jackson *(F & SF)*

1956 **'The Man Who Came Early'**
Poul Anderson *(F & SF)*

1957 **'The Mile-Long Spaceship'**
Kate Wilhelm *(Astounding SF)*

1958 **'Two Dooms'**
Cyril M. Kornbluth *(Venture)*

1959 **'The Pi Man'**
Alfred Bester *(F & SF)*

1960 **'The Lost Kafoozalum'**
Pauline Ashwell *(Analog)*

1961 **'The Sources of the Nile'**
Avram Davidson *(F & SF)*

1962 **'Where Is The Bird of Fire?'**
Thomas Burnett Swann *(Science Fantasy)*

1963 **'Stand-by'**
Philip K. Dick *(Amazing Stories)*

1964 **'Now Is Forever'**
Thomas M. Disch *(Amazing Stories)*

1965 **'All The King's Men'**
Barrington J. Bayley *(New Worlds)*

1966 **'Light of Other Days'**
Bob Shaw *(Analog)*

1967 **'The Star Pit'**
Samuel R. Delany *(Worlds of Tomorrow)*

1968 **'The Barbarian'**
Joanna Russ *(Orbit 3)*

1969 **'Sundance'**
Robert Silverberg (F & SF)

1970 **'The Island of Doctor Death and Other Stories'**
Gene Wolfe *(Orbit 7)*

1971 **'Vaster Than Empires, and More Slow'**
Ursula K. LeGuin *(New Dimensions)*

1972 **'Painwise'**
James Tiptree, Jr. *(F & SF)*

1973 **'My Brother Leopold'**
Edgar Pangborn *(An Exaltation of Stars)*

1974 **'Pale Roses'**
Michael Moorcock *(New Worlds)*

1975 **'Retrograde Summer'**
John Varley *(F & SF)*

1976 **'Piper at the Gates of Dawn'**
Richard Cowper *(F & SF)*

1977 **'Aztecs'**
Vonda N. McIntyre *(2076: The American Tricentennial)*

1978 **'The Very Slow Time Machine'**
Ian Watson *(Anticipations)*

STANLEY SCHMIDT'S 10 SF BOOKS FOR SCIENTISTS

B42

Stanley Schmidt is the current editor of science fiction's leading magazine, *Analog,* having taken over from Ben Bova in 1978. He commented on the following lists by stating that neither is intended to be definitive.

1. **The Mote in God's Eye**
Jery Pournelle & Larry Niven
2. **Dune**
Frank Herbert
3. **The Moon is a Harsh Mistress**
Robert A. Heinlein
4. **The Daleth Effect**
Harry Harrison
5. **More Than Human**
Theodore Sturgeon
6. **The World of Null-A**
A.E. van Vogt
7. **The Foundation Trilogy**
Isaac Asimov
8. **Tau Zero** (or **The People of the Wind,** or...) Poul Anderson
9. **Mission of Gravity**
Hal Clement
10. **The Black Cloud**
Fred Hoyle

STANLEY SCHMIDT'S 20 FAVOURITE STORIES FROM ASTOUNDING/ANALOG

B43

When I asked Stan if he could select his ten favourite he retorted 'Impossible, sir!', but proceeded to do two sets of ten. The first below represents those that he personally likes and which also enjoy wide popularity, and the second ten are some that he liked but seem generally relatively unknown.

1 **The Lotus Eaters**
Stanley G. Weinbaum (April 1935)
2 **Placet is a Crazy Place**
Fredric Brown (May 1946)
3 **E For Effort**
T.L. Sherred (May 1947)
4 **Ex Machina**
Lewis Padgett (April 1948)
5 **In Hiding**
Wilmar Shiras (November 1948)
6 **Light of Other Days**
Bob Shaw (August 1966)
7 **The Dead Past**
Isaac Asimov (April 1956)
8 **City**
Clifford D. Simak (May 1944)
9 **The Cold Equations**
Tom Godwin (August 1954)
10 **Thunder and Roses**
Theodore Sturgeon (November 1947)

and then...
1 **The Chromium Helmet**
Theodore Sturgeon (June 1946)
2 **Transfusion**
Chad Oliver (June 1959)
3 **Now Inhale**
Eric Frank Russell (April 1959)
4 **Despoilers of the Golden Empire**
David Gordon (March 1959)
5 **Peek! I See You!**
Poul Anderson (February 1968)
6 **Hi Diddle Diddle**
Peter E. Abresch (September 1968)
7 **Gone With the Gods**
Andrew J. Offutt (October 1974)
8 **Ravenshaw of WBY, Inc**
W. Macfarlane (March 1970)
9 **Local Effect**
D.L. Hughes (April 1968)
10 **The Gentle Earth**
Christopher Anvil (November 1957)

Stanley Schmidt also drew attention to two recent stories by new writers that he considered remarkable and especially striking for one reason or another:
1 **Emergence**
David R. Palmer (January 5, 1981)
2 **Petals of Rose**
Marc Stiegler (November 9, 1981)

ROGER ZELAZNY'S 10 FAVOURITE MYSTERIES

B44

Roger Zelazny burst on the sf scene in the early sixties and within a few years was scooping up all the awards. He's at home in the sf field as he is in fantasy and anyone who has read such books as *My Name is Legion* will see how much he has been influenced by some of the greatest detective writers, hence the following list.

1. **The Bride Wore Black**
   Cornell Woolrich
2. **Drink to Yesterday**
   Manning Coles
3. **A Toast to Tomorrow**
   Manning Coles
4. **The Big Sleep**
   Raymond Chandler
5. **Some Buried Caesar**
   Rex Stout
6. **Rogue Male**
   Geoffrey Household
7. **Daughter of Time**
   Josephine Tey
8. **The Thief Who Couldn't Sleep**
   Lawrence Block
9. **Night of Wenceslaus**
   Lionel Davidson
10. **Dance Hall of the Dead**
    Tony Hillerman

Illustration From 'The Island Of Captain Sparrow' A36

SECTION C
THE RECORDHOLDERS

In which we learn who are the most prolific writers, who are the oldest, youngest, most pseudonymous, most honoured, and discover what is the longest and shortest work of sf, and many other record-breaking feats.

THE MOST PROLIFIC WRITERS

This is not an easy category to assess, and I must say straight away that I have made no attempt to gauge total output by wordage. What I have done is assessed output firstly by novels, then by short stories, and then combined the two. Novels cover all works over 40,000 words whether or not published in book-form. Works are only counted once, so that if a story is later revised as a novel, I've counted it once only as a novel and not as a story. Similarly if three or four short stories are revised to form a novel, that also counts as one novel and the stories are excluded from the story total. Where a novel has been substantially revised for a later publication I have included a separate entry, but it did have to constitute a major rewrite.

In the first two lists I've allocated one point to a solo novel or story, and half a point for a revised novel or one written in collaboration.

I have only counted science fiction, fantasy and the supernatural and have excluded mystery, horror and other output. I have tried to be accurate throughout but being only almost human I think it would be safe to allow for a one or two per cent error either way.

One word on Lester Dent. The *Doc Savage* magazine novels grew shorter over the years and when the magazine went digest they dropped to under 40,000 words. I've only counted therefore those over 40,000 and the remainder have been added in with short fiction. I've excluded the three novels known to have been ghosted for Dent by another writer. There may have been more.

THE 12 MOST PROLIFIC SF & FANTASY NOVELISTS C1

	Novelist	Solo Novels	Revisions	Collab. Novels	Total Novels	Points
1	**Lionel Fanthorpe**	121	—	—	121	121
2	**Lester Dent**	117	—	—	117	117
3	**John Russell Fearn**	117	—	—	117	117
4	**E.C. Tubb**	89	—	—	89	89
5	**Andre Norton**	76	—	5	81	78½
6	**Kenneth Bulmer**	77	—	2	79	78
7	**John Brunner**	55	9	—	64	59½
8	**Edgar Rice Burroughs**	56	—	—	56	56
9	**Lin Carter**	47	—	4	51	49
10	**Michael Moorcock**	48	—	2	50	49
11	**H. Rider Haggard**	48	—	1	49	48½
12	**Robert Silverberg**	46	2	2	50	48

In thirteenth place and clearly destined to rise higher is Poul Anderson with 47½ points out of forty-nine volumes. You may have noticed I have excluded

the German Perry Rhodan team from the listing for obvious reasons. A writing committee is equal to working with four or more collaborators and if one takes this into account their phenomenal output takes on less awesome proportions. Nevertheless on a single book-by-book count writers like Walter Ernsting and William Vortz would be way in excess of any on this list.

Luis Senarens is excluded because although he wrote in excess of 180 sf 'dime novels' they were under the 40,000 word limit.

Lionel Fanthorpe

THE 12 MOST PROLIFIC SF & FANTASY SHORT STORY WRITERS

C2

	Writer	Solo Stories	Collab. Stories	Total	Points
1	**Lord Dunsany**	415	—	415	374*
2	**Robert Silverberg**	301	33	334	317½
3	**Lionel Fanthorpe**	265	—	265	265
4	**Robert Bloch**	238	8	246	242
5	**Poul Anderson**	218	17	235	226½
6	**E.C. Tubb**	220	—	220	220
7	**Edmond Hamilton**	205	—	205	205
8	**Henry Kuttner**	187	32	219	203
9	**Brian W. Aldiss**	193	—	193	193
10	**Fritz Leiber**	190	—	190	190
11	**August Derleth**	171	37	208	189½
12	**Algernon Blackwood**	182	—	182	182

*Lord Dunsany's total output includes at least eighty-two stories that are only about a hundred or two hundred words. These squibs hardly count as stories and for that reason I've only allocated them a half point.

Some stories are credited as collaborations although the author is only acknowledging the source of the idea for the story. The writing was done wholly by the one person. This is true in the

Lord Dunsany

case of some 'collaborations' by August Derleth, Poul Anderson and Algernon Blackwood, and these stories are listed as solo efforts.

THE 12 MOST PROLIFIC SF & FANTASY WRITERS

C3

In combining the novel and short story outputs I've amended the points system to acknowledge the differential between writing a novel and a short tale. The columns and the points are as follows.

A: **Solo novels** — 3 points
B: **Revised novels** — 1½ points (half of A)
C: **Collaborative novels** — 1½ points
D: **Solo stories** — 1 point
E: **Collaborative stories**— ½ point

	Author	A	B	C	D	E	Total	Points
1	**Lionel Fanthorpe**	121	—	—	265	—	386	628
2	**John Russell Fearn**	117	—	—	164	—	281	515
3	**E.C. Tubb**	89	—	—	220	—	309	487
4	**Robert Silverberg**	46	2	2	301	33	384	461½
5	**Lord Dunsany**	8	—	—	415	—	423	398
6	**Lester Dent**	117	—	—	45	—	162	396
7	**Poul Anderson**	46	—	3	218	17	284	369
8	**Kenneth Bulmer**	77	—	2	91	1	171	325½
9	**Edmond Hamilton**	39	—	—	205	—	244	322
10	**John Brunner**	55	9	—	116	—	180	294½
11	**Robert Moore Williams**	31	—	—	177	—	208	270
12	**Murray Leinster**	35	—	—	156	—	191	261

To give Fanthorpe's output even greater significance it should be borne in mind that all his work was written in his spare time whilst all the others in the list (except Dunsany) are (or were) full-time writers. Furthermore the bulk of it was written in a period of about eight years whereas the others are the result of twenty, thirty or even more years active writing. Even the German writers must acceed to the fact that Lionel Fanthorpe is the most prolific sf and fantasy writer in the world.

John Russell Fearn

THE 10 FASTEST OR MOST COMPULSIVE WRITERS

C4/5

1 **Barry Malzberg**
Malzberg must hold the record for the quickest short story ever written. In an interview conducted by Charles Platt and published in Platt's *Who Writes Science Fiction?* (Savoy Books, 1980), Malzberg claims that his story 'Uncoupling' was written between 8.15 and 8.50 on Saturday, January 14th 1973. That's thirty-five minutes for a story of 4,200 words or 120 words a minute! A phenomenal speed for a copy typist, let along composing a story. And to sustain it for thirty-five minutes is quite incredible. I can only believe that the story was written from pure inspiration, and cannot have been consciously conceived. Nevertheless, Malzberg was a compulsive writer. In the seven years between 1968 and 1975 he wrote 25 sf novels and 200 short stories, with another 50 non-sf novels atop that. His quickest novel (non-sf) was written in sixteen hours on February 13th and 14th 1969, totalling 60,000 words — a modest 62½ words a minute. His fastest sf novel was *Phase IV* — a book of the film — written in three days in July 1973, whilst an original novel, *In The Enclosure,* took four days in July 1971. 'If these be records you can have them', Malzberg commented in a private letter. 'I am not proud of these statistics.' Malzberg's most productive year was 1973, with 16 novels, 30 short stories and a poem, which put him in the million-words a year bracket.

2 **Lionel Fanthorpe**
Fanthorpe has an enviable ability for instant composition. He probably holds the record for the fastest novel ever written: *Radar Alert,* published under the Karl Zeigfreid alias in 1963. 'I started this in the early hours and posted it before the post office closed on the same day. The day was Saturday, November 3rd 1962.' Post offices closed at 5pm on Saturdays in those days, and Fanthorpe's day usually began at

6am, which means this 50,000 word novel was completed in, at the most, *eleven hours* — or nearly 76 words a minute. Fanthorpe had assistance, however, in the form of a battery of typists. He would dictate a novel and as each tape was finished so he would feed it to each successive typist until his requisite wordage was complete. This was not an isolated example. *Atomic Nemesis* took eighteen hours, *Legion of the Lost* thirty hours, and a collection *The Frozen Tomb* also thirty hours. Fanthorpe's peak period was in the three full years 1961 to 1963 when he wrote 89 books totalling 4,500,000 words — and all this *in his spare time.* Fanthorpe adds: 'Given enough tape-recorders and typists used to my style of dictating, I have no doubt at all that I could still do it in the time. If any publisher has the spare cash to set up the production line and will also promise to publish the result at normal rates, I'll take up the gauntlet tomorrow!'

3 Lester Dent

Lester Dent, under the alias Kenneth Robeson, wrote most of the Doc Savage novels in the pulp magazine of the same name. This isn't all he wrote, as he often filled whole issues of the pulps with his stories. Robert K Jones, in his book *The Shudder Pulps* (Fax, 1975), reports that Dent is reputed to have produced 56,000 words as a day's work, 32,000 by dictaphone and 24,000 by typewriter. Philip Jose Farmer reports that Dent often worked an eighteen hour day, so this output would average 52 words a minute. Dent's average annual output was probably between 1.5 and 2 million words.

4 Arthur J Burks

Again in *The Shudder Pulps*, Robert Jones says that Burks 'may have been the most compulsive writer ever'. Apparently Burks aimed at a regular 18,000 words a day, day after day. What is exceptional about Burks is that his output was predominantly short fiction, and it is considerably harder to maintain a high production rate when having to conceive new plots and characters every five or six thousand words. Burks total output is unknown, but at least one story, possibly apocryphal, has become legend about his work. Apparently when Harry Bates was preparing to launch *Astounding Stories* in 1929 he asked Burks for a serial, but he specified he wanted something properly plotted, not turned out overnight. Burks went home and wrote *Earth, The Marauder* in less than three days, and at only 30,000 words, this must have been easy for Burks. He then set it aside for a couple of weeks before taking it to Bates. Bates read the manuscript and then congratulated Burks: 'See how much better you do when you take your time.'

5 Michael Moorcock

As will be seen elsewhere in this book, Moorcock already rates as one of fantasy's most prolific novelists, in a career of less than twenty years. His memory betrayed him when I asked him which book he had completed the quickest. 'I've never timed myself exactly', he responded. 'One of the 'Mars' books took two days.' The 'Mars' books were the trilogy *Warriors of Mars, Blades of Mars* and *Barbarians of Mars* published under the pen name of Edward P. Bradbury by Compact Books in 1965. They have since been reprinted under Moorcock's own name by other publishers under the titles *City of the Beast, Lord of the Spiders* and *Masters of the Pit.*

6 Robert Silverberg

Silverberg is almost certainly the most prolific writer that science fiction has produced if you take into account all his writings outside the field. He talks casually about his output as if it were all a matter of course. 'I often wrote 10,000 words a day,' he said in a recent letter. 'If you do that five days a week that gives you two and a half million words a year, so I never felt the need to write novels in a weekend. Once, under unusual pressure, I wrote one in 3½ days (I don't remember which one! Not sf), but usually I took five or six for the potboilers, and two weeks or more for the serious projects.' Nevertheless, Silverberg's production rate is awesome. He was only just into his twenties when he was hitting a million words a year, which he maintained through to 1966. His record production in one day was 16,000 words. His peak years were 1962-64 when he wrote 5,759,000 words, with a high of 1,977,000 in 1963. Little of this, however, was science fiction. He reckons his total output is now 21 million words.

7 E.C. Tubb

The fastest novel Tubb wrote was *Menace From the Past* published under the Carl Maddox pen name in 1954. It took him 32 hours spread over four days. Tubb could maintain a sustained output, even when holding a full-time job. In one period of eleven days in February 1953, Tubb wrote *Dynasty of Doom* followed instantly by *The Tormented City,* two short novels totalling 76,000 words in evenings and weekend-afternoons. Tubb's quickest rate for a short story was for 'Sword of Tormain', a total of 9,000 words. 'It was produced in a rush one afternoon and was so easy I thought it had to be bad so I submitted it as 'Eric Storm' to *Planet* who bought it by return.'

8 **John Brunner**
Although Brunner is one of Britain's most prolific sf writers his quality output is the result of a steady and controlled production. His quickest novel, at 71,000 words, took one week, one day and one-and-a-half hours. This was his black-magic thriller *Black is the Colour* published by Pyramid Books in 1969.

9 **Luis Senarens**
In the last half of the nineteenth century the direct ancestor of the pulp magazine reigned — the dime novel. These had their mega-wordsters just like the pulps, and the one most closely associated with sf was Luis Senarens who produced the Frank Reade Jr. series of invention stories. In his chapter on Senarens in *Explorers of the Infinite* (World, 1963), Sam Moskowitz summarises Senarens' career. 'In a bit more than thirty years, he wrote some forty million words and fifteen hundred individual stories under twenty-seven pseudonyms.' And this, don't forget, was in long-hand, though he later transferred to a typewriter. He frequently wrote twelve to fourteen hours at a stretch, and apparently invented a special device of his own to avoid writer's cramp.

10 I reserved tenth place for the names of several prolific writers for whom I have been unable to ascertain precise statistics. A number of writers were noted for their composing and production speeds, but it is not easy, now, to prove it. Amongst them are Norvell Page, who wrote 116 *Spider* novels in ten years plus countless other stories and novels in the 1930s, L. Ron Hubbard, who regularly churned out long stories overnight, and claims his speed is greater now than ever, and George F. Worts, who wrote several quasi-sf novels and maintained an output of 25,000 words a day on an electric typewriter.

THE 10 MOST PSEUDONYMOUS SF WRITERS

C6

The following list is restricted to pseudonyms used within the science fiction field. There are some writers, like H. Bedford-Jones and Frederick Faust who used many pen-names but adopted only one or two for their sf stories. All those below, however, will be found on stories or books within the sf world. Writers like Silverberg and Fearn used other pseudonyms outside sf, but these have not been included. For the record, Fearn comes top here with seventy-three identified pseudonyms as of 1981 (so I am reliably informed by Philip Harbottle, literary agent for Fearn's estate).

1 **E.C. Tubb 45**
Stuart Allen + Anthony Armstrong + Ted Bain + Alice Beecham + Anthony Blake + L.T. Bronson + Raymond L. Burton + Julian Car(e)y + Morley Carpenter + Norman Dale + Robert D. Ennis + James Evans + R.H. Godfrey + Charles Grey/Gray + Volsted Gridban + Alan Guthrie + D.W.R. Hill + George Holt + Gill Hunt + Alan Innes + Gordon Kent + Gregory Kern + King Lang + Nigel Lloyd + Robert Lloyd + Frank T. Lomas + Ron Lowam + Arthur Maclean + Carl Maddox + Phillip Martyn + John Mason + Colin May + Carl Moulton + L.C. Powers + Edward Richards + John Seabright + Brian Shaw + Roy Sheldon + Eric Storm + Andrew Sutton + Ken Wainwright + Frank Weight + Douglas West + Eric Wilding + Frank Winnard

2 **John Russell Fearn 40**
Geoffrey Armstrong + Thornton Ayre + Hugo Blayn + Morton Boyce + Denis Clive + John Cotton + Polton Cross + Mark Denholm + Douglas Dodd + Sheridan Drew + Max Elton + Preston Foxe + Geoffrey Grayson

E.C. Tubb

+ Volsted Gridban + Griff + Malcolm Hartley + Conrad G. Holt + Noel Jackson + Preston James + Frank Jones + Nat Karta + Marvin Kayne + Herbert Lloyd + Paul Lorraine + Astron del Martia + Jed McCloud + Dom Passante + Alex O. Pearson + Francis Rose + Lawrence F. Rose + Ward Ross + John Russell + Bryan Shaw + Astroea Starforth + Vargo Statten + K. Thomas + Earl Titan + John Wernheim + G.L. Wilson + Ephriam Winiki

3 **Lionel Fanthorpe 26**
Neil Balfort + Othello Baron + Erle Barton + Lee Barton + Thornton Bell + Leo Brett + Bron Fane + Mel Jay + Marston Johns + L.P. Kenton + Victor La Salle + Oben Lerteth + John E. Muller + Elton T. Neef(e) + Phil Nobel + Peter O'Flynn + John Raymond + Lionel Roberts + Rene Rolant + Deutero Spartacus + Robin Tate + Neil Thanet + Trebor Thorpe + Pel Torro + Olaf Trent + Karl Zeigfreid

4 **Robert Silverberg 25**
Gordon Aghill + Robert Arnette + T.D. Bethlen + Alexander Blade + Ralph Burke + Dirk Clinton + Richard Greer + E.K. Jarvis + Ivar Jorgensen + Warren Kastel + Calvin M. Knox + Dan Malcolm + Webber Martin + Alex Merriman + Clyde Mitchell + David Osborne + George Osborne + Robert Randall + Ellis Robertson + Eric Rodman + Leonard G. Spencer + S.M. Tenneshaw + Hall Thornton + Gerald Vance + Richard F. Watson

5 **John S. Glasby 22**
John Adams + R.L. Bowers + Berl Cameron + Max Chartair + Randall Conway + Ray Cosmic + John Crawford + J.B. Dexter + Michael Hamilton + J.J. Hansby + Victor LaSalle + Peter Laynham + Rand Le Page + H.K. Lennard + Paul Lorraine + John C. Maxwell + A.J. Merak + John Morton + John E. Muller + J.L. Powers + Alan Thorndyke + Karl Ziegfried

6 **Roger P. Graham 19**
Clinton Ames + Robert Arnette + Franklin Bahl + Alexander Blade + Craig Browning + Gregg Conrad + P.F. Costello + Sanandana Kumara + Charles Lee + Milton Mann + Inez McGowan + Rog Phillips + Melva Rogers + Chester Ruppert + William Carter Sawtelle + Alfred R. Steber + Gerald Vance + John Wiley + Peter Worth

7 **Henry Kuttner 18**
Edward J. Bellin + Paul Edmonds + Noel Gardner + Will Garth + James Hall + Keith Hammond + Hudson Hastings + Peter Horn + Kelvin Kent + Robert O. Kenyon + C.H. Liddell + Hugh Maepann + K.H. Maepann + Scott Morgan + Lawrence O'Donnell + Lewis Padgett + Woodrow Wilson Smith + Charles Stoddard

8 **Randall Garrett 16**
Gordon Aghill + Grandall Barretton + Alexander Blade + Ralph Burke + David Gordon + Richard Greer + Ivar Jorgensen + Darrell T. Langart + J.B. McKenzie + Seaton McKettrig + Clyde Mitchell + Mark Phillips + Robert Randall + Leonard G. Spencer + S.M. Tenneshaw + Gerald Vance (Garrett is also attributed with the pseudonym Walter Bupp, but this is denied by Garrett himself).

9 **Forrest J. Ackerman 16**
(Most of Ackerman's pseudonyms have been used in the fan field) Dr Acula + Silvestre Aldeano + Les Angeleano + Nick Beal + Carl F. Burke + Morris Chapnick + Walter Chinwell + J. Forrester Eckman + Jacques DeForest Erman + Alden Lorraine + Aime Merritt + Spencer Strong +

Fisher Trentworth + Hubert George Wells + Robert Wright + Weaver Wright

10 **Cyril M. Kornbluth 13** Gabriel Barclay + Arthur Cooke + Cecil Corwin + Walter C. Davies + Simon Eisner + Kenneth Falconer + S.D. Gottesman + Cyril Judd + Paul Dennis Lavond + Scott Mariner + Martin Pearson + Ivar Towers + Dirk Wylie

THE 10 MOST AWARDED SF & FANTASY WRITERS

C7

Rather than list the most-honoured persons, which would include awards received outside the sf field, I have limited this list to awards presented within the genre. I've excluded national awards with the one exception of the American Book Awards, and the reckoning includes the International Fantasy Awards, the Hugo (including associated Special Awards and the Gandalf Awards), the John W. Campbell Memorial Award, the Nebula, the Jupiter, the World Fantasy, the British Fantasy, the British Science Fiction, the Ditmar International and the Locus Awards. I have included all of the Locus categories (except the all-time polls) rather than just the fiction ones, because the Locus Poll is probably the best barometer of appreciation in the field due to the size of the vote, usually well in excess of that for the Hugo or Nebula.

1 **Harlan Ellison 23 Awards** (7 Hugos, 2 Hugo Specials, 3 Nebulas, 8 Locus, 2 Jupiters, 1 British Fantasy)

2 **Edward L. Ferman 17 Awards** (5 Hugos, 12 Locus)

3 **Ursula K. LeGuin 16 Awards** (4 Hugos, 1 Gandalf, 3 Nebulas, 5 Locus, 3 Jupiters)

4 **Frank Kelly Freas 15 Awards** (10 Hugos, 5 Locus)

5 **Fritz Leiber 15 Awards** (6 Hugos, 1 Gandalf, 1 Hugo Special, 3 Nebulas, 2 World Fantasy, 2 British Fantasy

6 **Richard E. Geis 13** (11 Hugos, 2 Locus)

7 **Frederik Pohl 12 Awards** (5 Hugos, 2 Nebulas, 3 Locus, 1 Campbell, 1 ABA)

8 **Poul Anderson 11 Awards** (6 Hugos, 1 Gandalf, 2 Nebulas, 1 Locus, 1 Derleth Fantasy)

8 **Robert Silverberg 11 Awards** (2 Hugos, 4 Nebulas, 4 Locus, 1 Jupiter)

8 **Isaac Asimov 11 Awards** (3 Hugos, 1 Hugo Special, 2 Nebulas, 4 Locus)

A few words of explanation for those raised eyebrows. Firstly the award-counts for Edward Ferman and Frederik Pohl include the awards for Best

Harlan Ellison

Magazine when they were the editors. Secondly, you'll see that the recipient of the most Hugos has been Richard Geis, a name none too well known in Britain. Geis has received the award six times as editor of the Best Fanzine (Amateur Magazine) and five times as the Best Fan Writer.

THE 15 NOVELISTS WITH THE MOST HUGO & NEBULA NOMINATIONS C8

It's one thing to know who has won the most Awards, but this overlooks the many authors who have near misses time after time, making them consistently popular. The following list isolates those writers who had novels nominated for Hugo and Nebula Awards regardless of whether or not they won.

	Author	Hugo	Nebula	Total
1	**Robert Silverberg**	11	9	20
2	**Robert A. Heinlein**	8	2	10
	Larry Niven	7	3	10
5	**Poul Anderson**	4	4	8
6	**Roger Zelazny**	4	3	7
	Samuel R. Delany	3	4	7
8	**Philip K. Dick**	2	4	6
	Ursula K. LeGuin	3	3	6
	John Brunner	3	3	6
	Jerry Pournelle	4	2	6
12	**Clifford D. Simak**	4	1	5
	Arthur C. Clarke	3	2	5
	David Gerrold	2	3	5
	Kate Wilhelm	1	4	5

THE 7 MOST CONSISTENT HUGO & NEBULA AWARD LOSERS C9

Some authors are nominated time and again for the Hugo and Nebula Awards but are always pipped at the post. From the latest edition of *A History of the Hugo, Nebula and Fantasy Awards* compiled by Donald Franson and Howard DeVore, I have drawn up a list of the seven most consistent losers.

	Author	Hugo	Nebula	Total
1	**Michael Bishop**	5	7	12
2	**Gardner Dozois**	4	6	10
3	**Thomas M. Disch**	3	6	9
4	**David Gerrold**	3	4	7
	Norman Spinrad	3	4	7
6	**Piers Anthony**	5	1	6
	Keith Laumer	2	4	6

THE 10 OLDEST PEOPLE TO RECEIVE A HUGO OR NEBULA AWARD C10

1 **Murray Leinster.**
60 years 2 months
1956 Hugo for Best Novelette with *Exploration Team.*

2 **R.A. Lafferty.**
58 years 9 months
Co-winner of the 1973 Hugo for Best Short Story with *Eurema's Dam.*

3 **James Tiptree, Jr.**
57 years ? months
Winner of the 1973 Nebula (in 1974) for Best Short Story with *Love Is the Plan, the Plan is Death.*

4 **Wilson (Bob) Tucker.**
55 years 9 months
Winner of the 1970 Hugo for Best Fan Writer.

5 **Clifford D. Simak.**
55 years 1 month
Winner of the 1959 Hugo for Best Novelette with *The Big Front Yard.* Simak had previously won the International Fantasy Award in 1953 for *City* when he was a mere 48 years 8 months. In 1981 he carried off both the Nebula and the Hugo Awards for his short story *Grotto of the Dancing Deer* making him at 77 years the oldest writer to win such an award.

6 **Frederik Pohl.**
53 years 9 months
Co-winner fo the 1973 Hugo for Best Short Story with *The Meeting,* the completion of a story by Cyril Kornbluth. Pohl had, technically, won a Hugo in 1966 whilst editor of the Best Professional Magazine *If* when a youthful 46 years 9 months.

7 **Theodore Sturgeon.**
53 years 2 months
Winner (in 1971) of the 1970 Nebula for Best Novelette with *Slow Sculpture.* Sturgeon had earlier won the 1954 International Fantasy Award for Fiction with *More Than Human* when a little over 36 years.

8 **P. Schuyler Miller.**
51 years 6 months
Winner of a 1963 Special Hugo for his Book Reviews in *Analog.*

9 **Eric Frank Russell.**
50 years 8 months
Winner of the 1955 Hugo for Best Short Story for *Allamagoosa.*

10 **William Rotsler.**
49 years 2 months
Winner of the 1975 Hugo as Best Fan Artist.

The oldest recipient of any Hugo Award was Chesley Bonestell who received a Special Committee Award at the 1974 World Convention for his beautiful and scientifically accurate artwork. Bonestell was 87.

Clifford D. Simak

THE 10 YOUNGEST PEOPLE TO RECEIVE A HUGO OR NEBULA

I've included the John W.Campbell Award for Best New Writer as this used to be a Hugo category, but otherwise I've only counted awards that are for current work. All retrospective awards such as the Grand Master and certain special Hugos are excluded. Of the 120 or so people who have received Hugo Awards there were only about a dozen whose birth-dates I was not able to trace, and a few more, like John Varley, whose complete date of birth eluded me. So my apologies to those who may belong in the list but are missing.

1 **Ron Ellik.**
20 years 11 months
Co-winner with Terry Carr of the 1959 Hugo for Best Fanzine, *Fanac.* Ron was a prominent fan during the 1960s and with Bill Evans was co-compiler of *The Universe Of E.E.Smith* (1968). He was killed in a car accident in January 1968 the day before he was to have married.

2 **Robert Silverberg.**
21 years 7 months
1956 Hugo for Best New Writer

3 **Lisa Tuttle**
22 years 3 months
Co-winner with Spider Robinson of the 1974 John W Campbell Award for Best New Writer

4 **Terry Carr**
22 years 6 months
Co-winner with Ron Ellik above of the 1959 Hugo for Best Fanzine, *Fanac.*

5 **Tim Kirk**
23 years ? months
1970 Hugo as Best Fan Artist.

6 **Samuel R. Delany.**
25 years 0 months
Winner (in 1967) of the 1966 Nebula Award for Best Novel with *Babel-17,* thus making Delany the youngest writer to win an award for a specific piece of work and Delany went on to win two more Nebulae the following year, making him the youngest writer to win three awards.

7 **Susan Wood.**
25 years ? months
Co-winner of the 1973 Hugo for Best Fanzine with her then husband Michael Glicksohn for *Energumen.* The following year she had the Hugo all to herself as Best Fan Writer.

Robert Silverberg (aged 21)

8 **Spider Robinson.**
25 years 10 months
Co-winner with Lisa Tuttle of the 1974 John W. Campbell Award for Best New Writer.

9 **Vonda N. McIntyre.**
26 years ? months
Winner (in 1974) of the 1973 Nebula for Best Novelette with *Of Mist, and Grass and Sand.*

10 **Rick Sternbach.**
26 years ? months
Winner of the 1977 Hugo for Best Professional Artist.

THE 20 OLDEST SF & FANTASY WRITERS

C12

1 **Adolphe De Castro**
100 years 1 month
February 1859 — March 1959
Real name Gustaf Danziger, de Castro was not prominent in the fantasy field and is remembered only for his collaboration with Ambrose Bierce (*The Monk and the Hangman's Daughter* 1892) and his contributions to *Weird Tales* (revised by H.P. Lovecraft) such as *The Electric Executioner* (1930).

2 **Eden Phillpotts**
98 years 1 month
November 1862 — December 1960
Phillpotts wrote more sf than most people realise, although it was a small portion of his 250 books. An early novel was *A Deal With the Devil* (1895) whilst many books came later (*Address Unknown* 1949).

3 **E. Douglas Fawcett**
94 years 1866 — April 1960
An early disciple of Jules Verne, Fawcett wrote three sf novels: *Hartmann the Anarchist* (1893), *Swallowed By An Earthquake* (1894) and *The Secret of the Desert* (1895); plus several works on philosophy.

S. Fowler Wright

4 **E.H. Visiak**
94 years 1 month
July 1878 — August 1972
Although better known as an expert on Milton, Visiak wrote a number of fantasies of which the best known tells of a bizarre sea voyage, *Medusa* (1929).

5 **Laurence Housman**
93 years 7 months
July 1865 — February 1959
A much neglected fantasist who wrote scores of allegorical fairy tales. Some will be found in *The Field of Clover* (1898) and *Ironical Tales* (1926). His sister, Clemence, only wrote one work of fantasy, *The Were-Wolf* (1890), so is not included in this list even though she too lived to be 94.

6 **Elliott O'Donnell**
93 years 2 months
February 1872 — May 1965
Better known for his non-fiction studies of the paranormal, O'Donnell wrote a number of short stories plus a few novels of which the best known was *The Sorcery Club* (1912).

7 **S. Fowler Wright**
91 years 1 month
January 1874 — February 1965
The oldest of the more dedicated sf writers, Wright produced one of the classics of the field with *The World Below* (1924).

8 **John Cowper Powys**
90 years 8 months
October 1872 — June 1963
Powys wrote a number of mystical novels like *Morwyn* (1937) and some sf like *Up and Out* (1957).

9 **Gertrude Atherton**
90 years 7 months
October 1857 — June 1948
A noted writer whose fiction includes some weird, some ghost, and some sf, like *Black Oxen* (1923).

10 **Greye La Spina**
89 years 2 months

Greye La Spina

July 1880 — September 1969
A popular contributor to *The Thrill Book* and *Weird Tales*. One of her serials was published in book form as *Invaders From The Dark* in 1960.

11 **Julian Hawthorne**
88 years June 1846 — July 1934
The son of Nathaniel Hawthorne, Julian wrote a fair quota of sf and fantasy such as the stories in *Ellice Quentin* (1880) and a space opera *The Cosmic Courtship* serialised in *All-Story* in 1917.

12 **Oliver Onions**
88 years 1873 — April 1961
Regarded as one of the best supernaturalists in the English language with such stories as *The Beckoning Fair One* and *Phantas*. He also wrote a few fantasy novels such as *The Tower of Oblivion* (1921) about immortality.

13 **Robert Nathan**
88 years + January 1894 —
A prolific and still active fantasist, author of such books as *Portrait of Jennie* (1940) and *The Mallot Diaries* (1965).

14 **Robert William Wood**
87 years 3 months
May 1868 — August 1955
A remarkable American physicist, Wood collaborated with Arthur Train on two sf novels, *The Man Who Rocked the Earth* (1915) about atomic power, and a sequel *The Moon Maker*, not issued in book-form until 1958.

15 **Miriam Allen deFord**
86 years 10 months
August 1888 — July 1975
Probably better known in the mystery field, Miss deFord turned more to sf from the 1950s onwards, with many short stories, some collected as *Xenogenesis* (1969).

16 **David H. Keller**
85 years 6 months
December 1880 — July 1966
One of the greats of the early sf pulps, Keller wrote well over 100 short sf and fantasy stories, plus a number of neglected novels.

17 **Stanton A Coblentz**
85 years + August 1896 —
Another of the great oldtimers from the pulps, Coblentz is still writing and has another novel in the works as I write this.

Stanton A. Coblentz

18 **George C. Wallis**
85 years 1871 — September 1956
Now all but forgotten Wallis was a prolific contributor to the US and British pulps and boys magazines. His published books range from *Children of the Sphinx* (1901) to *The Call of Peter Gaskell* (1947).

19 **Arthur Machen**
84 years 9 months
March 1863 — December 1947
Possibly the best known of all the writers so far mentioned, Machen was a fine supernaturalist whose work influenced, among others, H.P. Lovecraft.

20 **Naomi Mitchison**
84 years + November 1897 —
A noted novelist, and sister of J.B.S. Haldane, she has written several sf novels and stories, notably *Memoirs of a Spacewoman* (1962) and *Solution Three* (1975).

If I had stretched the limits of coverage a little further I could have included writers like E.M. Forster (91y 5m), Martin Armstrong (91y 4m), and Paul Eldridge. I've been able to find no recent information on Mr Eldridge who may well still be alive, aged 93. Eldridge wrote the Three Immortals trilogy with G.S. Viereck.

Other active octagenarians include Vera Chapman (born May 1898), E. Hoffman Price (July 1898) and Jorge Luis Borges (August 1899). Other octagenarians include A. Hyatt Verrill (83y 3m), Walter de la Mare (83y 1m), Hugo Gernsback (83y), Algernon Blackwood (82y 8m), H.F. Heard (81y 10m), J.R.R. Tolkien (81y 8m), Harry Bates (81y), Seabury Quinn (80y 11m), Dennis Wheatley (80y 10m) and George Macdonald (80y 9m).

THE 10 LONGEST SF WRITING CAREERS

C13

In keeping within some form of frame of reference for the following I have reckoned from an author's first sf sale (and thus excluded earlier non-sf sales) through to his last sf sale, or his death if he was still active in his final days. I have also excluded early non-professional publications (see Frank Belknap Long below) and in doing so have excluded David H. Keller from the list who might otherwise have topped it. Keller's earliest fantasies appeared in a college amateur magazine in 1902. Keller was co-editor. Sixty-four years later at the time of his death Keller was still dabbling with his stories, updating and revising his work. However, Keller's career in sf can only be reckoned to start from 1928.

1 **Curt Siodmak 62 years**
I was tempted to reckon Siodmak's career as starting in 1910 when, at the age of eight, he had a story published in a German children's magazine. Siodmak's first professional fantasies, however, started to appear in *Das Magazin* in 1919. Siodmak is still alive and writing occasionally, his last sighted story being *The P Factor* (*F & SF* September 1976).

2 **Robert Nathan 58 years**
Nathan's first story was published in 1915, but his first fantasy, *The Puppet Master*, did not appear until 1923. He is still active and writing, though his last published fantasy was *Heaven and Hell and the Megas Factor* (1975).

3 **Frank Belknap Long 57 years**
Long had stories in the amateur magazines as long ago as 1919 and these brought him into contact with H.P. Lovecraft who was one factor in helping Long make his first professional sale, *The Desert Lich* to *Weird Tales* in 1924. Long is still very active, his latest story, *The Autumn Visitors*, appeared in the January 1982 *Twilight Zone*.

Frank Belknap Long

4 **Murray Leinster 57 years** Leinster was selling epigrams to *Smart Set* as long ago as 1915 but his first professional sale was *Oh, Aladdin!* published in *Argosy* in 1919. He was still active in the field at the time of his death in June 1975.

5 **E. Hoffman Price 56 years** Price's fantasy career can be said to have started with his second story, *The Rajah's Gift*, published in *Weird Tales* in 1924. Over the years he has written hundreds of stories in many fields, though his heart has always remained close to the fantasy genre, and he has now returned to writing in the field with two recent novels *The Devil Wives of Li Fong* (1979) and *Operation Misfit* (1980).

6 **Manly Wade Wellman 54 years** Wellman's first story, *Back to the Beast*, appeared in *Weird Tales* in 1927 and was an sf story about reversed evolution. Still active, he has long since carved himself a niche in the fields of sf, fantasy, mystery and historical fiction, and is working on a number of new stories and novels. His latest in print is *Nobody Ever Goes There* in the Fall 1981 *Weird Tales.*

7 **Eden Phillpotts 54 years** I have reckoned Phillpotts's career from his early novel *A Deal with the Devil* (1895) to one of his last books *Address Unknown* (1949). It is entirely possible that Phillpotts had sold earlier fantasy short stories as yet untraced, and that he planned further sf in his latter years.

8 **George C. Wallis 54 years** Wallis's earliest known sf stories appeared in 1896, though there may be some earlier. He was known to be still active in 1950 when he was in contact with Walter Gillings, though his last published works appeared in 1947. He died in 1956.

9 **Stanton A. Coblentz 53 years** Coblentz sold his first story in 1919, but he did not enter the sf field until *Amazing Stories Quarterly* published *The Sunken World* in the Summer 1928 issue. Coblentz is currently completing a new sf novel.

10 **Jack Williamson 53 years** Just a few months behind Coblentz, Williamson's first story, *The Metal Man*, made the December 1928 *Amazing Stories*. He too is as active as ever with many new stories in the pipeline

I might just add that also with fifty-three years sf service was Jules Verne who started it all in 1851 and kept on going until 1904.

THE 12 WRITERS WHO SOLD AN SF STORY BEFORE 16 C14

There are three important moments in the life of a short story (aside from its conception and actually being read) — the day it is completed, the day it is bought by the editor, and the day it is published. Wherever possible I've endeavoured to establish these dates to get a full chronology, but it hasn't always been possible. The writers listed below are those who genuinely wrote a story for submission, rather than those infants whose parents or friends submitted the story as a novelty item. Robin Sturgeon (the son of Theodore) had an essay *Martian Mouse* in the September 1962 F & SF when he was 10, and Mildred Posselt had a rather chilling story *The Flower* in the May 1961 F & SF when she was 11. I have records of stories by Paul Bowles when he was nine and Kurt Siodmak when he was eight, but these usually constitute precocious pieces of prose to children's corners in newspapers. The following were 'adult' sales to adult magazines or publishers.

1 **Anthony Weller** *Antiquity, Infinity 3* edited by Robert Hoskins (New York, 1972) Weller is the son of George Weller who won a Pulitzer Prize in 1943 for his reporting of an emergency operation on board a submarine. Weller was twelve years, eleven months when he completed *Antiquity* in August 1970. He submitted it as an after-thought along with another story to Robert Hoskins at Lancer Books. Hoskins rejected the story but bought *Antiquity.* 'Publishing it was totally his idea,' Weller recalled to me in a letter in April 1979. 'I included it in the envelope without correcting it at all – it was written as is on the typewriter...'

2 **Kenneth Sterling** *The Brain-Eaters of Pluto, Wonder Stories* March 1934. Sterling was thirteen years, seven months old when the story was published and remains the youngest writer to see his story in print. 'This opus was done largely during the summer, partly before and partly after my thirteenth birthday,' Sterling recalled. That would be the summer of 1933. 'It was not my first submission to *Wonder Stories* but I was truly astonished to receive a letter of acceptance above the signature of Charles D. Hornig some time in the Fall followed by the quite prompt publication.' Unlike Weller, Sterling sold further sf stories, including a collaboration with H.P. Lovecraft, before his time was eclipsed by academic pursuits at medical school, and later in medical research.

3 **Lohr Miller** *Paddlewheel on the Styx, If* October 1968. At the time the story appeared editor Frederik Pohl who had selected it for *If* said of the author: 'Lohr Miller is a Baton Rouge high-school student whose special interests are Napoleonic history, astronomy, weaponry — and science fiction.' Miller was thirteen years and ten months old when the story appeared, and could have been as much as a year younger when he completed it.

4 **Ted Reynolds** *Just Imagine, Beyond* November 1953. 'Misty memories,' replied Reynolds when I asked him about the origin of the story. 'I wrote *The Figment* (never cared for the editor's title) in Japan, so it was after Fall of 1950, and much more likely it was in 1952. I wrote it for my family, but my mother sent it secretly to her literary agent. I seem to remember the story as an attempted refutation of Descartes — but I can't have been *that* precocious!' As Reynolds was born in October 1938 he was just fifteen when the story appeared in print but was clearly a year or two younger when he wrote it.

5 **Jane Gaskell** *Strange Evil* (London, 1957) Jane Gaskell, a distant relative of the Victorian novelist Mrs Gaskell, is the youngest novelist on our list. *Strange Evil* was published in August 1957 when she was sixteen years and one month old, but the story had been written two years earlier in a school exercise book. Not only that, she had already completed a second novel, *The King's Daughter,* written when she was fifteen and published in 1958.

6 **Terry Pratchett** *The Hades Business, Science Fantasy* August 1963. Born in April 1948 Terry Pratchett was fourteen-and-a-half when he completed *The Hades Business* in October 1962. 'Getting my first story published was probably a bad thing,' he now believes. 'I'd arrived without quite knowing how I'd got there'. Pratchett has since, after a few years silence, sold a couple of impressive sf novels.

7 **Anthony Boucher** *Ye Goode Olde Ghoste Storie, Weird Tales* January 1927. Boucher's real name was William Anthony Parker White, but so well known was he by his pen-name that he hoped that his first sale would be

forgotten. Not so. Forrest Ackerman produced the evidence and Boucher confessed. 'When I was fifteen', he wrote in 1950, 'I sold a story to *Weird Tales'*. It was awful, and it should never have been bought. It was not only vile writing, but an outright, if innocent, steal from Mrs Bland's *Number 17,* which I'd heard as oral tradition'. Thus he absolved himself. The story appeared in print when Boucher was fifteen years, three months old, so he probably sold the story before he was fifteen.

8 **Charles Cloukey** *Sub-Satellite, Amazing Stories* March 1928. Writing in his history of fandom, *All Our Yesterdays* (1969), Harry Warner, Jr. said of Cloukey, '...Cloukey had made his first sale to *Amazing* when only fifteen. The Edison Scholarship Contest had shown Cloukey to be the seventh highest participant from the entire nation's schools.'

9 **Robert Spencer Carr** *The Composite Brain, Weird Tales* March 1925. Carr, brother of the noted detective writer John Dickson Carr, shot to premature fame with his novel *The Rampant Age* (1926) about teenagers in the 1920s. Earlier he had sold several stories to Farnsworth Wright at *Weird Tales* who encouraged and advised Carr in his work. His first sale was made when he was fifteen and he made five further sales to *Weird Tales* before being lured away by Hollywood.

10 **Bruce McAllister** *The Faces Outside, If* July 1963. For many years Bruce McAllister was wrongly credited as being tory stayed in the inventory for many months.

11 **Robert Payes** *Target Practice, Vertex* December 1974. Payes, the son of writer Rachel Cosgrove Payes, made his first sale a month before his sixteenth birthday. *Target Practice* had been written when he was fifteen years, four months. An earlier story, *Final Bomb*, written in the month after his fifteenth birthday, also appeared in *Vertex*, although that had not sold until Payes was passed sixteen.

12 **August Derleth** *Bat's Belfry, Weird Tales* May 1926. Derleth was born in February 1909. As he himself wrote in his bibliography *100 Books by August Derleth* (1962): 'Began writing at thirteen, sold first story to *Weird Tales* at fifteen, saw it published April 1, 1926...'. Derleth was thus seventeen by the time it appeared, and he probably made the sale in 1924 at the time when *Weird Tales* nearly folded, and the story stayed in the inventory for many months.

Ted Reynolds

6 OF THE OLDEST 'NEW' WRITERS

So many sf writers start in their twenties and thirties that it is easy to forget that there are those who didn't turn to the field until much later in life. Here are a few of them in reverse order. Ages are at date of debut.

1 **R.A. Lafferty.**
45 years 1 month
Worked in the electrical industry from 1935 to 1971 and did not turn to writing until 1959. His first sf, *The Day of the Glacier* appeared in January 1960 *Science Fiction Stories.*

2 **A. Hyatt Verrill.**
45 years ? months
For nearly fifty Verrill was one of the top explorers and archaeologists in South America. He became one of the earliest contributors to *Amazing Stories* with the serial *Beyond the Pole* (1926). As you can imagine most of his output revolved around stories of lost races and he had earlier published a novel of such intrigue in *The Golden City* (1916), his earliest work of fantasy fiction.

3 **David H. Keller.**
47 years 2 months
Keller was a leading physician and an early psychologist as well as a prolific writer. Although he had amateur stories published in the 1890s his first professional sale was — *The Revolt of the Pedestrians* to *Amazing Stories* where it made the February 1928 issue.

4 **James Tiptree, Jr.**
51 years ? months
One of the greatest and most delightful surprises in the sf world in recent years was when it was revealed that James Tiptree, Jr., that mysterious but powerful new writer was not a he, but a she, Alice Hastings Sheldon, an experimental psychologist. Within one week she sold a story to John Campbell and another to Harry Harrison and the first to appear was *Birth of a Salesman* in the March 1968 *Analog.*

5 **Winifred Kearns.**
72 years ? months
After her retirement in 1967 Winn Kearns took to writing sf and made her first sale to Thomas M. Disch and Charles Naylor's *New Constellations* anthology published in 1976. A little over a year later she died of cancer.

6 **Vera Chapman.**
77 years
The grande dame of fantasy fiction is Vera Chapman, founder of the British Tolkien Society, and for many years Member of the Order of Bards, Orates and Druids. Born on May 7th 1898, Mrs Chapman's first work of fiction, *The Green Knight,* was published in 1975. She has since completed the trilogy of which that novel formed the first part, and now available in one volume as *The Three Damosels,* plus other novels and stories.

Vera Chapman

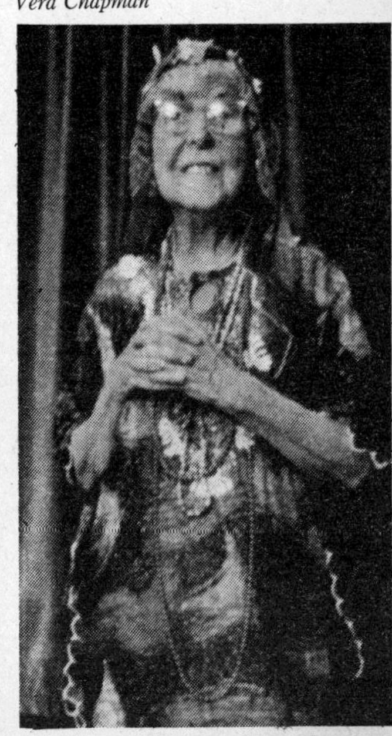

THE 6 SHORTEST SF WRITING CAREERS

C16

Career perhaps isn't the best word because until recently very few writers could survive simply by writing and selling sf and fantasy. In considering the following I have excluded those writers whose early sales were in the sf field but who later chose to leave it for other pastures because I feel sf was only a stepping stone for them. The following are all those who would, had not nature or other circumstances intervened, have established themselves firmly in the sf genre. Indeed, one could say that with the exception of two of them, they are already immortalised.

1 **David R. Daniels** Daniels first appeared in the May 1935 *Astounding Stories* with *Stars* and followed it up with five further quick sales. One, *The Far Way,* was nominated as one of the three best stories *Astounding* had published in 1935. For reasons known only to himself, however, on April 17th 1936 Daniels took his own life, almost a year to the day after his debut.

2 **Winifred Kearns** Winn Kearns became one of the oldest debutantes when she sold *The Rape of OOOOOOO* to Thomas Disch and Charles Naylor for their anthology *New Constellations* published in November 1976. She was seventy-two. Although working on other stories she made no further sales and died on December 29th 1977, fourteen months later.

3 **Susan C. Petrey** Sold her first story to *The Magazine of Fantasy & Science Fiction* where *Spareen Among the Tartars* appeared in the September 1979 issue. Sales began to accumulate and Petrey was nominated for the John W. Campbell Award as Best New Writer in 1981, coming third in the final ballot. Alas, she had died on December 5th 1980 of an accidental overdose of anti-depressants. She was thirty-five.

4 **Stanley G. Weinbaum.** Now a legend of early magazine sf, Weinbaum sold his first story, *A Martian Odyssey* to *Wonder Stories* where it made the July 1934 issue. Over the next eighteen months Weinbaum made over twenty sales to the magazines, especially *Astounding,* and few would doubt that he was not the best sf writer of his day. He knew his days were numbered, however, and he died on December 14th 1935 of throat cancer.

Tom Reamy

5 **Tom Reamy.** Tom Reamy was a much-loved and accomplished sf fan whose fanzines *Nickelodeon* and *Trumpet* were much respected. In 1972 he turned to writing sf and fantasy, his third sale, *Twilla,* being the first in print in the September 1974 *Magazine of Fantasy & Science Fiction. Twilla* was nominated for a Nebula Award

but though it did not win, the following year Reamy's *San Diego Lightfoot Sue* carried off the Best Novelette Nebula. He also received the John W. Campbell Award as Best New Writer. Three years and two months after his first appearance, however, on November 4th 1977, Reamy died of a heart attack.

6 **Charles Cloukey** Most of Cloukey's life, which was exceedingly short, is now forgotten in the mists of time. He made his first sale to *Amazing Stories, Sub-Satellite,* when only fifteen and within five years, at about the age of twenty, he had died, after an output of eight stories and one novel. Something of a boy genius, Cloukey had a vivid imagination, and had life allowed him the time to combine experience with vision he could have been as revered as others of his generation.

THE 12 MOST PROLIFIC ANTHOLOGISTS OF ALL TIME

C17

I've listed twelve because the placings between tenth and twelfth are so close that it seemed safer to list them than risk leaving them out. As with the novelists and short story writers I've used the same point system. I've also included not only anthologies but single author volumes edited by another, as in the case of *The Best of Cyril Kornbluth,* which was assembled by Frederik Pohl. I've not extended this to include in-house editors, such as August Derleth at Arkham House.

	Anthologist	Solo Anths.	Coll Anths.	Author Vols	Total Vols	Points
1	**Robert Silverberg**	60	8	—	68	63⅔
2	**Donald A. Wollheim**	47	20	1	68	58
3	**Roger Elwood***	48	16	2	66	54
4	**Peter Haining**	49	—	5	54	54
5	**Terry Carr**	44	8	—	52	48
6	**Damon Knight**	47	1	—	48	47⅓
7	**Groff Conklin**	36	3	—	39	37½
8	**Sam Moskowitz***	13	21	6	40	34¾
9	**Lin Carter**	24	—	10	34	34
10	**Michel Parry**	32	—	—	32	32
11	**Frederik Pohl**	25	7	1	33	29
12	**John Carnell**	29	—	—	29	29

*In the case of Roger Elwood, those anthologies credited jointly with Virginia Kidd, Vic Ghidalia and Sam Moskowitz were for the most part assembled by the co-editor, not Elwood, so in assessing the points I have allowed him only 25% instead of 50%. Conversely, most of Moskowitz's collaborations were in fact fully edited by Moskowitz, including some which Moskowitz ghost-edited. Here I've allowed 75% of the points.

THE 10 MOST PRODIGIOUS SF MAGAZINE EDITORS

C18

Who has edited the most issues of a science fiction magazine? The following (which is as at December 1981 for current editors) excludes *Doc Savage's* editor John Nanovic as that magazine did not require the same kind of editorship as a normal sf magazine.

	Editor	Total Issues
1	**John W. Campbell** (*Astounding/Analog* 409; *Unknown* 39)	448
2	**Raymond A. Palmer** (*Amazing* 117; *Fantastic Adventures* 90; *Other Worlds* 46; *Science Stories* 4; *Universe* 10; *Mystic* 16) *Mystic* 16)	283
3	**John Carnell** (*New Worlds* 141; *Science Fantasy* 62; *SF Adventures* 32)	235
4	**Robert A.W. Lowndes** (*Future* 61; *SF Quarterly* 36; *Dynamic* 6; *Science Fiction Stories* 38; *Magazine of Horror* 36; *Famous SF* 9; *Startling Mystery Stories* 18; *Bizarre Fantasy* 2; *Weird Terror Tales* 3)	209
5	**Edward L. Ferman** (*F & SF* 201; *Venture* 6)	207
6	**Farnsworth Wright** (*Weird Tales* 179; *Oriental Stories/Magic Carpet* 14)	193
7	**Frederik Pohl** (*Astonishing* 16; *Super Science* 16; *Star* 1; *Galaxy* 47; *If* 69; *Worlds of Tomorrow* 23; *International SF* 2)	174
8	**Hugo Gernsback** (*Amazing* 37; *Amazing Annual/-Quarterly* 6; *Air Wonder* 11; *(Science) Wonder* 78; *Wonder Quarterly* 14; *Scientific Detective* 10; *SF Plus* 7)	163
9	**Cele Goldsmith** (*Amazing* 79; *Fantastic* 79)	158
10	**Horace L. Gold** (*Galaxy* 115; *Beyond* 10; *If* 14)	137

John W. Campbell

The only person who can reasonably challenge Campbell's record is Edward L. Ferman who, assuming he continues to publish and edit *F & SF* on its monthly schedule will equal Campbell's 448 in January 2002, two months before Ferman's sixty-fifth birthday. Stanley Schmidt would have to edit *Analog* until mid-2013 to equal it.

THE 10 YOUNGEST MAGAZINE EDITORS

C19

The age is given, where known, at the time the editor was appointed. Where this is not known the age is for three months prior to the cover date on existing magazines and six months prior for new magazines.

1 **Charles D. Hornig. 17 years 4 months**
Hornig was a young fan who sent his fanzine *The Fantasy Fan* to Gernsback just at the time that the previous editor, David Lasser, was leaving. Gernsback was so impressed with the fanzine that he called Hornig in and, despite being taken aback at his age, hired him. Hornig took over *Wonder Stories* from the November 1933 issue.

2 **Peter Hamilton. 18 years 0 months**
Peter Hamilton stepped into editorial shoes straight from school when, through his own efforts, he succeeded in convincing his family printing firm into issuing a regular science fiction magazine, *Nebula,* the first, and so far only, native Scottish magazine. The first issue was dated Autumn 1952, but Hamilton had officially started work on the magazine in mid-May, just two weeks after his eighteenth birthday.

3 **Frederik Pohl. 19 years 9 months**
With the boom in pulp magazines in the late 1930s Pohl chanced his arm at Popular Publications and was given the chance of editing his own new sf magazines. The first was *Astonishing Stories* in February 1940.

4 **Laurence M. Janifer. 20 years 2 months**
Although not credited it was Janifer, under the control of Scott Meredith who compiled and edited the four issues of *Cosmos* starting with the issue for September 1953.

5 **Mort Weisinger 21 year 2 months**
One of the leading fans of the 1930s Weisinger had not long been in the employ of Standard Magazines when they acquired Gernsback's *Wonder Stories* and reissued it as *Thrilling Wonder Stories* with Weisinger as editor in August 1936.

6 **Beatrice Mahaffey 23years 4 months**
At the World SF Convention in Cincinnati in 1949 Ray Palmer announced that he was going to hire Bea Mahaffey as an assistant editor on his new magazine *Other Worlds.* A few months later the accident-prone Palmer had another accident which suddenly left Mahaffey alone at the helm.

7 **Michael Moorcock. 24 years 2 months**
At the age of seventeen Moorcock had been the editor of a juvenile magazine *Tarzan Adventures.* Seven years later at the point when it seemed that Britain's leading sf magazine, *New Worlds,* was about to cease publication, a new publisher stepped in to the fray and salvaged it and with Moorcock as the new editor it was re-launched in May 1964.

8 **Robert A.W. Lowndes. 24 years 4 months**
In 1940, at the instigation of Donald Wollheim, Lowndes wrote to Blue Ribbon magazines, the publishers of *Future Fiction,* saying how bad the magazines were and how much better he could edit them. Louis Silberkleit took him at his word (and a lower salary than the previous editor, Charles Hornig) and hired him from the April 1941 issue.

9 **Donald A. Wollheim. 24 years 11 months**
Like his fellow Futurians, Frederik Pohl and Robert Lowndes, Wollheim was also on the look-out for editorial possibilities and his trail ended with Jerry Albing who gave Wollheim a minute budget and the chance to edit two new magazines. The first was *Stirring Science Stories* in February 1941. Wollheim is today the successful publisher of DAW Books in New York.

10 **Walter Gillings. 25 years**
The youngest of the British editors, Walter Gillings, is the father of British magazine sf. He fought hard and long during the 1930s to interest a publisher in bringing out a British science fiction magazine and finally succeeded with Worlds Work who gave him the opportunity to assemble *Tales of Wonder* issued in thc Summer of 1937.

THE 10 OLDEST SF MAGAZINE EDITORS

C20

	Editor	Date of Last Issue Under Direct Editorial Control	Age
1	**T.O. Conor Sloane** Sloane was also the oldest new editor. When Gernsback appointed him on the first issue of *Amazing* in April 1926 he was already seventy-four years old.	*Amazing Stories* April 1938	86y 4m
2	**Hugo Gernsback** Although Sam Moskowitz and Harvey Gernsback had the greater editorial control over *SF Plus*, Hugo always involved himself more than usual with his sf magazines and his influence on this one was no different.	*SF Plus* December 1953	69y 2m
3	**Ejler Jakobssen**	*Galaxy* May 1974	62y 3m
4	**John W. Campbell** Campbell died on July 11th 1971.	*Analog* December 1971	61y 1m
5	**Leo Margulies** Like Gernsback and Cohen, Margulies was both publisher and editor.	*Satellite* May 1959	59y ?m
6	**Sol Cohen** Cohen remained as publisher for another eight years.	*Amazing Stories* Nov 1969	58y ?m
7	**Lester del Rey**	*Worlds of Fantasy* Fall 1970	55y
8	**Robert A.W. Lowndes**	*Magazine of Horror* April 1971	54y 5m
9	**Sam Moskowitz**	*Weird Tales* Summer 1974	53y 7m
10	**John Carnell**	*New Worlds* April 1964	51y 10m

THE 20 MOST PROLIFIC SF MAGAZINE COVER ARTISTS

C21

The artist is always hard done by in the SF field because until recently his work was seldom credited — certainly not on book covers. Much more research is required before it would be possible to ascertain who has illustrated the most book covers. However, as a rule, the SF magazines have been more generous. The following shows the twenty most prolific artists together with the first magazine cover they painted, the total number of covers they painted, and the magazine which has featured most of their covers (with the number in brackets).

		Cover Debut	No. Covers	Chief Mag	No.
1	**Ed Emshwiller**	Galaxy Jun 51	275	F & SF	(71)
2	**Kelly Freas**	Weird Tales Nov 50	185	Analog	(111)
3	**Frank R. Paul**	Amazing Apr 26	183	Wonder	(77)
4	**Earle K. Bergey**	Strange Stories Aug 39	153	Thrilling Wonder	(59)
5	**Jack Gaughan**	Fantasy Book 6, 1950	120	Galaxy	(38)
6	**Virgil Finlay**	Weird Tales Feb 37	106	FFM	(27)
7	**Leo Morey**	Amazing Feb 30	103	Amazing	(77)
8	**Robert Gibson Jones**	Fantastic Adventures Aug 42	100	Fantastic Adventures	(46)
9	**Ed Valigursky**	Fantastic Adventures Nov 51	90	Amazing	(49)
	Howard V Brown	Astounding Oct 33	90	Astounding	(53)
11	**Alex Schomburg**	Thrilling Wonder Oct 51	87	Amazing	(18)
12	**Brian Lewis**	New Worlds Jul 57	81	New Worlds	(41)
13	**Mel Hunter**	Galaxy Feb 53	75	F & SF	(31)
	John Schoenherr	SF Adventures Jan 58	75	Analog	(72)
15	**Margaret Brundage**	Oriental Stories Spr 32	72	Weird Tales	(66)
16	**Gerard Quinn**	New Worlds Jan 52	68	New Worlds	(36)
17	**Hans Wessolowski**	Amazing Stories Quarterly Fall 29	60	Astounding	(41)
18	**Malcolm Smith**	Amazing Jan 42	59	Imagination	(21)
	Hubert Rogers	Astounding Feb 39	59	Astounding	(58)
20	**Harold McCauley**	Fantastic Adventures Sep 39	57	Fantastic Adventures	(17)

Brian Lewis and Gerard Quinn are the only two British artists to make the list.

'F & SF' March 1962

THE LONGEST RUNNING SF MAGAZINES

C22

I'm counting 'longest-running' as meaning the greatest number of issues rather than 'oldest', although the terms give almost the same results. I've limited myself to English language magazines because of the almost total unavailability of foreign language magazines, although I would mention the defunct Romanian magazine *Colectia Povestiri* which reached 373 issues and the current Swedish magazine *Jules Verne Magasinet* now just in excess of 373 issues, as some idea of their measure. For the purposes of this list I've included *Doc Savage* because although most of the short stories in that magazine were non-fantasy, the lead novel which took up almost 90% of it, usually was. All figures below relating to current magazines are as at December 1981.

1 **Analog** January 1930 — current. (formerly *Astounding Stories* then *Astounding SF*) *614 issues.*

2 **Amazing Stories** April 1926 — current. *502 issues.*

3 **Mag. F & SF** Fall 1949 — current. *367 issues.*

4 **Weird Tales** March 1923 — current. (ceased in 1954 but revived twice since and now a regular paperback magazine) *286 issues.*

5 **Galaxy** October 1950 — (in limbo) *254 issues.*

6 **New Worlds** Summer 1946 — (in limbo) (the only British title in the list) *217 issues.*

'Analog' 50th Anniversary Issue

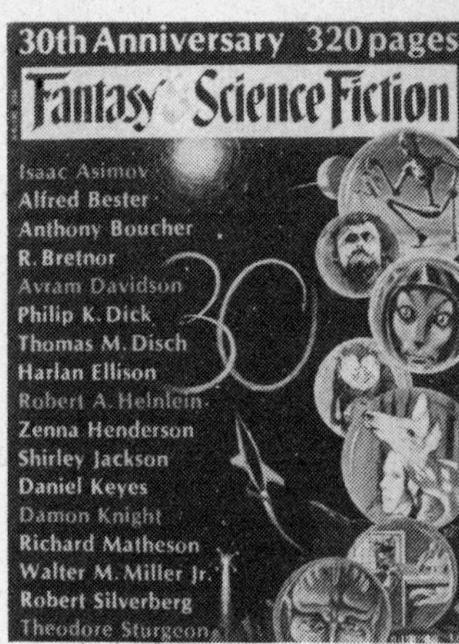

'F & SF' 30th Anniversary Issue

7 **Fantastic** Summer 1952 — October 1980 (*Fantastic* was for a while the companion to and then absorbed *Fantastic Adventures.* If that magazine's run of 129 issues is taken into account then *Fantastic* would total 337 issues and be placed fourth) *208 issues.*

8 **(Thrilling) Wonder** June 1929 — Winter 1955 (began as *Science Wonder Stories,* became *Wonder Stories* and finally *Thrilling Wonder Stories.* My total excludes the two reprint samplers issued in 1957 and 1963) *189 issues.*

9 **Doc Savage** March 1933 — Summer 1949 *180 issues.*

10 **If** March 1952 — December 1974 *175 issues.*

THE 7 SHORTEST SF STORIES

Fredric Brown (1906-72), who wrote more short-short stories than anyone else, traditionally gave birth to the microyarn in this untitled story which ran as a prologue to *Knock* (1948):

> The Last Man on Earth sat alone in a room. There was a knock on the door...

In the years since then, writers have progressively chipped away at those seventeen words and here, in reverse order, are some of the shortest of them all.

7 *The Shortest Science Fiction Love Story Ever Written* by Jeff Renner (*F & SF* March 1964, © Mercury Press, 1964)

Boy Meets Girl,
Boy Loses Girl,
Boy Builds Girl.
9 words

6 *The Shortest Science Fiction Story Ever Told* by Roger Deeley (*Generation* edited by David Gerrold, Dell Books, New York, 1972, © Roger Deeley, 1972)

Time Ended. Yesterday.
18 letters

5 *Sign At The End Of The Universe* by Duane Ackerson (*Alternities* edited by David Gerrold, Dell Books, New York, 1974, © Duane Ackerson, 1974)

This Side Up.
9 letters

4 *Cosmic Report Card* by Forrest J Ackerman (*Vertex* June 1973, © Forrest J Ackerman, 1973)

F
1 letter

In all truth this is cheating because the story cannot be understood as it stands, not even with the help of the title. One must refer to a host of ancillary information included on the *Cosmic Report Card* itself, and hence I feel it does not qualify. I include it because so many people refer to it. Instead Ackerman should consider the next story...

3 *Atomigeddon* 2419 *A.D.* by Forrest J Ackerman (*Vertex* June 1973, © Forrest J Ackerman, 1973)

The End.
6 letters

Title and story this time do blend together and are comprehensive. In fact as the title helps so much in the understanding of these microyarns, especially the next two, Ackerman's story here in four words including the title, remains the shortest title-story combination.

2 *If Eve Had Failed To Conceive* by Ed Wellen (*Orbit 15* edited by Damon Knight, Harper & Row, New York, 1974, © Ed Wellen, 1974)

.
1 period

Think about it.

1 *Why Booth Did Not Shoot Lincoln* by Ed Wellen (*Orbit 15* edited by Damon Knight, Harper & Row, New York, 1974, © Ed Wellen, 1974)

total blank

I'm not sure I get this one, myself. No doubt it's crystal clear to our American readers. It is arguable that a complete blank cannot be a story, but at the same time we all know how dramatic in acting total silence can be so, what's the difference?

THE 10 LONGEST SF & FANTASY NOVELS

C24

The dividing line between a single unified novel and a continuous interrelated series is rather blurred. Some works published as trilogies are to all intents a single story and may be more unified than some novels published in one volume. For the following, therefore, I have considered those series which must be read as a whole and not in part and where each successive volume can only be read in sequence, with each volume complementing the others. You may disagree with the selection, but I have provided supporting evidence where I can.

On the matter of word-count, I have averaged out several pages and multiplied by the whole, allowing for blank spaces between chapters or for artwork. Knowing the vagaries of publishing, however, and the inconsistencies in the lengths of words, I think one should allow a plus-or-minus of at least 5,000 words on all of the following.

1 **The Chronicles of Thomas Covenant, The Unbeliever**
Stephen Donaldson. 510,000 words.
Three volumes that lead undeniably to a climax in the final book. Individual titles are *Lord Foul's Bane, The Illearth War* and *The Power That Preserves* (all 1977). Donaldson is at present at work on *The Second Chronicles,* with all three volumes likely to be in print by 1983, and boding to be even longer.

2 **Mistress of Magic**
Marion Zimmer Bradley. 492,000 words.
As yet unpublished. An Arthurian fantasy told from a woman's viewpoint, with Morgan LeFay as the heroine. If published uncut and unedited it may prove to be the longest single-volume novel.

3 **The Riverworld Saga**
Philip Jose Farmer. 453,000 words.
Originally planned and written as a single novel in 1954, the then entitled *I Owe For The Flesh* was never published, and it was not until 1964 that Farmer began to rewrite and considerably expand the novel with sections appearing separately as serials and short stories. Although elements of the series can stand alone, they all contribute toward the whole which consists of four books: *To Your Scattered Bodies Go* (1971), *The Fabulous Riverboat* (1971), *The Dark Design* (1977) and *The Magic Labyrinth* (1980).

4 **The Lord of the Rings**
J.R.R. Tolkien. 450,000 words.
Originally published as three separate volumes in 1954-55, it was eventually issued as a single volume in 1968, and cannot be considered as anything other than one continuous story.

5 **The Dune Trilogy**
Frank Herbert. 439,000 words.
When interviewed in 1973, Herbert said: 'I plotted a much longer work than *Dune*...I cut it up into three parts and held out more than a third of it for the first book.' Now available as one book, the trilogy first appeared as *Dune* (1965), *Dune Messiah* (1969) and *Children of Dune* (1976). Herbert has since completed *God-Emperor of Dune* (1981), but this is a true sequel to the original concept, not a part of it.

6 **Man: The Endangered Species**
L. Ron Hubbard. 438,000 words.
This is the working title for the first novel in over thirty years by the founder of Dianetics. The estimate is Hubbard's and was reported in *Locus* in March 1981. It may be that the final book, when edited and published, will be shorter.

7 **Camber of Culdi**
Katherine Kurtz. 407,000 words.

Another trilogy published as *Camber of Culdi* (1976), *Saint Camber* (1978) and *Camber the Heretic* (1981). Miss Kurtz wrote the trilogy because of the success of her first Deryni series, the events of which take place two centuries later. That trilogy, which ran *Deryni Rising* (1970), *Deryni Checkmate* (1972) and *High Deryni* (1973), itself totals 300,000 words.

8 **Circle of Light**
Niel Hancock. 403,000 words.
One of the many *Lord of the Rings* imitations which has proved surprisingly popular in the United States but has yet to appear in Britain. Like *Rings* it appeared as separate volumes, but is a continuous story. The books are *Greyfax Grimwald* (1977), *Faragon Fairingay* (1977), *Calix Stay* (1977) and *Squaring the Circle* (1977).

9 **The Chronicles of Amber**
Roger Zelazny. 400,000 words.
A continuous story that can only be understood if read in sequence, and even then the final volume leaves enough loose threads to allow for further episodes. The books are *Nine Princes in Amber* (1970), *The Guns of Avalon* (1972), *Sign of the Unicorn* (1975), *The Hand of Oberon* (1976) and *The Courts of Chaos* (1977).

10 **The Lensman Series**
E.E. Smith. 385,000 words.
As with Herbert's *Dune,* Smith originally planned *Children of the Lens* as a novel, but could not relate it without 300,000 words of introductory material. Later two other novels, *Tri-planetary* (1948) and *First Lensman* (1950), were worked into the series, but I have not treated those as part of the original sequence. The main 'novel' considered here runs *Galactic Patrol* (1937), *Gray Lensman* (1939), *Second-Stage Lensman* (1941) and *Children of the Lens* 1947.

Other novels which come close in the reckoning are *The Foundation Trilogy* by Isaac Asimov which, with the new book in the series, *Lightning Rod,* now nearing completion, brings the total wordage to 340,000 words; *Islandia* by Austin Tappin Wright, published posthumously in 1942 and totalling around 300,000 words, and several trilogies by Piers Anthony. Anthony reckons his own *Cluster* trilogy runs to 349,000 words, but my calculations make it 286,000 words. His *Tarot* triple-decker runs to 240,000 words. At a stretch one could include his *Xanth* sequence. The original three novels, *A Spell For Chameleon* (1977), *The Source of Magic* (1979) and *Castle Roogna* (1979) total 330,000 words, and recently Anthony completed a fourth, *Centaur Aisle* (1982). But this series is rather too loosely connected to be realistically considered.

6 OF THE LONGEST SF STORY TITLES

C25

1 **The Mad Merger Meets the Gorn from Sucker at some Indefinite Time in the Future when Things are in a Hell of a Mess but Everything Turns out All Right in the End with the Death of the Hero** by David Andrews (*Unique Tales* 1, 1974) 140 letters; 38 words. Published in a fanzine it is doubtful that had the story sold professionally the title would have survived. Editors and publishers are notorious at changing titles, so no doubt many potential mega-titles have been crushed at birth.

2 **Hot Wireless Sets, Aspirin Tablets, The Sandpaper Sides of Used Matchboxes, and Something that might have been Castor Oil** by D.G. Compton (Michael Joseph, 1971). 100 letters; 19 words. Actually this was a retitling. The English publisher didn't like the original US title *Chronocules* and took a gamble on a more gimmicky title. The gamble didn't work. It remains, however, the longest title for a book, if you exclude sub-titles.

3 **The Season the Lemmings Worshipped the Slime-God and Daisy Jack Found the Factory had Swallowed His Quicksand People** by Harlan Ellison. 98 letters; 19 words.

4 **Adrift Just off the Islets of Langerhans: Latitude 38° 54' North, Longitude 77° 00' 13" West** by Harlan Ellison (*F & SF* October 1974). 75 letters (including symbols); 16 words.

5 **An Occurrence on the Mars-To-Earth Run No 128, At Approximately 2400 Hours, 21 January 2038** by William Dean (*F & SF* August 1971). 72 letters; 16 words.

6 **'I Had Vacantly Crumpled It into my Pocket...But By God, Eliot, It was a Photograph from Life!'** by Joanna Russ (*F & SF* August 1964). 71 letters; 18 words.

THE 4 SHORTEST SF STORY TITLES

C26

In reverse order of publication:

1 **Z** by Charles L. Fontenay (*If* June 1956)

2 **T** by Brian W. Aldiss (*Nebula* November 1956)

3 **●** by Gahan Wilson (*Again, Dangerous Visions* edited by Harlan Ellison, 1972)

4 **I** by Ed Weller (*Alfred Hitchcock's Mystery Magazine* February 1975 — and it is sf as well as a mystery as it concerns a computer that plays detective).

THE 10 LONGEST-RUNNING SF & FANTASY SERIES

C27

I've been selective in the following for two reasons. If I listed just the top ten series of all time, they would nearly all be of German origin. I take my hat off to the Germans. They cannot be touched when it comes to long-running series. *Crossroads* has nothing on them. The one trouble is that most of the series are totally unknown outside Germany, and a list of such titles as *Sun Koh, der Erbe von Atlantis,* won't mean very much. So, I hope the Germans will excuse me if I limit the list to just one-and-a-half (yes, one-and-a-half) German series, and acknowledge that they dominate the field. Secondly I've also excluded all juvenile series. Perhaps I should say *intentionally* juvenile, before you cast your eyes below. Otherwise, from the Frank Reade Jr., series of a hundred years ago, up to the *Dr Who* spin-off books of today, the following list would also be dominated by all the Tom Swifts of this world. So what you're left with really are the ten longest non-German non-juvenile series of all time.

1 **Perry Rhodan** 1039 novels as at 1981. This is the champion of all time and must surely be unbeatable. Ever since 1961 on a schedule that has been monthly, fortnightly and even weekly, Perry Rhodan, Overlord of the Universe, has battled all manner of foe. The series was created by Walter Ernsting and Karl-Herbert Scheer, and is written by a team of writers. Until recently Ernsting, writing as Clark Darlton, had written the bulk of the series, but at present the authorship of the 1039 novels is split as follows: William Voltz 193, Ernsting 171, H.G. Ewers 164, Kurt Mahr 155, Hans Kneifel 87, H.G. Francis 71, Ernst Vlcek 69, Scheer 51, Kurt Brand 37, Marianne Sydow 17, Peter Terrid 10, Peter Griese 6, W.W.Shols 4, Conrad Shepherd 3 and Harvey Patton 1. Rhodan has a companion series *Atlan,* featuring some of the same characters and written by the same team. Currently that stands as the second longest running series at 512 novels. The Rhodan books have been translated into many languages including English, but have not met with the same popularity elsewhere as they have in Germany.

2 **Doc Savage** 181 novels. Created by Henry Ralston of the publishers Street & Smith, Doc Savage became one of the most popular heroes of the pulps. The adventures of the Man of Bronze, Fighter against Evil were written mostly by Lester Dent, although as a rule the series bore the by-line, Kenneth Robeson, a house-pseudonym. Dent wrote 165 of the novels, Norman Daniels 9, Alan Hathway 4, and William Bogart 3. The magazine ran from March 1933 to Summer 1949. In 1964 Bantam Books began to re-issue the series in paperback form to a new readership and currently 106 of the adventures have been reprinted. George Pal also made a feature film of the first novel *The Man of Bronze* in 1974.

3 **Ki-Gor** 57 novels. Ki-Gor was probably the most successful of the many Tarzan imitation characters. His novel-length adventures were printed in *Jungle Stories* from January 1939 through to April

1954. The novels bore the by-line John Peter Drummond, a publishing convenience which hid the identities of many authors few of whom are known today.

4 **Cap Kennedy** 42 novels. Cap Kennedy, Secret Agent of the Spaceways, was conceived by British author E.C. Tubb along with his American publisher Donald Wollheim. Kennedy was clearly modelled on the popular pulp character of Captain Future, and set up as a rival to Perry Rhodan. The books appeared under the house name of Gregory Kern which was leased to the German publisher Bastei Verlag who changed the character's name to Commander Scott and brought in their own team of writers to add to the series. Tubb wrote seventeen of the Kennedy novels, all of which were translated, whilst the remainder were the work of Horst Pukallus and Ronald Hahn. The series ran from 1974 to 1977.

5 **Richard Blade** 33 novels and still going. Blade was conceived by Lyle Kenyon Engel and the adventures were initially written by a team of writers, although recently Roland Green has written most of them, all under the house pseudonym of Jeffrey Lord. The first book was *The Bronze Axe* (1969) and the series continues at the rate of two or three a year. Dark Shadows 32 novels. This is the first of the series (non-German, non-juvenile!) to be written by one man alone, and not a team. William E.D. Ross, writing under his wife's name as Marilyn Ross, produced this television-spawned series of supernatural novels featuring the popular Barnabas Collins. The original TV series, *Dark Shadows*, was broadcast in the States five nights a week but was initially almost a flop until the character of Collins was introduced, when it promptly attracted a pulp following. The first Barnabas Collins book is number six of the series. The TV series has the distinction of having more episodes than any other fantasy series — a thousand in all, from 1966-1972.

6 **Dark Shadows** 32 novels. This is the first of the series (non-German, non-juvenile!) to be written by one man alone, and not a team. William E.D. Ross, writing under his wife's name as Marilyn Ross, produced this television-spawned series of supernatural novels featuring the popular Barnabas Collins. The original TV series, *Dark Shadows*, was broadcast in the States five nights a week but was initially almost a flop until the character of Collins was introduced, when it promptly attracted a pulp following. The first Barnabas Collins book is number six of the series. The TV series has the distinction of having more episodes than any other fantasy series — a thousand in all, from 1966-1972.

7 **Tarzan** 30 novels. Probably one of the best known fictional characters of all time, the original stories and novels by Edgar Rice Burroughs fill twenty-four books from *Tarzan of the Apes* to *Tarzan*

and the Castaways. In 1966 Fritz Leiber wrote the one official non-Burroughs Tarzan novel *Tarzan and the Valley of Gold*. There have been a number of unauthorised Tarzan novels most notably the five by Peter T. Scott and Peg O'Neill Scott and published in Connecticut in 1964/5 all under the alias Barton Werper.

8 **Dray Prescott** 26 novels and still going. For a long time the identity of the author of this space opera series, Alan Burt Akers, was a well kept secret though the novels are now known to be the work of British writer Kenneth Bulmer. A complicated and well-conceived series the books are nevertheless clearly inspired by Burroughs's Martian series. The first novel was *Transit to Scorpio* in 1972 and the latest as I write is *Allies of Antares*.

9 **Dumarest of Terra** 25 novels and still going. This is the first series so far listed which is not only all the work of one man but is actually published under his own name, E.C. Tubb. Tubb is thus the only author to have two series in the top ten. Dumarest is probably Tubb's most popular character: a doomed hero on his relentless quest to find old Earth. The series began with *The Winds of Gath* in 1967 and the latest is *The Terridae*.

10 **Golden Amazon** 15 novels and 9 novellas. The Golden Amazon series about Violet Ray, a Super-Woman, was written by John Russell Fearn. An original sequence of four novelettes written during 1939-41, was entirely revamped into a series of novels and published in the Canadian *Star Weekly* from 1944 to 1961, finishing on Fearn's death.

A special note should be added on the longest-running series in terms of time-span. *The Jameson Satellite*, published in *Amazing Stories* in July 1931 introduced the character of Professor Jameson, conceived and written by Neil R. Jones. Thirty-six years later when the stories were being brought out in book-form, Jones added two new ones, bringing the total to twenty-three novelettes. Several more exist completed but as yet unpublished.

Similarly, Fritz Leiber's Gray Mouser series has been running since *Two Sought Adventure* appeared in *Unknown* in August 1939 and is still going.

THE 10 MOST REPRINTED SF SHORT STORIES

C28

I applied several restrictions to this category, so the following statistics will seem far lower than you might anticipate. It is all but impossible to trace the reprinting of all SF stories, especially those by Wells, Clarke and Bradbury in all manner of books and magazines, so my first limitation was to restrict the selection to genre anthologies only. I also excluded reprintings where the author and editor were one and the same, hence it excluded stories reprinted in author collections or where an editor has included one of his own stories in an anthology. The bulk of this information was derived from William Contento's invaluable *Index to Science Fiction Anthologies and Collections* (Boston, 1978) updated where possible, but this is a category that would change dramatically with further research (which is continuing).

1	**Nightfall** Isaac Asimov	16
2	**'Repent Harlequin!' Said the Ticktockman** Harlan Ellison	14
	The Cold Equations Tom Godwin	14
4	**The Star** H.G. Wells	13
5	**The Nine Billion Names of God** Arthur C. Clarke	12
6	**Nine Lives** Ursula K. LeGuin	11
	Billenium J.G. Ballard	11
8	**Day Million** Frederik Pohl	10
	Arena Frederic Brown	10
	The Star Arthur C. Clarke	10

THE 10 HIGHEST ADVANCES PAID FOR AN SF NOVEL

C29

The following information was taken from news releases published in *Locus* and *SF Chronicle.* They are listed in reverse order.

10 **The Vision** $130,000 by Dean R. Koontz — paperback rights purchased by Bantam Books.

9 **Rendezvous With Rama** $150,000 by Arthur C. Clarke — paperback rights purchased by Ballantine Books.

8 **Imperial Earth** $200,000 by Arthur C. Clarke — paperback rights purchased by Ballantine Books.

7 **Lucifer's Hammer** $236,500 by Larry Niven & Jerry Pournelle — purchased by Fawcett Books at auction.

Carl Sagan

6 **The Book of the Dun Cow** $280,000 by Walter Wangerin – paperback rights purchased by Pocket Books.

5 **The Number of the Beast** $500,000 by Robert A. Heinlein – purchased by Fawcett Books at open auction.

4 **Footfall** estimated $600,000 by Larry Niven & Jerry Pournelle – purchased by Fawcett Books at auction.

3 **God-Emperor of Dune** $750,000 by Frank Herbert – purchased by Berkley/Putnam.

2 **2010: Space Odyssey 2** $1 million by Arthur C. Clarke – purchased by Ballantine Books.

1 **Contact** $2 million by Carl Sagan – purchased by Simon & Schuster.

THE BEST-SELLING BOOKS IN BRITAIN IN 1980

C30

1980

1 **The Hitchhiker's Guide to the Galaxy**
Douglas Adams

2 **The Empire Strikes Back**
Donald F. Glut

3 **The Wounded Land**
Stephen Donaldson

4 **The Last Enchantment**
Mary Stewart

5 **The Master Mariner**
Nicholas Montserrat

6 **The Dark**
James Herbert

7 **The Stand**
Stephen King

8 **More Tales of the Unexpected**
Roald Dahl

9 **The Spear**
James Herbert

10 **The Dead Zone**
Stephen King

Close runners-up were *White Dragon* by Anne McCaffrey and *The Fountains of Paradise* by Arthur C. Clarke.

...AND 1981

C31

1981

1 **The Hitchhiker's Guide to the Galaxy**
Douglas Adams

2 **The Restaurant at the End of the Universe**
Douglas Adams

3 **Duncton Wood**
William Horwood

4 **Girl in a Swing**
Richard Adams

5 **The Jonah**
James Herbert

6 **Firestarter** Stephen King

7 **The Day of the Triffids**
John Wyndham

8 **Down to the Sunless Sea**
David Graham

9 **Dragondrums**
Anne McCaffrey

10 **The Wounded Land**
Stephen Donaldson

The above lists are calculated from the Bestsellers list as published weekly in *The Bookseller* and calculated in collaboration with the *Sunday Times.*

THE 10 FASTEST-SELLING SF AND FANTASY BOOKS IN THE UK IN 1981

C32

This list was derived from Alex Hamilton's excellent compilation of bestsellers published in *The Guardian* at the end of 1981. It was limited to books that saw their first UK publication in paperback in 1981, so excludes such other bestsellers as *The Restaurant At The End of the Universe.* I've amended the list slightly to take into account the number of months the book was on sale, so that a book that sold 20,000 in one month would feature higher than one that took four months even if in the end they sold the same total. The number of months on sale follows in brackets after the title, then average monthly sales and finally total home sales for 1981. Export sales are excluded.

1	**The Jonah** (3) James Herbert	93,215	279645
2	**Duncton Wood** (4) William Horwood	48,917	195667
3	**Clan of the Cave Bear** (3) Jean Auel	29,408	88225
4	**The Girl in a Swing** (6) Richard Adams	28,848	173086
5	**Firestarter** (5) Stephen King	26,458	132292
6	**Omen 3** (4) Gordon McGill	25,357	101428
7	**Raiders of the Lost Ark** (7) Campbell Black	20,830	145808
8	**Clash of the Titans** (6) Alan Dean Foster	9,275	55649
9	**Effigies** (10) William Wells	8,666	86663
10	**The Number of the Beast** (9) Robert A. Heinlein	6,898	62081

(My thanks to Mrs Alex Hamilton for her help in the compilation of the above)

9 ACTORS WHO HAVE APPEARED IN THE MOST SF/FANTASY FILMS

C33

The following list was supplied by bibliophile and bookdealer Richard Dalby whose knowledge of the deep, dark recesses of matters bibliographic and 'filmographic' are prodigious. He is the co-author of *The Dervish of Windsor Castle* (a biography of Arminius Vambery, the man who inspired Bram Stoker into writing *Dracula*), and has collected together *The Best Ghost Stories of H. Russell Wakefield.*

1	**John Carradine**	63
2	**Christopher Lee**	57
3	**Peter Cushing**	53
4	**Boris Karloff**	51
5	**Bela Lugosi**	40
6	**Lon Chaney, Jr.**	35
7	**Vincent Price**	33
8	**Donald Pleasance**	24
9	**Michael Gough**	17

This includes appearances both in starring and supporting roles.

John Carradine

10 OF THE RAREST AND MOST COLLECTIBLE SF BOOKS/MAGAZINES

C34

Every fan and collector has his one pride or prize in his collection or that one book that he has sought for years but which always eludes him. Books and magazines can command high prices for a variety of reasons, not necessarily rarity. They may contain first or scarce stories by a particular author or illustrations by a particular artist, or have some other significance. If you have any or all of the following items, however, I'd make sure that your house-contents insurance has sufficient cover.

1 **Dawn of Flame and Other Stories** by Stanley G. Weinbaum. Also known as the Weinbaum Memorial Volume. After Weinbaum's tragic death in 1935 a group of fans sponsored the publication of this collection, featuring the first publication anywhere of the title novel. Conrad H. Ruppert printed 500 copies, but only 250 were bound, the remaining sheets being destroyed by water in Raymond Palmer's basement. It exists in two variants. The rarer contains an unsigned introduction by Raymond A. Palmer and only five copies are known to exist, prepared specially for the sponsors: Ruppert, Palmer, Julius Schwartz, Lawrence Keating and Margaret Weinbaum. The other copies contain an introduction by Keating.

2 **The Shunned House** by H.P. Lovecraft. In 1928 Lovecraft's friend W. Paul Cook set in type Lovecraft's novelette 'The Shunned House' with the intention of publishing a limited edition. Sources differ on the number of copies printed. Lloyd Currey specifies 300, Sam Moskowitz believes that 'it could not have exceeded one hundred'. The book was never bound, however, but six sets of unbound sheets were circulated. In 1934 Robert H. Barlow secured the sheets and subsequently bound a handful of copies, some in boards others in paper. Currey reports that no more than seven copies are believed to exist, although de Camp refers to 'about a dozen' copies. It is these Barlow-bound copies, with Cook's 1928 copyright notice overprinted with Barlow's 1935 notice that are the rarities. There is just one copy presented to Lovecraft that was bound in full brown leather. Later Arkham House bound about a hundred sets and though rare, are not so sought after. Beware of a forged set that is known to exist, photo-offset from the Arkham House binding, although this has a collector's value of its own. Watch for the watermark. Cook's original bears the watermark 'Canterbury Laid', while the forgery is simply 'Chantry'.

3 **The Outsider and Others** by H.P. Lovecraft. This isn't an especially rare item. It was the first book published by August Derleth and Donald Wandrei's Arkham House and appeared in 1939 selling for $5.00. It carried a dustjacket by Virgil Finlay. Surprisingly it took years to sell out its print run of 1268 copies, but now it it one of the most sought after of collectors' items. Just how many still survive is not known but those collectors who have copies keep hold of them so that the book rarely comes on to the market.

4 **Poems and The Dream of X** by William Hope Hodgson. Hodgson took great care to ensure that the copyright on his books was protected in the United States and that no pirated editions of his books could appear unchallenged. When his massive *The Night Land* failed to find an American publisher, Hodgson rewrote the novel in a considerably reduced form as *The Dream of X.* Along with a dozen poems and another item it was printed privately in New York by Hodgson's agent R. Harold Paget in 1912. A corresponding copy was endorsed by Hodgson's English agent A.P. Watt. Just how many bound copies of these printings exist is not known but there are certainly only a few as Hodgson had to pay for the cost of production himself. It wasn't the first time he had produced such an edition. Equally rare, and perhaps more sought after, is *Carnacki, the Ghost Finder and a Poem,* a summary of four of the Carnacki cases, printed by Paul R. Reynolds in New York in 1910. Reynolds had earlier printed *The Ghost Pirates a Chaunty and Another Story* in 1909.

5 **The Cheetah Girl** by Christopher Blayre. As already mentioned under the List of Banned Books, the story of 'The Cheetah Girl' was to be included in Blayre's collection *The Purple Sapphire* published by Philip Allan in 1921. At the last moment, after the book had been set in proof, the publisher decided the story too risque to include and it was removed. Blayre, the pseudonym of Edward Heron-Allen, had twenty copies of the story bound for private circulation in 1923.

6 **The Ship that Sailed to Mars** by William M. Timlin. Published in London by George Harrap in 1923, bookdealer Richard Dalby says that in his experience this is the most beautiful and most sought-after sf and fantasy book. It was profusely illustrated in colour by the British-born South African author/artist William M Timlin, in a variety of styles reminiscent of Rackham, Dulac and Heath Robinson. 2,000 copies were published and retailed at 42/- *fifty years ago.* 12 inches high and 2 inches thick it is bound in half-vellum; the text is adorned with hand lettering, and the 49 full-colour illustrations are each separately mounted on matte paper.

7 **The History Of Civilisation** by E.E. Smith. This was a six-volume special edition boxed set of 'Doc' Smith's famous Lensman series: *Triplanetary, First Lensman, Galactic Patrol, Gray Lensman, Second Stage Lensman* and *Children of the Lens.* Published by Lloyd A Eshback's specialist imprint Fantasy Press during 1953-55, only 75 sets exist. Lloyd Currey details that each volume has a numbered leaf signed by the author inserted. They were issued without dustjackets.

8 **The Homunculus** by David H Keller. Aside from the general trade issue of this novel published in Philadelphia by Prime Press in 1949, a special deluxe boxed edition of only 112 copies was released, both numbered and signed. Many of Keller's books are available only in limited edition printings, and of special interest is *The Sign of the Burning Hart* published in a signed edition of 250 copies by the National Fantasy Fan Federation in 1948. Keller also published some of his own work including a poetry collection *Songs of a Spanish Lover* issued under the alias Henry Cecil in 1924 in an edition of only 50 copies.

9 **Nine Princes In Amber** by Roger Zelazny. Apparently shortly after Doubleday had published Zelazny's novel in 1970, but before stocks were released from the warehouse, a decision was made to pulp

Zelazny's previous book *Creatures of Light and Darkness* published by Doubleday in 1969. It seems the directive was misunderstood, so that not only *Creatures* but also *Nine Princes in Amber* was pulped. The mistake was discovered too late, and the whole print run had to be reprinted. Just how many of the first edition survived is not known, although several review copies were sent out. Check your copy.

10 **New Worlds** 21 May 1953
Don't panic. There is an issue of *New Worlds* 21 issued in May 1953 that is relatively common. Is yours digest-sized with 128 pages, cover price 1/6 and a cover by Alan Hunter illustrating E.R. James's 'Ride the Twilight Rail'. Oh well, never mind. So is everyone else's. All bar one copy, that is. For in 1953 *New Worlds* underwent a number of changes in format, linked with the plans to publish a series of paperback novels. The plans suddenly coalesced earlier than anticipated with the result that the originally planned *New Worlds* 21, in a slightly larger format, 96 pages and priced 2/-, was scrapped. At least one copy is known to exist, however, and there may be more. A similar scarcity applies to the June 1959 issue of the American magazine *Satellite SF*, which was never published. Sam Moskowitz reports, however, that a few sets of page proofs were run off and still exist as collectors' items.

'In Caverns Below' A40

SECTION D
ODDITIES AND ENTITIES

In which we discover
some of the peculiarities
and specialities of
science fiction.

30 LEADING SF WRITERS AND THEIR FIRST PUBLISHED WORKS

D1

1 **Jack Williamson** *The Metal Man, Amazing Stories* December 1928. Earlier Williamson had had an editorial entitled *Scientifiction, Searchlight of Science* published in the Fall 1928 issue of *Amazing Stories Quarterly* as the result of a contest.

2 **Clifford D. Simak** *The World of the Red Sun, Wonder Stories* December 1931. Simak had earlier sold *The Cubes of Ganymede* to *Amazing Stories* but it was never published.

3 **Eric Frank Russell** *The Saga of Pelican West, Astounding Stories* February 1937.

4 **Isaac Asimov** *Marooned Off Vesta, Amazing Stories* March 1939.

5 **Alfred Bester** *The Broken Axiom, Thrilling Wonder Stories* April 1939.

6 **A.E. Van Vogt** *The Black Destroyer, Astounding SF* July 1939. Van Vogt had previously sold a number of non-sf pieces to the confession magazines since 1932.

7 **Robert A. Heinlein** *Life-Line, Astounding SF* August 1939.

8 **Fritz Leiber** *Two Sought Adventure, Unknown* August 1939. Leiber had earlier sold *The Automatic Pistol* to *Weird Tales* but it was not published until May 1940.

9 **Theodore Sturgeon** *Ether Breather, Astounding SF* September 1939. Sturgeon had earlier sold a number of non-sf stories to the McClure syndicate since 1937.

10 **Frederik Pohl** *Before the Universe, Super Science Stories* July 1940. Frederik Pohl's early appearances are complicated. His first published work was a poem, *Elegy to a Dead Planet: Luna* in the October 1937 *Amazing Stories* as Elton Andrews. Two years later, acting as part agent-part collaborator, Pohl partially rewrote two stories by Milton Rothman and the first appeared as *Heavy Planet* in the August 1939 *Astounding SF* under the alias 'Lee Gregor'. The above listed story was a collaboration with Cyril Kornbluth and appeared under the alias 'S.D. Gottesman' but was published in *Super Science Stories* which Pohl himself edited. Pohl's first solo effort, *The Dweller in the Ice*, appeared under the pseudonym of 'James MacCreigh' in the January 1941 *Super Science* (still edited by Pohl). Pohl's first sale to a magazine not edited by himself was *A Prince of Pluto* in the April 1941 *Future Fiction* (edited by his friend Robert Lowndes) but this was also a collaboration with Kornbluth and appeared under the alias Paul Dennis Lavond! Pohl's first solo appearance in a magazine edited by another was with *Conspiracy on*

Illustration For 'The Metal Man'

Callisto in the Winter 1943 *Planet Stories* under the alias 'James MacCreigh'.

11 **Damon Knight** *Resilience, Stirring Science Stories* February 1941.

12 **Ray Bradbury** *Pendulum, Super Science Stories* November 1941. Bradbury had earlier had a non-sf story, It's Not the Heat, It's the Hu — in *Script Magazine* for 2 November 1940. Pendulum was a rewrite by Henry Hasse of an original by Bradbury that he had published in his own fan magazine *Futuria Fantasia* for Fall 1939. Bradbury did appear solo in the July 1942 *Astounding SF* with *Eat, Drink and Be Wary* but this was in the fan-orientated Probability Zero column which was more of a reader department than a true sale. His next appearance, *The Candle* in *Weird Tales* for November 1942 had actually been completed by Henry Kuttner. So we find that Bradbury's first true solo sale was *The Piper* published in the February 1943 *Thrilling Wonder Stories*. This story had also seen a prior appearance in Bradbury's *Futuria Fantasia* in the issue for Summer 1940.

13 **Jack Vance** *The World-Thinker, Thrilling Wonder Stories* Summer 1945.

14 **Arthur C. Clarke** *Loophole, Astounding SF* April 1946. Clarke had earlier sold a non-fiction article, *Man's Empire of Tomorrow* to *Tales of Wonder* and it appeared in the Winter 1938 issue.

15 **Poul Anderson** *Tomorrow's Children, Astounding SF* March 1946. Although the story bears the name of co-author F.N. Waldrop, the story was written entirely by Anderson from an idea suggested by Waldrop.

16 **Gordon R. Dickson** *Trespass! Fantastic Story Quarterly* Spring 1950. This story was a collaboration with Poul Anderson. Dickson's first solo story was *The Friendly Man, Astounding SF* February 1951.

17 **Harry Harrison** *Rock Diver, Worlds Beyond* February 1951.

18 **John Brunner** *Galactic Storm* (Curtis Warren, 1951) as 'Gill Hunt'.

19 **Frank Herbert** *Looking for*

Amid the deceit, the intrigue, the treachery marking the Earthmen's scheme to conquer the world of Ozagen, Hal Yarrow broke every taboo to love his Jeannette....

The LOVERS

A Novel by PHILIP JOSE FARMER

12

Foreword

DURING the day, the dreadnaught *Gabriel* squatted in a park in the center of the city of Siddo, on the planet Ozagen. From sunrise to sunset the *Gabriel's* personnel ventured out among the Ozagenians —or wogglebugs, as they were familiarly and contemptuously called—learning all they could of Ozagen's history, customs, language and other things.

The "other things," though the Earthmen did not mention this to the wogglebugs, were Ozagen's technologies. As far as could be seen, the wogs had progressed, roughly speaking, to the level of Earth's early 20th-century science. Logically, there should be nothing to fear from them. But the

13

Something?, Startling Stories April 1952. Herbert had previously appeared with a non-sf story *Survival of the Cunning* in the March 1945 *Esquire.*

20 **Philip K. Dick** *Beyond Lies the Wub, Planet Stories* July 1952.

21 **Philip Jose Farmer** *The Lovers, Startling Stories* August 1952. Farmer had a non-sf story, *O'Brien and Obrenov* in the March 1946 issue of *Adventure.*

22 **Marion Zimmer Bradley** *Keyhole, Vortex* 2, 1953.

23 **Robert Silverberg** *Gorgon Planet, Nebula SF* February 1954. Silverberg had an earlier article *Fanmag* in the December 1953 *Science Fiction Adventures.*

24 **Brian W. Aldiss** *Criminal Record, Science Fantasy* July 1954. Aldiss had earlier had a non-sf story, *A Book in Time* in *The Bookseller* for 13 February 1954 and, earlier still, had sold *T* to *Nebula* but that did not appear until November 1956.

25 **Michael Moorcock** *Peace on Earth, New Worlds* December 1959. This story was a collaboration with Barrington Bayley and appeared under the alias Michael Barrington. Moorcock had earlier sold several stories to the juvenile magazine *Tarzan Adventures* starting with *Sojan the Swordsman* in 1957. His first solo adult fantasy story was *The Dreaming City*, the first of the Elric stories, in *Science Fantasy* June 1961.

26 **Roger Zelazny** *Passion Play, Amazing Stories* August 1962. Zelazny had earlier entered a National Scholastic High School story contest and was successful in selling a story *Mister Fuller's Revolt* published in the October 1954 *Literary Cavalcade.*

27 **Ursulà K. Leguin** *April in Paris, Fantastic* September 1962.

28 **Larry Niven** *The Coldest Place, If* December 1964.

29 **Joan D. Vinge** *Tin Soldier, Orbit 14* edited by Damon Knight (1974)

30 **John Värley** *Picnic on Nearside, F & SF* August 1974. Varley also sold *Scoreboard* to *Vertex* and it appeared in the concurrent August 1974 issue.

4 RECIPIENTS OF POSTHUMOUS AWARDS

D2

1 **Richard M. McKenna** Better known outside the sf field for his novel *The Sand Pebbles* (1962), McKenna died in 1964 at the age of fifty-one. In 1967 his story *The Secret Place* (published posthumously in 1966 in Damon Knight's *Orbit 1*) received the Nebula Award for Best Short Story.

2 **Cyril M. Kornbluth** Kornbluth died in 1958 of a heart attack. A first class writer in his own right he was also well known for his collaborations with Frederik Pohl. In 1972 Frederik Pohl completed *The Meeting* from notes made by Kornbluth and the story won the 1973 Hugo for Best Short Story.

3 **J.R.R. Tolkien** The revered scholar and author of *The Lord of the Rings* died in 1973. In 1974 Lin Carter initiated a Grand Master of Fantasy Award (called the Gandalf after the wizard in *Rings*) for contributions to the fantasy genre and the first recipient was Tolkien. Carter later added a second, short-lived category, the Best Booklength Fantasy and this was won in 1978 again by Tolkien for *The Silmarillion.*

4 **Susan Wood** A very talented writer in the fan press Susan Wood had been the winner of three Hugos: in 1973 with her then husband Michael Glicksohn, for Best Fanzine *Energumen*, and in 1974 and 1977 as Best Fan Writer.

In 1981 she won the award again, but Susan had alas died in November 1980 aged only thirty-two. Her death was apparently caused by an accidental overdose of two drugs — aspirin and naproxen.

Susan Wood

10 STORIES BY ONE AUTHOR COMPLETED/REWRITTEN BY ANOTHER

D3

1 **The Lighthouse** by Edgar Allan Poe and Robert Bloch.
The Lighthouse was a story left incomplete by Poe at the time of his death; he had written a little more than 600 words. Just over a hundred years later the fragment was handed to Robert Bloch to complete and the story, now with 5,000 words of pure Bloch added, appeared in the January 1953 issue of *Fantastic*. It will also be found in the Sam Moskowitz anthology *A Man Called Poe* (1970).

2 **Nekht Semerkeht** by Robert E. Howard and Andrew J. Offutt.
Howard will go down in history as the most prolific posthumous collaborator of all-time. There seems no end to the story fragments that he left behind him and which, since the Howard boom of the mid-1960s, have been completed by others. This story is of particular interest as it was the very tale Howard was working on when he shot himself. Offutt included it in his 1977 anthology *Swords Against Darkness*. 'It's Howard's plot,' Offutt wrote. 'Most of it is Howard's writing. Dear God I hope this is close to the way he'd have done it.'

3 **The Black Wheel** by Hannes Bok and A. Merritt.
Abraham Merritt ranked as one of the most popular, if not the most popular fantasy writers of the first half of this century. One of his most devoted followers was Hannes Bok who, after Merritt's death in 1943, had the opportunity to complete two of Merritt's unfinished works. *The Black Wheel* was Merritt's last novel which he was working on at the time of his death, with 20,000 words done. Bok added 65,000 and the book

was published in 1947. *The Fox Woman* was a 15,000 word fragment that Merritt had toyed with but with no satisfaction and he gave it up. Although it has been published separately it is incomplete. Bok added his own epilogue as *The Blue Pagoda*, and the novel was published under the combined titles in 1946.

4 **The Hag Seleen** by Theodore Sturgeon and James H. Beard.
It is quite common for an editor having received a story with a good idea but which is poorly written, to hand that story over to another writer to add the final polish. James H. Beard was one such man who could not quite get his ideas adequately on paper. He had only one story accepted as it stood, *Five Fathoms of Pearls* , published in the December 1939 *Unknown*. The editor of *Unknown*, John W. Campbell, handed over the manuscripts of *The Bones* and *The Hag Seleen* to Theodore Sturgeon to bring up to standard, and both subsequently appeared in *Unknown Worlds*. A fourth story, *Carillon of Skulls*, was completed by Lester del Rey and published in the magazine under the pseudonym Philip James.

5 **The Black Kiss** by Robert Bloch and Henry Kuttner.
This was originally a story by Kuttner but, when it failed to sell, he passed it to Bloch to see if he could re-work it as a collaboration. Bloch revised it so substantially that although it was first published in the June 1937 *Weird Tales* as a collaboration, Kuttner felt that his name should be removed because it was too much the work of Bloch. Most subsequent reprintings have credited it to Bloch alone.

6 **The Little Man on the Subway** by Isaac Asimov and James MacCreigh.
MacCreigh was one of Frederik Pohl's pseudonyms used extensively during the 1940's. Pohl wrote the original draft of this story without success and so he passed it to Asimov who rewrote it. It still took a while to sell and only eventually appeared in the small circulation magazine *Fantasy Book* in 1950.

7 **Empire** by Clifford D. Simak.
According to Lloyd Currey in his *Science Fiction and Fantasy Authors* (1979), *Empire* was originally written by John W. Campbell, Jr. when in his teens. When Campbell became the editor of *Astounding* he gave the story to Simak to revise. Simak totally re-wrote it. 'I may have taken a few of the ideas and action, but I didn't use any of his words,' Simak commented. When Simak returned the manuscript to Campbell, he rejected it!

8 **The Utmost Abomination** by Clark Ashton Smith and Lin Carter.
When Smith died in 1961 he left behind a number of draft story outlines and notes. Lin Carter took it upon herself to attempt to imitate Smith's unique style and complete the more major outlines. *The Utmost Abomination*, completed from a 400-word fragment, was the first, and appeared in the Fall 1973 *Weird Tales*. Carter has completed five further fragments since then: *The Double Tower, The Scroll of Morloc, The Stairs in the Crypt, The Light From the Pole* and *The Descent Into the Abyss*

9 **The Meeting** by Frederik Pohl and Cyril M. Kornbluth.
Pohl and Kornbluth were the best of friends and the best of collaborators when Kornbluth was alive. After his death in 1958 he left behind him several outlines for stories, and Pohl completed all those he felt worthy — *The Quaker Cannon, The World of Myrion Flowers* and *Critical Mass*. That, it seemed, was that. And then,,in 1972 appeared *The Meeting*, completed from another remaining outline . The story won a Hugo in 1973 for Best Short Story.

10 **Deus Irae** by Philip K. Dick and Roger Zelazny.
Dick had started this novel in the early 1960s but became bogged down because, as he put it, 'my lack of knowldege of theology'. Meeting Zelazny in 1968, Dick asked him if he would help with the book and after much arduous agonising the book was finished and published in 1976, 12 years after its conception.

6 ROUND ROBIN STORIES

D4

Round-robin stories are those started by one writer who produces a certain quota of words and then passes it to another writer who continues for a further quota and then so on along the line until one writer is lumbered with writing a conclusion. It's only to be expected that written in this manner the stories lack for quality what they possess in novelty and ingenuity.

1 **Cosmos** (1933-35)
published as a supplement to the fan magazine *Science Fiction Digest* (later retitled *Fantasy Magazine*). Seventeen episodes written by: 1 Ralph Milne Farley; 2 David H. Keller; 3 Arthur J. Burks; 4 Bob Olsen; 5 Francis Flagg; 6 John W Campbell, Jr.; 7 Rae Winters (Raymond A. Palmer); 8 Otis Adelbert Kline & E. Hoffman Price; 9 Abner J. Gelula; 10 Raymond A. Palmer; 11 A. Merritt; 12 J. Harvey Haggard; 13 E.E. Smith 14 P. Schuyler Miller; 15 Lloyd A. Eshbach; 16 Eando Binder; 17 Edmond Hamilton.

2 **The Challenge from Beyond — I**
Commissioned by *Fantasy Magazine* in 1935, there were two round-robins of the same name, one sf and one fantasy. The sf sequence was by five authors: 1 Stanley G. Weinbaum; 2 Donald Wandrei; 3E.E. Smith; 4 Harl Vincent; 5 Murray Leinster.

3 **The Challenge from Beyond — II**
The fantasy sequence was also in five parts by: 1 C.L. Moore; 2 A. Merritt; 3 H.P. Lovecraft; 4 Robert E. Howard; 5 Frank Belknap Long.

4 **The Great Illusion**
A further *Fantasy Magazine* sequence published in 1936, this had the added novelty of having been written backwards, so that of the five authors listed here, Fearn wrote the ending first, and then Gallun picked up the threads and so on until Binder had to write the beginning! 1 Eando Binder; 2 Jack Williamson; 3 Edmond Hamilton; 4 Raymond Z. Gallun; 5 John Russell Fearn.

5 **The Covenant**
Commissioned by Cele Goldsmith and published in the July 1960 *Fantastic*. Sequence was written in order by: 1 Poul Anderson; 2 Isaac Asimov; 3 Robert Shekcley; 4 Murray Leinster; 5 Robert Bloch.

6 **Othuum**
Commissioned by Gerald Page, editor of *Witchcraft & Sorcery* and published in the tenth and final issue in 1974. In five parts, written by: 1 Brian Lumley; 2 David Gerrold; 3 Emil Petaja; 4 Miriam Allen deFord; 5 Ross Rocklynne.

10 SEQUELS TO BOOKS BY ONE WRITER WRITTEN BY ANOTHER

D5

It's only natural when a story or series is popular that fans would wish it to continue, even after the writer's death, as witness the many Sherlock Holmes pastiches. Certain sf and fantasy stories and series are no different as the following list shows.

1 **Conan** Created by Robert E. Howard, Conan the Cimmerian first flexed his muscles in *The Phoenix on the Sword* (*Weird Tales*

December 1932). Sixteen further Conan adventures appeared in *Weird Tales* with the last, a serial – *Red Nails*, having only just started when Howard killed himself. He left behind him many notes and outlines and when these were later discovered by L. Sprague de Camp, he revised, edited and added to the series to flesh out Conan's life. Of the paperback editions of the complete Conan, the only volumes that are wholly by Robert E. Howard are *Conan the Warrior* and *Conan the Conqueror*. The remainder consist mostly of fragments completed or rewritten by L. Sprague de Camp or Lin Carter. Further, totally new adventures have been written by de Camp and Carter along with Bjorn Nyberg, and most recently other writers have been drafted in to add to the saga. Recent books include *The Sword of Skelos* (1979) by Andrew Offutt, *The Road of Kings* (1979) by Karl Edward Wagner and *Conan the Rebel* (1980) by Poul Anderson. The Conan saga at present runs to 18 volumes.

2 **The Cthulhu Mythos** Although it was never called by that name in his day, H.P. Lovecraft began to write a series of stories with a connected background of which the first major tale was *The Call of Cthulhu* (*Weird Tales* February 1928). The basic idea soon captured the imagination of other writers and Lovecraft encouraged their involvement. The first was Frank Belknap Long who added to the Mythos with *The Hounds of Tindalos* (*Weird Tales* March 1929). In the intervening fifty years many writers have contributed to the Mythos, including Robert E. Howard, Clark Ashton Smith, August Derleth, Robert Bloch and Henry Kuttner. More recently novel-length works have appeared including *The Philosopher's Stone* (1969) by Colin Wilson, *The Transition of Titus Crow* (1975) and others by Brian Lumley, and *Strange Eons* (1979) by Robert Bloch. There have been anthologies containing reprinted and new stories edited by August Derleth, Lin Carter, Edward P. Berglund and Ramsey Campbell.

3 **Cugel the Clever** In 1965-66 Jack Vance published a series of stories about a cunning rogue called Cugel, collected in book form as *The Eyes of the Overworld* (1966). Cugel was one of Vance's most fascinating creations and his adventures were set against a background originally used by Vance in his sequence *The Dying Earth* (1950). *The Eyes of the Overworld* ended almost where it began and begged a sequel, but none was forthcoming. Eventually, Michael Shea obtained Vance's permission to use the character and the background in an adventure of his own, with only the one condition that Shea didn't kill Cugel off. The adventure appeared as *A Quest for Simbilis* (1974). Since then Vance has written a few more Cugel and Dying Earth stories and it is to be hoped that a further book will appear before long.

4 **Frankenstein** *Frankenstein* is probably second only to *Dracula* in the number of sequels and parodies that have appeared from other hands. Ignoring the many film spin-off novels, perhaps the most interesting from an sf viewpoint is *Frankenstein Unbound* (1973) by Brian W. Aldiss, set in a parallel

world where Mary Shelley and Victor Frankenstein co-exist.

5 **Lemuel Gulliver** The immediate success of Jonathan Swift's *Gulliver's Travels* (1726) spawned a host of imitations such as *Memoirs of the Court of Lilliput* (1727) by 'Captain Gulliver', and *Lilliput* (1796) by 'Lemuel Gulliver Jr'. Of more recent interest however are the two sequels written by Hungarian Frigyes Karinthy in 1916 and 1922 and published in English in 1966 as *Voyage to Faremido and Capillaria.* Furthermore in the pages of the American magazine *Fantastic*, Dr Joseph Wassersug, a New England medical-school teacher, writing under the alias Adam Bradford, wrote four modern sequels, *Lilliput Revisited* (December 1963), *Return to Brobdingnag* February 1964), *Gulliver's Magic Islands* (May 1964) and *Land of the Yahoos* (August 1964).

6 **Gray Lensman** Edward Elmer Smith's most popular story series are almost certainly those about the Lensmen. The core series runs *First Lensman, Galactic Patrol, Gray Lensman, Second Stage Lensman* and *Children of the Lens*, with a few other peripheral novels. Before Smith's death, fan William B. Ellern obtained permission to set an adventure in the same world as the Lensmen, and subsequently wrote a new novel *New Lensman* (1977). In 1980 David A. Kyle wrote a further addition *The Dragon Lensman.*

7 **Phileas Fogg** Phileas Fogg was the intrepid traveller in Jules Verne's *Around the World in Eighty Days* (1874). A century later Philip Jose Farmer retold the story — or rather told the real behind-the-scenes story — in *The Other Logg of Phileas Fogg* (1973). Farmer, more than any other writer, has added new novels to old adventures. *The Wind Whales of Ishmael* (1971) for instance is a direct sequel to Herman Melville's *Moby Dick*, whilst *Hadon of Ancient Opar* (1974), is set in the same setting but centuries earlier as Burroughs's *Tarzan and the Jewels of Opar* (1918).

8 **Arthur Gordon Pym** Edgar Allan Poe's The Narrative of Arthur Gordon Pym of Nantucket (1838), ends so abruptly and inconclusively that several writers have attempted their own version of the real events omitted from the narrative. Probably the best know is Jules Verne's *Le Sphinx des glaces* (1897) *The Sphinx of the Icefields,* translated as *An Antarctic Mystery*). To Some extent H.P. Lovecraft's *At the Mountains of Madness* (1936) is his own extension of the mystery.

9 **Tarzan** The Edgar Rice Burroughs Estate holds such a strong tie on the rights of Tarzan that only one authorised non-Burroughs Tarzan novel exists, *Tarzan and the Valley of Gold* (1966) by Fritz Leiber. A few unauthorised sequels have been written and published (see Banned Books), and only Philip Jose Farmer has had special permission for his variations on the Tarzan saga with books such as *Lord Tyger* (1970) and *The Adventures of the Peerless Peer* (1974).

10 **The Time Machine** All who have read H.G. Well's *The Time Machine* (1895), know that our intrepid hero returned to the future, and the narrator awaits his return. Wells had no intention of writing a sequel, but in Austria, sometime during the 1920s or 30s, Egon Friedell, a Viennese dramatist, penned his own sequel. The book was never published during Friedell's lifetime and may well have been unauthorised by Wells. Friedell, of Jewish descent, committed suicide when the Nazis entered Austria in 1938. His book first appeared in print in 1946 as *Die Reise mit der Zeitmaschine*, but an English edition did not appear until 1972 with a translation by Eddy Bertin as *The Return of the Time Machine.*

10 AMERICAN SF WRITERS BORN IN EUROPE

D6

1 **Piers Anthony** born at Oxford in England in 1934 (within six weeks and almost as many miles of John Brunner), reached America viä Spain while still a youngster and took out American citizenship in 1958.

2 **Algis Budrys** Full name Algirdas Jonas Budrys is still a Free Lithuanian citizen as he was born under diplomatic passport in Konigsberg, East Prussia, Germany in January 1931. His father, Jonas Budrys, was Consul General of Lithuania in East Prussia until 1936, and then in New York City from 1936 to his death in 1964. 'U.S.A. never recognised the Red Army occupation of 1940 or subsequent changes of *de facto* regime,' Budrys asserts. 'Ergo, Lithuania exists *de jure.* I have been a resident in the U.S. under that same passport, since 1936.'

3 **Arsen Darnay** was born in Budapest, Hungary in the 1930s and came to the United States after the War when he was 15.

4 **Hugo Gernsback** the Father of Magazine Science Fiction, was born in Luxembourg in August 1884 and came to the United States in February 1904. By the next year he was publishing a radio catalogue which metamorphosed into the technical magazine *Modern Electrics* in 1908 and so germinated the seed that would sprout 18 years later into the first true sf magazine *Amazing Stories.*

5 **Willy Ley** was born in Berlin, Germany, in October 1906. An early interest in science fiction and rocketry caused him to write a treatise *Die Fahrt ins Weltall* (A Trip Into Space, 1926). A member of the German Rocket Society from the start, Ley can be counted as one of the true pioneers of space travel. Ley left Germany in 1935 travelling to the United States via England, and he never returned. Within a couple of years he was writing stories and articles for the sf magazines and rapidly became a much respected and popular contributor to the field.

6 **Hans Stefan Santesson** was better known as an editor than a writer, editing *Fantastic Universe* during its heyday in the late 1950s. Santesson had been born in Paris, France in 1914.

7 **James H. Schmitz** was born in Hamburg, Germany in October 1911 and came to the United States at the outbreak of World War II, selling one story to John Campbell (*Greenface* in *Unknown Worlds* August 1943) before being drafted.

8 **Kurt Siodmak** was born in Dresden, Germany in August 1902, and had already sold sf stories and novels in Germany before he went to England in 1933 and subsequently the U.S. in 1937 where he soon established himself as a film director and writer. The

John Taine

July 1926 *Amazing Stories* had featured a translation of Siodmak's early story *The Eggs From Lake Tanganyika.*

9 **John Taine** was the sf pseudonym of Eric Temple Bell, a Professor of Mathematics who was born at Peterhead in Scotland in February 1883 and who came to the United States in 1902, later becoming a naturalised citizen. His sf began to appear in 1924 with the publication of his lost race novel *The Purple Sapphire.*

10 **George Zebrowski** was born in Villach, Austria in December 1945 and was raised in the Tyrol and in England before settling in the United States. He sold his first sf in 1970.

20 SF WRITERS WHO MARRIED EACH OTHER

D7

1 **7 June 1940 Henry Kuttner and C.L. Moore**
Perhaps one of the most popular writing teams of sf. Both Kuttner and Moore had established themselves individually as writers before their marriage but after, their combined talents masked behind such pseudonyms as Lewis Padgett and Lawrence O'Donnell produced such classics as *Fury* (1947) and *The Fairy Chessmen* (1946). Kuttner died in 1958 and Catherine Moore has since re-married.

2 **31 December 1946 Edmond Hamilton and Leigh Brackett**
Both popular writers in their own right, they advised each other on their work but they never outwardly collaborated. That is, until their last story *Stark and the Star Kings* where, at the request of Harlan Ellison for his *magnum opus The Last Dangerous Visions*, they combined their two great heroes Eric John Stark and John Gordon. Hamilton died on February 1st 1977, Leigh died on March 18th 1978, whilst working on the screenplay of *The Empire Strikes Back*.

3 **17 May 1947 James Blish and Virginia Kidd**
Blish's first marriage and Virginia's second. In the shadow of her husband's writing career, Virginia concentrated on her activities as a ghost-writer, but the two collaborated at least once on the story *On the Wall of the Lodge* (1962). The couple divorced in 1963, and James Blish remarried. Virginia Kidd established her own literary agency.

4 **1948 Frederik Pohl and Judith Merril**
In both cases this was their second marriage. Judith Merril had been born Josephine Judith Grossman

Kate Wilhelm/Damon Knight

and from her first marriage had become Judith Zissman. Later this combination of maiden and matrimonial names caused Damon Knight to pen this golden rhyme:

Juliet Grossman Zissman Pohl
Hated her name from the bottom of her soul;
Went to court in imminent peril;
Changed her name to Judith Merril.

Pohl and Merril were divorced in 1953 and both have subsequently re-married.

5 **29 September 1962 Michael Moorcock and Hilary Bailey**
By 1962 Moorcock was starting to establish himself in *Science Fantasy* as the writer of the Elric stories. Hilary, a journalist, had yet to make the grade, though within a year her first story, *Breakdown*, had appeared in *New Worlds*. Shortly after Moorcock had become editor of *New Worlds*, he published one of Hilary's best stories, *The Fall of Frenchy Steiner* (1964). Moorcock and Bailey separated in 1973 and were subsequently divorced.

6 **23 February 1963 Damon Knight and Kate Wilhelm**
Damon Knight's third marriage and Kate Wilhelm's (nee Meredith) second, brought together two of sf's best talents. Both had already established themselves as writers in the 1950s though after their marriage Knight concentrated more on the editing side of the business, whilst Kate wrote success after success.

7 **4 June 1969 Alexei Panshin and Cory Seidman**
By 1969 Panshin had already established himself as both a writer and critic, his novel *Rite of Passage* carrying off the 1969 Hugo for Best Novel. Since their marriage Alexei and Cory frequently write together with both by-lines adorning the books, most recently *Earth Magic* (1978).

8 **17 January 1972 Vernor Vinge and Joan Dennison**
Vernor Vinge, a professor of mathematics, had sold his first story in 1965 and notched up several more sales including *Grimm's World* (1969) and *The Witling* (1976). After their marriage, and at Vernor's prompting, Joan turned her hand to writing, and within a very short space of time Joan D. Vinge established herself as one of the big new writers of the 1970s. Joan and Vernor were subsequently divorced and Joan has now remarried.

9 **2 September 1972 Stephen Goldin and Kathleen Sky**

Goldin had made his first sale at the age of seventeen to Frederik Pohl at *If*, and made several notable sales in the years immediately after. He has since taken on the task of chronicling the Family d'Alembert saga from an outline prepared by E.E. Smith. Since their marriage Kathleen Sky has become a writer with several stories and such novels as *Birthright* (1975) and *Ice Prison* (1976).

10 **30 November 1973 Isaac Asimov and Janet Jeppson** Asimov's second marriage. Janet Jeppson is a doctor and psychiatrist who, at the time of the marriage, had completed her first novel *The Second Experiment* (1974). In fact, it sold to the publisher on the day they were married. Since then she has written a number of stories and another novel. On one occasion Asimov offered to help her out on a particular short story. By-lined as a collaboration, Asimov submitted it to his own magazine – *Isaac Asimov's SF Magazine* – and the editor, George Scithers, rejected it! When Janet later sold a story to Scithers, Asimov conceded that 'she's better off on her own than with my help.'

10 PARENT-CHILDREN WRITERS

D8

1 **Edgar Rice Burroughs and John Coleman Burroughs** The famed creator of Tarzan and John Carter of Mars had three children including two boys, John Coleman, who became both writer and illustrator, and Hulbert, who collaborated with his brother on several sf stories in the pulps in the late 1930s. John is also suspected of having written either on his own, or with his father, the story of *John Carter and the Giant of Mars.*

2 **Howard and Jonathan Fast** Howard Fast is better known to the non-sf world as the author of *Spartacus*, but his first ever sale was a science fiction story, and thirty-three years later his son Jonathan sold his first story, *Decay*, to *F & SF.*

3 **Fred and Geoffrey Hoyle** One of the better known father-son writing teams, father Fred had written a couple of novels on his own; *The Black Cloud* (1957), and *Ossian's Ride* (1959)) plus the two television serials with John Elliot (*A For Andromeda* (1962), and *The Andromeda Breakthrough* (1964), before drafting his son in to help starting with the *Fifth Planet* (1963) and continuing thereafter.

4 **Fritz and Justin Leiber** Justin Leiber was born in 1938, but until 1980 his activities in the sf field had been restricted to fanzine publishing and writing a few articles. 1980, however, saw his first novel *Beyond Rejection.* Fritz Leiber could not avoid commenting in his column *On Fantasy* in *Fantasy Newsletter:* 'I try to allow for parental bias, but I must say that the day I read *Beyond Rejection* was the proudest of my life so far.'

5 **Richard and Richard Christian Matheson** Richard Matheson's first story, *Born of Man and Woman* appeared in 1950. Twenty-seven years later his son's first story, *Graduation*, appeared in *Whispers*. Since then Richard the Younger has been a regular contributor to the fantasy magazines and anthologies, and father and son collaborated on the story *Where There's a Will* in Kirby McCauley's blockbusting anthology *Dark Forces* (1980).

6 **Rachel and Robert Payes** Mother-and-son teams are rare in sf and fantasy. Rachel Cosgrove Payes (who for many years used the pseudonym E.L. Arch on her sf books) has been writing sf and fan-

tasy since 1950 when she delighted fans of the Oz saga by adding a new title to the series with *Hidden Valley of Oz*. Her son Robert started his sales early in life and in fact you'll find him in the listing of all-time youngest sf writers.

7 **William Murray Graydon and Murray Roberts** Murray Roberts is a name fondly remembered amongst fans of old boy's books. Roberts wrote the Captain Justice sf series for *Modern Boy* in the 1930s, which had an influence on several impressionable young lads, not least Brian W. Aldiss. His father, William Murray Graydon, was also a prolific writer, mostly of Sexton Blake detective stories, but he turned his hand to sf in the novel *The River of Darkness* (1890; book 1902), an adventure in the world beneath Africa, to which he provided a sequel, *Over Africa* (1891). Graydon outlived his son who died, relatively young, in 1937. Graydon died in 1946 aged eighty-two.

8 **Milton and Tony Rothman** Milton Rothman is a long-time fan of science fiction who has sold more non-fiction to the sf magazines than fiction, but places his stories under the alias Lee Gregor. He has had no novels published as yet. His son, Tony, however, jumped in at the deep end with his first novel, *The World Is Round* in 1978.

9 **Clifford and Richard Simak** Richard Simak's name has only appeared on one item of fiction to date, and that a collaboration with his father, the hauntingly simple tale *Unsilent Spring* in Judy-Lynn del Rey's anthology *Stellar 2* (1976).

10 **Manly Wade and Wade Wellman** Wade Wellman, a professor of English, usually confines his appearances in the sf field to poetry, but occasionally experiments with prose. His first such sally is especially memorable. A collaboration with his father, *The Adventure of the Martian Client (F & SF* December 1969) looks at what became of Sherlock Holmes, Dr Watson *and* Professor Challenger during the Martian invasion of Earth described in Wells's *The War Of The Worlds.*

15 SF WRITERS WHO HAVE ALSO EDITED SF MAGAZINES

D9

1 **Anthony Boucher**
was co-editor of *F & SF* with J Francis McComas from its first issue in 1949 until 1954, and then continued solo until 1958.

2 **Ben Bova**
was editor of *Analog* in succession to John W. Campbell, from 1971 to 1978, and had scarcely left *Analog* to return to writing than he became Fiction Editor (and subsequently Executive Editor) of *Omni.*

3 **John W. Campbell, Jr.**
was editor of *Astounding* from the end of 1937 to his death in 1971. He also edited *Unknown* from 1939 to 1943.

Ben Bova

4 **Avram Davidson**
served a few years as executive editor of *F & SF* from his home in Mexico from 1962 to 1964.

5 **Lester Del Rey**
edited four magazines during the period 1952-53, *Space SF, SF Adventures, Fantasy Fiction* and *Rocket Stories.* He edited the first two issues of *Worlds of Fantasy* in 1968/70.

6 **Horace L. Gold**
had served an apprenticeship as assistant editor on a number of pulps during the 1940s before becoming founding editor of *Galaxy* in 1950 where he remained until ill-health forced his retirement in 1961. In 1981 he became Fiction Editor of *Quest/Star.*

7 **Harry Harrison**
took over from Lester del Rey as editor of *SF Adventures* and *Rocket Stories* during 1953/4. He also edited *Amazing Stories* and *Fantastic* for five issues a piece during 1967/68, having only a year earlier been Editor-in-Chief of the British magazine *Impulse,* which he also saw through five issues until it folded.

8 **Damon Knight**
was an assistant editor on *Super Science Stories* before becoming editor of *World Beyond* for its three issues in 1950/51. He later edited another three issues of *If* in 1958/59.

9 **Samuel Merwin**
edited *Thrilling Wonder Stories* and *Startling Stories* from 1945 to 1951 as well as being founder editor of the companion magazines *Fantastic Story Quarterly* and *Wonder Story Annual* in 1950. He later served briefly as editor of *Fantastic Universe* (1953) and *Satellite* (1956).

10 **Michael Moorcock**
succeeded John Carnell as editor of *New Worlds* in 1964 and saw it through several traumas and incarnations until it wasted away in 1977. The magazine is currently in limbo, but may well reappear some day.

11 **Raymond A. Palmer**
became editor of *Amazing Stories* in 1938 and soon created a legend. He was founder editor of *Fantastic Adventures* in 1939 and left both magazines in 1949 to publish and edit his own magazines *Fate* and *Other Worlds;* he later added *Imagination, Universe, Mystic* and *The Hidden World* to the fold.

12 **Keith Roberts**
was Managing Editor of *Impulse* under Harry Harrison in 1966/67, but as Harrison was in Italy for most of this period, it was Roberts who deserves the credit.

13 **E.C.Tubb**
served as editor of *Authentic* for twenty issues in 1956/57 until the publishers decided to quash it and concentrate on paperbacks.

14 **Frederik Pohl**
started editing in 1940 with *Astonishing Stories* and *Super Science Stories* which he guided until 1942. In 1958 he edited the one-shot magazine issue of his paperback anthology series *Star SF,* and in 1962 he took over officially from Horace Gold as editor of *Galaxy* and *If,* adding *Worlds of Tomorrow* (1963) and *International SF* to the stable. He left the magazines when they changed publisher in 1969.

15 **Ted White**
worked wonders when he took over as editor of *Amazing Stories* and *Fantastic* in 1969. Against large odds he raised the standard of the magazines significantly, but finally gave up in 1978 when it was clear there was to be a change in the publishing circumstances.

7 SF WRITERS WHO HAVE APPEARED IN FILMS

D10

1/2 **Charles Beaumont and William F. Nolan**
The Intruder

3 **Stephen King**
Creepshow

4 **Fritz Leiber**
Camille (the Greta Garbo version) and Equinox.

5 **Richard Matheson**
Somewhere in Time

6 **Tom Reamy**
The Goddaughter

7 **Forrest J. Ackerman**
The Farmer's Daughter ('extra' behind Loretta Young in political rally sequence)
This Is the Army (as himself, soldier on bench when busload of recruits is unloading)
The Time Travellers (Technician No. 3 in Android Factory) Queen of Blood (Basil Rathbone's assistant)
Dracula vs Frankenstein (Dr Beaumont)
Schlock (aka The Banana Monster; 'frozen face' cameo in movie theatre)
Hollywood Boulevard (toaster: 'To Hollywood!')
Kentucky Fried Movie (juror)
The Howling (as self, browsing in bookshop, laying out Tarot cards to spell SCIFI)
The Aftermath (curator of the last museum on Earth)

10 WRITERS WHO ARE ALSO ILLUSTRATORS

D11

1 **Hannes Bok**
A student of Maxfield Parrish, Bok was a friend of Ray Bradbury's, and illustrated Bradbury's early fanzine *Futuria Fantasia* in 1939/40. It was through Bradbury that Bok got his first professional commissions for art with Farnsworth Wright at *Weird Tales,* his first cover adorning the December 1939 issue. It was clear that Bok could not survive by illustrating alone and he turned to writing, heavily influenced by the work of A. Merritt. He had stories in *Weird Tales, Unknown, Future* and other pulps, and he completed three novels. Only two have appeared in book form, *The Sorceror's Ship* (1942; book 1969) and *Beyond the Golden Stair* (1948 as *The Blue Flamingo;* book, 1970). Bok died in 1964 of a heart attack, two months before his fiftieth birthday.

2 **John Coleman Burroughs**
The younger son of Edgar Rice Burroughs, he illustrated many of his father's stories and books, including a short-lived John Carter comic strip. Starting in 1939 he and his brother Hulbert wrote two short stories for *Thrilling Wonder* and a novel, *The Bottom of the World* for *Startling Stories.* John also collaborated with his wife on a short story for *Thrilling Mystery,* but of greater import is the rumour that has never been satisfactorily proved or denied that John wrote the story *John Carter and the Giant of Mars* (*Amazing* January 1941) that was credited to his father. It was not until 1967 that JCB's first book appeared, *Treasure of the Black Falcon,* but he did not pursue writing. He died in 1981.

3 **Jack Gaughan**
One of science fiction's most popular and prolific artists,

Gaughan has been illustrating books and magazines since 1948. After thirty years he turned his hand to writing and his first story *One More Time* appeared in the November-December 1978 issue of *Isaac Asimov's SF Magazine.* Within three years he followed it up with *The Wind From the Seven Suns* in the 16 March 1981 *Asimov's.*

4 Harry Harrison
Harrison was a freelance commercial artist from 1946 to 1955 working mostly in the comic book field. In 1949 Harry was illustrating Damon Knight's magazine *World Beyond* but a serious throat infection left him too weak to draw but didn't stop him typing. So he turned out a story, *I Walk Through Rocks,* which Knight promptly bought and published as *Rock Diver* in the third and last issue of *Worlds Beyond* in February 1951. Within a few years Harrison said good-bye to his art studio and became a full-time writer.

5 Laurence Housman
Writer-Artists were less rare in the Victorian days, and one of the best in the fantasy field was Laurence Housman, brother of the noted poet A.E. Housman. Laurence began his professional career as an artist, and had several exhibitions, influenced strongly by Pre-Raphaelites like Rossetti and Morris. Failing eyesight however foreshortened his career and he turned, instead, to writing poems, plays and tales. Amongst the books he illustrated were the 1900 Blackie edition of George Macdonald's *The Princess and the Goblin* and R. Nisbet Bain's *Weird Tales From the North* (1893). His own books include *The Field of Clover* (1898), which he illustrated, right through to *Strange Ends and Discoveries* (1948), which he didn't!

6 Frederick T. Jane
Who'd have thought that the man behind *Jane's Fighting Ships* and such similar definitive tomes was both a writer and illustrator of science fiction. He was, first and foremost, an illustrator and in the sf field his best known work accompanies E. Douglas Fawcett's novel *Hartmann the Anarchist* (1893). Jane wrote and illustrated his own future-war novel *Blake of the Rattlesnake* (1895), but his best known work of sf is *To Venus in Five Seconds* (1897) where our hero is kidnapped and transported to Venus by matter-transmitter.

7 Damon Knight
Knight was never a prominent

Illustration by Fred T. Jane For 'Worlds Apart'

illustrator, always being an editor and writer first. However, he produced and illustrated his own fanzine, *Snide,* and illustrated stories in *Future* and *SF Quarterly* in the 1940s.

8 **William Morris**
Perhaps the best known and most collected of all writer-artists, Morris tried to drag the industrial Victorian world back to an imaginary, perfect past, both through his activities as a Socialist, and as a writer. His sf includes *News From Nowhere* (1890), set in a utopian future, and the similar *A Dream of John Ball* (1888). Morris's best known works of fiction, however, are his later fantastic romances such as *The Wood Beyond the World* (1894), *The Well at the World's End* (1896) and *The Water of the Wondrous Isles* (1897). The first editions Morris published himself wih his Kelmscott Press at Hammersmith. Morris, along with his friend Edward Burne-Jones, produced some of the most beautiful books ever published in Britain.

9 **Keith Roberts**
Long before he was a writer, Roberts was an animator and background artist in cartoon films, and is now an advertising copywriter. He began to sell fiction in 1964 and has since produced some of Britain's best sf, including the *Pavane* cycle of stories. His stories and illustrations appeared in the two British sf magazines of the 1960s, *New Worlds* and *Science Fantasy.*

10 **Lawrence Todd**
Not prolific in the sf field, Todd has produced a few memorable short stories, usually accompanied by his own illustrations. They include *Flesh and the Iron* in *If* (September 1968) and *The Warbots* (*Galaxy* October 1968). Todd occasionally teamed up with his college friend Vaughn Bode in producing artwork.

8 SF WRITERS WHO ARE ALSO MUSICIANS OR COMPOSERS

D12

When I came to compile this list I was astonished at just how many writers had an affinity with music and how many played some kind of instrument.

1 **Jerome Bixby**
An occasional sf writer and editor during the 1950s, Bixby has drifted from the field in recent years in favour of painting and composing. He writes his own music and has composed some symphonies.

2 **Lloyd Biggle, Jr.**
A musicologist, Biggle taught Music Literature and History at the University of Michigan before becoming a full-time writer. Music is evident in many of his stories and novels such as *The Still, Small Voice of Trumpets* (1968) and *The Metallic Muse* (1972).

3 **John F. Burke**
A popular British sf writer of the 1950s, Burke is now more active in other spheres of writing though still produces the occasional story of the supernatural. Music is a sideline interest and he is proficient on the piano and clarinet.

4 **Laurence M. Janifer**
When not writing and reviewing or acting as literary agent, Janifer has been an MC, an actor, a theatrical producer, and most particularly a pianist and accompanist having performed, back in the 1950s, in a dance band.

5 **John Kippax**
Another dance band musician of the 1950s, as well as a club comedian and a teacher, Kippax

(real name John Hynam, 1915-74) was particularly proficient in playing the saxophone.

6 **Sam Lundwall**
Sweden's sf jack-of-all-trades Lundwall is a professional photographer, editor, writer, television director, singer and recording artist. He has had a number of best-selling records in Sweden and of particular relevance to the sf field is the song cycle related to his novel *The King Kong Blues* (1974). Released as a record album to accompany the book in 1974 they both became best-sellers.

7 **Barry N. Malzberg**
Malzberg is as frenetic a violinist as he is a writer. He played second violin on the premier performance of Somtow Sucharitkul's *Starscapes*

8 **Michael Moorcock**
Moorcock has been intensely active in the rock music scene, performing both with the rock bank Hawkwind and forming his own group Deep Fix. Some of his own songs have been included in albums from Hawkwind and Blue Oyster Cult, and a number of Moorcock's stories, such as *A Dead Singer*, about Jimi Hendrix, centre on the music scene.

20 WRITERS WHO HAVE STARS OR CRATERS NAMED AFTER THEM

D13

Lunar Craters:
1 **Hugo Gernsback**
2 **Willy Ley**
3 **H.G. Wells**
Martian Craters:
1 **John W. Campbell**
2 **Stanley G. Weinbaum**
3 **H.G. Wells**
Stars
(My thanks to Forrest J. Ackerman for providing this list as I had no idea any stars were named after the following):
1 **Forrest J. Ackerman**
2 **Wendayne Ackerman**
3 **Isaac Asimov**
4 **Ray Bradbury**
5 **Edgar Rice Burroughs**
6 **E. Everett Evans**
7 **Hugo Gernsback**
8 **L. Ron Hubbard**
9 **Fritz Lang**
10 **George Pal**
11 **Frank R. Paul**
12 **Gene Roddenberry**
13 **Takumi Shibano**
14 **Olaf Stapledon**
15 **William F. Temple**
16 **Stanley G. Weinbaum**
17 **Tetsu Yano**
18 **H.G. Wells**

9 SF WRITERS WHO ARE ALSO MEDICAL DOCTORS

D14

1 **T.J. Bass**
Real name Thomas J. Bassler, author of *Half Past Human* (1971) and *The Godwhale* (1974). A qualified pathologist he is editor of the *American Medical Joggers Newsletter.*

2 **Miles J. Breuer**
A popular contributor to the Gernsback magazines in the 1920s

F. Paul Wilson

and 30s, author of *The Appendix and the Spectacles* (1928).

3 **Arthur Conan Doyle**
Studied medicine at Edinburgh University and set up in his own practice for a few years before concentrating on writing.

4 **David H. Keller**
Probably the most popular of the early Gernsback authors. An early student in psychology, and a pioneer authority on shell-shock, Keller introduced many medical matters into his stories, such as *Life Everlasting* and *The Abyss.*

5 **Alan E. Nourse**
With a surname that's pronounced 'Nurse', perhaps a medical career wasn't so surprising. Nourse was a fairly prolific writer in the 1950s, and his medical sf stories were collected as *Rx for Tomorrow* (1971), whilst *Star Surgeon* (1960) explored the medium at greater length.

6 **Kenneth F. Sterling**
Sterling was a writer first, and then physician, having to give up writing to pursue his medical career. (See List C14).

7 **Leonard Tushnet**
A New Jersey G.P. Tushnet had written many medical articles before turning to fantasy and sf in 1964 and produced a number of short stories, including *In Re Glover* in *Again, Dangerous Visions,* before his death in 1973.

8 **F. Paul Wilson**
Another New Jersey family G.P., Wilson began to sell stories in the 1970s, including a novel *Healer* (1976) about an immortal psychiatric healer.

9 **Joseph A. Winter**
A none-too prolific writer who contributed two stories and a few articles to *Astounding* from 1948 to 1953, but is probably better known for having gone overboard in support of L. Ron Hubbard's Dianetics.

20 SF WRITERS AND THEIR FORMER (OR CURRENT) OCCUPATIONS

D15

1 **Greg Benford**
Professor of Physics (1971-to date)

2 **Ed Bryant**
Disc jockey then radio news director then shipping clerk, then teacher at an experimental High School.

3 **Jack L. Chalker**
History instructor

4 **A. Bertram Chandler**
Ship's master (became an apprentice) in 1928 and worked his way up)

5 **Arthur C. Clarke**
Civil Service auditor 1936-40, then radar officer in RAF, 1941-46.

6 **David Gerrold**
Assistant manager of a toy department and then clerk in a dirty book store.

7 **Charles L. Harness**
Attorney

8 **Robert A. Heinlein**
U.S. Naval Officer, 1929-1934

9 **Frank Herbert**
Newspaper reporter, editor and

photographer; also oyster-diver and oenologist, before turning full-time writer in 1970.

10 **Daniel Keyes**
Professor of English

11 **Sterling E. Lanier** Research historian, editor and sculptor.

12 **Keith Laumer**
Captain in U.S. Air Force 1952-57, 1960-65; Third Secretary, U.S. Embassy in Burma 1957-59.

13 **William F. Nolan**
One-time greetings-card designer.

14 **Andre Norton**
Children's librarian 1934-50

15 **Chad Oliver**
Professor of Anthropology

16 **Jerry Pournelle**
Former Professor of History and Political Science; former political campaign manager.

17 **Joanna Russ**
Professor of English

18 **Clifford D. Simak**
Newspaper reporter (retired 1976)

19 **Wilson Tucker**
Electrician and cinema projectionist

20 **Roger Zelazny**
Claims representative (social security) and subsequently claims policy specialist until turning full-time in 1969.

(Information derived from *Science Fiction and Fantasy Literature Volume 2: Contemporary Science Fiction Authors II* by R. Reginald, Detroit,1979,Gale Research Co.)

10 SF WRITERS WHOSE CAREERS WERE CUT SHORT

D16

The following writers all died either at the height of their fame or just as their star was rising. They are listed in the order of their death.

1 **William Hope Hodgson**
was killed at Ypres in the First World War in 1918. He was 40.

2 **Stanley G. Weinbaum**
died of throat cancer in 1935. He was 35.

3 **Bryan Berry**
died suddenly in 1955, aged 25.

4 **Cyril Kornbluth**
died of a heart attack in 1958, aged 35.

5 **Henry Kuttner**
died of a heart attack in 1958, aged 42.

6 **Charles Beaumont**
died after a long, wasting illness in 1967. He was 38.

7 **Walter F. Moudy**
died in 1973, aged 43.

8 **Vaughn Bode**
the artist and cartoonist, died after an unfortunate accident in 1975, four days before his 34th birthday.

9 **David McDaniel**
died as the result of a fall in his shower in 1977, aged 38.

10 **Tom Reamy**
died of a heart attack in 1977, aged 42.

Stanley G. Weinbaum

One other, rather more mysterious death can be added to the list; that of Homer Eon Flint, a writer from the pre-*Amazing* era of sf. His body was found under a car with the rear axle impaling his stomach. The car had apparently been used a few weeks earlier in a bank robbery. Sam Moskowitz gives the known but puzzling facts of Flint's death in his book *Under the Moons of Mars* (1970). And it is stranger than any fiction. Flint, by the way, was 32.

8 SF & FANTASY WRITERS WHO TOOK THEIR OWN LIVES

1 **Dr John Polidori** (1795-1821)
Polidori's name has been saved from oblivion by a series of circumstances. He was Lord Byron's personal physician and friend and was present at that historic moment in 1916 when Byron along with Percy Bysshe Shelley and his young wife Mary Shelley challenged each other to write a convincing horror story. By rights it should have been Byron and Shelley who delivered the goods, but their enthusiasm soon faded. It was Mary Shelley who made her reputation as a result of that challenge with *Frankenstein* (1818). But Polidori also finished his attempt. *The Vampyre; A Tale* (1819), is at best a rather undistinguished work but it is important as the first vampire story written in English. Polidori now set to establish himself as a writer but nothing came of it. Heavily in debt, he poisoned himself when only 26.

2 **Edward Lucas White** (1866-1934)
White was a noted American novelist, mostly in the vein of historical fiction, but he has carved himself a niche in the annals of fantasy fiction with a number of powerful supernatural stories, not least *Lukundoo* (1925) and *The House of the Nightmare* (1927). All his life White suffered from intense migraines and came the day in March 1934 when he gassed himself.

3 **David R. Daniels** (?-1936)
Daniels had sold five stories to *Astounding* and one to *Wonder Stories* and seemed all set for a promising career when, in April 1936 he killed himself.

4 **Robert E. Howard** (1906-1936)
Fifty six days after Daniels killed himself, Robert E. Howard took his own life. One of the great fantasy writers for *Weird Tales,* Howard had everything going for him with sales building up in all the pulps. In the fantasy field he is best remembered for his creation of that mighty barbarian swordsman Conan of Cimmeria, and today Howard must rate as one of the biggest selling writers in the field. Howard was, however, obsessed with his mother and could not reconcile himself to the thought of life without her. When he understood that she had entered a terminal coma he walked out to his car, and shot himself through the head. A strip of paper in his pocket bore these lines:
All fled — all done, so lift me on the pyre —
The Feast is over and the lamps expire.

5 **H. Beam Piper** (1904-1964)
Piper was a popular contributor to *Astounding/Analog* whose work has only recently found a wider readership. He is best known for two series of stories, the *Fuzzy* episodes and the *Paratime Police.* In 1964 however, Piper's agent committed suicide, leaving various papers in turmoil. Piper, worried by the financial outlook, took the final step. He had a valuable collection of over 100 weapons. Selecting a .38-calibre pistol he shot himself. His death note ended with these grim words: 'I don't like to leave messes when I go away, but,if I could have cleaned up any of this mess, I wouldn't be going away.'

6 **Stephen Southwold** (1887-1964)
A prolific writer in many fields, Southwold wrote a fair proportion of sf, most of ients, was active in the French resistance and later held several ambassadorial posts. In December 1980 Gary shot himself. His suicide note left the impression that he had written all he could, having expressed himself completely in his autobiography *The Night Will Be Peaceful*, and that there was nothing left to say.

7 **Peter George** (1924-1966)
George could best be described as a futurophobe — he feared what the future would bring. He was obsessed with the horror of nuclear war and brought this into all his work, which he wrote under the

alias Peter Bryant. His best known was *Two Hours to Doom* (1958), published in the States as *Red Alert* and later made into the film *Dr Strangelove* by Stanley Kubrick. In the end fear of the future was too much for George and in June 1966, he shot himself.

8 **Romain Gary** (1914-1980) Although better known outside the sf field, Gary used many fantasy elements in his books which include *Tulipe* (1946), *The Dance of Genghis Cohn* (1968), *The Gasp* (1973) and the story collection *Hissing Tales* (1964). Gary, born Romain Kacewgari in Russian Georgia of Polish parents, was active in the French resistance and later held several ambassadorial posts. In December 1980 Gary shot himself. His suicide note left the impression that he had written all he could, having expressed himself completely in his autobiography *The Night Will Be Peaceful*, and that there was nothing left to say.

Other suicides associated with the field include Robert H. Barlow, who had been H.P. Lovecraft's literary executor, but who later absented himself from the genre to pursue a career in archeology. He took an overdose of sedatives in 1951 because he was being blackmailed for his homosexuality. Another was William B. Seabrook, a larger than life writer and journalist who wrote a few weird stories and a book about black magic. He took an overdose in 1945.

ONCE A YEAR — SF WRITERS BORN IN EACH YEAR OF THIS CENTURY

D18

1901 Ed Earl Repp
1902 Curt Siodmak
1903 John Wyndham
1904 Clifford D. Simak
1905 Eric Frank Russell
1906 Fredric Brown
1907 Robert A. Heinlein
1908 Jack Williamson
1909 Neil R. Jones
1910 Fritz Leiber
1911 Raymond Z. Gallun
1912 A.E. von Vogt
1913 Alfred Bester
1914 Wilson Tucker
1915 Lester del Rey
1916 George Turner
1917 Arthur C. Clarke
1918 Theodore Sturgeon
1919 Frederik Pohl
1920 Isaac Asimov
1921 James Blish
1922 Damon Knight
1923 Gordon R. Dickson
1924 Ray Russell
1925 Brian W. Aldiss
1926 Poul Anderson
1927 Randall Garrett
1928 Philip K. Dick
1929 Ursula K. LeGuin
1930 Fred Saberhagen
1931 Bob Shaw
1932 Ben Bova
1933 Jerry Pournelle
1934 Harlan Ellison
1935 Robert Silverberg
1936 S.J. Treibich
1937 Roger Zelazny
1938 Larry Niven
1939 Michael Moorcock
1940 Thomas M. Disch
1941 Greg Benford
1942 Samuel R. Delany
1943 Ian Watson
1944 Jack L. Chalker
1945 Gordon Eklund
1946 Alan Dean Foster
1947 John Varley
1948 Brian Stableford
1949 Adrian Cole
1950 Karl Hansen

In case you wonder what happened to 1900, that was the last year of the nineteenth century, but to save you wondering, you can add Wallace West for that year. Most years have an abundance of talent; 1934, for instance, also boasts John Brunner and Piers Anthony. I had the most trouble with 1936 which was a slack year for sf writers. S.J. Treibich, who died at the tragically young age of 36, was a friend and collaborator with Laurence M. Janifer who called him 'the finest storyteller I've ever known'.

24 AUTHORS AND THEIR SIGNS OF THE ZODIAC

D19

	Sign	Male	Female
1	**Aries**	James White	Joan D. Vinge
2	**Taurus**	Richard Cowper	Lee Killough
3	**Gemini**	Harlan Ellison	Kate Wilhelm
4	**Cancer**	Robert A. Heinlein	Jane Gaskell
5	**Leo**	Clifford D. Simak	Janet O Jeppson
6	**Virgo**	Orson Scott Card	Chelsea Quinn Yarbro
7	**Libra**	John Brunner	Ursula K. LeGuin
8	**Scorpio**	R.A. Lafferty	Zenna Henderson
9	**Sagittarius**	Poul Anderson	Rachel Cosgrove Payes
10	**Capricorn**	Robert Silverberg	Raylyn Moore
11	**Aquarius**	Philip Jose Farmer	Katherine MacLean
12	**Pisces**	Theodore Sturgeon	Patricia A. McKillip

20 WORKS WRITTEN BY FAMOUS NON-SF WRITERS

D20

There are many critics who look disdainfully at sf; considering it to be the work of childish minds for immature readers. They do not seem to realise, or wish to concede, that their own peers have written sf, often in copious quantities. The following list highlights some of the more obvious but deliberately leaves out the most obvious — George Orwell's *Nineteen-Eighty-Four* (1949) and Aldous Huxley's *Brave New World* (1932).

1 **Kingsley Amis**
The Alteration (1976)
Set in an alternate universe where the Spanish Armada was victorious. Amis, famous for such books as *Lucky Jim* and *Jake's Thing*, is a noted supporter and critic of science fiction and has edited a number of science fiction anthologies, such as the *Spectrum* series with Robert Conquest, and written a critical study of the field in *New Maps of Hell (1960)*.

2 **Anthony Burgess**
A Clockwork Orange (1962)
Set in a future London it follows the personality change of a young hoodlum who is brainwashed by the authorities. Filmed by Stanley Kubrick in 1971 it has become a cult work. Burgess wrote another

dystopian sf novel *The Wanting Seed (1962)*.

3 **Joseph Conrad**
The Inheritors (1901)
Written in collaboration with Ford Madox Hueffer (later better known as Ford Madox Ford) it depicts a new future race, 'the Dimensionists' who supersede mankind.

4 **J. Jefferson Farjeon**
Death Of A World (1948)
Better known as a writer of detective fiction, Farjeon produced this one sf novel about a dead Earth and its doom revealed in the diary of the last survivor to a visiting alien. Typical of the many post-nuclear disaster novels that were in abundance in the late 1940s.

5 **Howard Fast**
The Edge Of Tomorrow (1961)
A collection of science fiction stories such as *The First Men* and *The Large Ant* by the renowned author of *Spartacus* and *Freedom Road*. Fast's very first story sale *Wrath of the Purple* in 1932 was sf, and now his son Jonathan is also writing and selling science fiction.

6 **E.M. Forster**
The Machine Stops (1909)
The noted British novelist and essayest, best known for *Passage to India*, wrote this long story as a warning of a possible machine-dominated future.

7 **Robert Graves**
Seven Days in New Crete (1949)
About a poet who is transported to the future purposely to bring disorder to the utopian existence then prevailing so that the ideal life could be better appreciated. Graves is best known for *I, Claudius*. This book was published in the US as *Watch the Northwind Rise*.

8 **L.P. Hartley**
Facial Justice (1960)
The author of *The Go-Between* wrote this post-nuclear dystopian novel set after World War III. Hartley also wrote several notable ghost stories.

9 **Julian Huxley**
The Tissue Culture King (1926)
Unlike his younger brother Aldous, Julian Huxley only wrote one piece of fiction and it just happened to be sf, about a genetic engineering machine that transmits telepathic commands.

10 **McKinlay Kantor**
If The South Had Won the Civil War (1961)
Another alternate-world novel with a self-explanatory title. Kantor was a noted American novelist with a deep interest in the Civil War, the subject of his long novel *Andersonville*.

11 **Rudyard Kipling**
With the Night Mail (1905)
Set in the next century and concerning how aviation, governed by the Aerial Board of Control, had transformed the world. Kipling wrote a sequel in *As Easy as A.B.C.* (1912).

12 **Sinclair Lewis**
It Can't Happen Here (1935)
A notable portrayal of the United States under the control of a Nazi-like fascist dictator, written in the years immediately after Hitler came to power.

13 **Shepherd Mead**
The Big Ball of Wax (1954)
Mead is best known for *How to Succeed In Business Without Trying* but has written several sf works. This novel, set in the future, explores the possibilities of experiencing other people's sensory perceptions.

14 **J.B. Priestley**
Three Time Plays (1947)
Priestley has long been fascinated with the concepts of time and employed it not only in the three plays collected here but also in several short stories collected as *The Other Place (1953)*. Another sf/fantasy is *The Magicians (1954)*.

15 **R.C. Sherriff**
The Hopkins Manuscript (1939)
By the author of the popular play *Journey's End* (filmed in 1975 as *Aces High*), this is a disaster novel where the Moon crashes into the Atlantic Ocean.

16 **Nevil Shute**
On The Beach (1957)
Another post-nuclear disaster novel where all but Australia have been destroyed but now prepares for the end. Shute, known also for such works as *A Town Like Alice*, wrote another sf novel about a future

Australia in *In the Wet (1953)*.

17 **George R. Stewart**
Earth Abides (1949)
Regarded as one of the best of all disaster novels with mankind recovering from a plague that has wiped out most of humanity. Stewart has written a variety of works of fiction and non-fiction and in *Storm (1941)* was responsible for giving a personal name to the mighty storm — Maria — an idea which caught on and persists to this day.

18 **T.S. Stribling**
The Green Splotches (1920)
Stribling is not so well known in Britain as he was in America where he wrote a famous series about country life in the South of which *The Store* earned him the Pultizer Prize in 1933. In this early sf story Stribling tells a rousing story of a Geographical Society expedition to South America and the discovery of an atomic-powered spaceship.

19 **Anthony Trollope**
The Fixed Period (1882)
One of Trollope's lesser known works it concerns the establishment of a utopia on an island near Australia in the year 1980.

20 **Colin Wilson**
The Space Vampires (1976)
This prolific British writer and researcher has always professed an interest in the occult but not so obviously in sf. This novel, a bizarre space opera, is something of a blending of the two. Wilson has also written two Lovecraftian sf/fantasy novels *The Mind Parasites* (1967) and *The Philosopher's Stone* (1969).

15 SF WRITERS WHO HAVE RECEIVED NON-SF AWARDS

D21

1 **Isaac Asimov**
The Howard W. Blakeslee Award, 1960. Well known for his non-fiction works on the popularisation of science, Asimov received this Award presented by the American Heart Association for high standards of reporting on the heart and circulatory diseases for his book *The Living River* (Abelard-Schumann, 1960)

2 **Ray Bradbury**
The California Literature Medal Award, 1954. In 1954 Bradbury received the Best Fiction Gold Medal for his sf novel *Fahrenheit 451* (Ballantine, 1953). The same year he also received the National Institute and American Academy Award in Literature for creative achievement.

3 **John Christopher**
The Christopher Book Award, 1971. John Christopher (real name Sam Youd, just to prove that the coincidence of names is just that) has established himself as probably Britain's best writer of science fiction for children. The Christopher Society present a bronze medallion each year in recognition of the efforts of individuals to maintain high standards in the field of communications. The medallion is engraved with their motto 'Better to light one candle than to curse the darkness.' Christopher won the

award for his novel *The Guardians* (Hamish Hamilton, 1970).

4 **Arthur C. Clarke**
The Kalinga Prize, 1961. The Kalinga Prize is awarded annually by UNESCO to a science writer for outstanding interpretation of science to the general public and of strengthening cultural and scientific links between India and other nations. Other recipients also known in the sf field include Julian Huxley (1953), George Gamow (1956) and Fred Hoyle (1967).

5 **Stanton A. Coblentz**
The California Literature Medal Award, 1953. A prolific writer of sf in the 1920s and 30s, Coblentz also established himself as a poet and received the Commonwealth Club of California's Poetry Silver Medal for his volume of verse *Time's Traveller* (Wing's Press, 1952)

6 **L. Sprague de Camp**
The Drexel Award, 1978. De Camp, and his wife Catherine, received this award for Distinguished Contributions to Children's Literature. L. Sprague de Camp also received the Athenaeum of Philadelphia Literary Award for his historical novel *An Elephant for Aristotle* (Doubleday, 1958) in 1959.

7 **Thomas M. Disch**
The Union League Civic and Arts Foundation Prize for Poetry, 1972. Disch received this award for his contribution to *Poetry* magazine.

8 **Harlan Ellison**
The Mystery Writers of America Edgar, 1973. It may well be that before he's through Harlan Ellison will have received more awards in every field than anyone else in the world. In 1973 he received the Edgar for Best Short Story for *The Whimper of Whipped Dogs* from Thomas M. Disch's anthology *Bad Moon Rising* (Harper, 1973). He has also received the Writers Guild of America Award three times: for the Best Anthology Script, 1964-65 season for *Demon With a Glass Hand* (an episode in *The Outer Limits*) for best Dramatic Episode Script, 1966-67 season for *The City on the Edge of Forever* (from *Star Trek*) and again for the 1973-74 season for *Phoenix Without Ashes* (from *The Starlost*)

9 **Ursula K. LeGuin**
The Horn Book Award, 1969. Mrs LeGuin's Earthsea Trilogy received three awards for its separate volumes. *The Wizard of Earthsea* (Parnassus, 1968) won the Boston Globe Horn Book Award in 1969 for excellence in children's books. *The Tombs of Atuan* (Atheneum, 1971) received the Newbery Silver Medal in 1972 whilst *The Farthest Show* (Atheneum, 1972) won the 1973 National Book Award for Children's Literature.

10 **Chad Oliver**
The Western Writers of America Golden Spur, 1968. Less active in the sf field today than he was in the 1950s Oliver, a Professor of Anthropology, received the Golden

Spur for the Best Historical Novel with *The Wolf is My Brother* (NAL, 1967).

11 **Michael Resnick**
The American Dog Writer's Association, 1978. Resnick won this Award for the Best Short Fiction of the Year with his story *The Last Dog* from the June 1978 issue of *Hunting Dogs Magazine.*

12 **Michael Shaara**
The Pulitzer Prize, 1975. An above average writer of sf in the 1950s Shaara won this prestigious prize for his non-fantasy *The Killer Angels* (McGraw, 1974).

13 **John Taine**
The California Literature Medal Award, 1938. Although he wrote sf as John Taine, his real name was Eric Temple Bell and he was a Professor of Mathematics. He received this award for his book *Men of Mathematics* (Simon & Schuster, 1937).

14 **Jack Vance**
Mystery Writers of America Edgar, 1961. Under his proper name of John Holbrook Vance he won this Awardocket to the Moon – Now! (Summer 1939).

50 SF WRITERS WHO WERE PRO-VIETNAM, AND 50 WHO WERE ANTI

D22

In 1967 Judith Merril and Kate Wilhelm took the views of over 150 SF writers as to whether they were for or against the United States' involvement in Vietnam. The resultant lists appeared in most of the SF magazines during that year. There were seventy-two who believed the United States must remain in Vietnam to fulfill its responsibilities to the people of that country and eighty-two who opposed that view.'I have selected fifty of the better-known names from each of those lists.

	Pro-Vietnam	Anti-Vietnam
1	**Poul Anderson**	**Forrest J Ackerman**
2	**Harry Bates**	**Isaac Asimov**
3	**Lloyd Biggle Jr**	**Peter S. Beagle**
4	**Jesse F. Bone**	**Jerome Bixby**
5	**Leigh Brackett**	**James Blish**
6	**Marion Zimmer Bradley**	**Anthony Boucher**
7	**Reginald Bretnor**	**Ray Bradbury**
8	**Fredric Brown**	**Stuart J. Byrne**
9	**William R. Burkett Jr**	**Terry Carr**
10	**F.M. Busby**	**Theodore R Cogswell**
11	**John W. Campbell**	**Miriam Allen deFord**
13	**L. Sprague de Camp**	**Lester del Rey**
14	**Charles V. de Vet**	**Philip K. Dick**
15	**William B. Ellern**	**Thomas M. Disch**
16	**R.C. Fitzpatrick**	**Harlan Ellison**
17	**Daniel F. Galouye**	**Philip Jose Farmer**
18	**Raymond Z. Gallun**	**Ron Goulart**
19	**Robert M. Green Jr**	**Joseph Green**

20	Edmond Hamilton	Harry Harrison
21	Robert A. Heinlein	Daniel Keyes
22	Joe L. Hensley	Virginia Kidd
23	Dean Ing	Damon Knight
24	Jay Kay Klein	Ursula K. LeGuin
25	David A. Kyle	Fritz Leiber
26	R.A. Lafferty	Robert A.W. Lowndes
27	C.C. MacApp	Katherine MacLean
28	Norman Metcalf	Barry Malzberg
29	P. Schuyler Miller	Robert E. Margroff
30	Sam Maskowitz	Bruce McAllister
31	John Myers Myers	Judith Merril
32	Larry Niven	Robert P. Mills
33	Alan E. Nourse	Kris Neville
34	Gerald W. Page	Alexei Panshin
35	Rachel Cosgrove Payes	Emil Petaja
36	Lawrence Perkins	Arthur Porges
37	Jerry Pournelle	Mack Reynolds
38	Joe Poyer	Gene Roddenberry
39	E. Hoffman Price	Joanna Russ
40	Fred Saberhagen	James Sallis
41	George O. Smith	Hans Stefan Santesson
42	G. Harry Stine	T.L. Sherred
43	Dwight V. Swain	Robert Silverberg
44	Thomas Burnett Swann	Henry Slesar
45	Albert Teichner	Jerry Sohl
46	Theodore L. Thomas	Norman Spinrad
47	Jack Vance	Margaret St. Clair
48	Harl Vincent	Kate Wilhelm
49	Robert Moore Williams	Richard Wilson
50	Jack Williamson	Donald A. Wollheim

15 AUTHORS KNOWN BETTER BY THEIR PSEUDONYMS THAN REAL NAMES

D23

	Pseudonym	Real Name
1	**Piers Anthony**	**Piers Anthony Jacob**
2	**Christopher Anvil**	**Harry C. Crosby**
3	**Charles Beaumont**	**Charles Nutt**
4	**Hannes Bok**	**Wayne Woodard**
5	**Anthony Boucher** — Boucher also used the alias H.H. Holmes in the mystery field and on a few SF stories.	**William A.P. White**
6	**John Christopher**	**Christopher Samuel Youd**
7	**Hal Clement**	**Harry Clement Stubbs**
8	**Richard Cowper** — Murry uses the Cowper alias for his SF and fantasy and the names Colin Murry or Colin Middleton Murry for his non-SF.	**John Middleton Murry, Jr.**

9	**Lester Del Rey** —In his chapter on Del Rey in *Seekers of Tomorrow* (Chicago, 1966), Sam Moskowitz reports del Rey's full name as being Ramon Felipe San Juan Mario Silvio Enrico Smith Heathcourt-Brace Sierra y Alvarez del Rey y de los Uerdes.	**Ramon Alvarez-del Rey**
10	**Ralph Milne Farley**	**Roger Sherman Hoar**
11	**Murray Leinster** — Leinster concocted this alias to keep his identity as an SF writer distinct from his other writing activities. He also used the alias William Fitzgerald.	**William F. Jenkins**
12	**C.C. MacApp**	**Carroll M. Capps**
13	**J.T. McIntosh**	**James M. Macgregor**
14	**Charles Eric Maine**	**David McIlwain**
15	**John Wyndham** — Harris's full name was John Wyndham Parkes Lucas Beynon Harris so it's easy to see where the Wyndham alias came from as well as his other pen-names John Beynon, Johnson Harris, Lucas Parkes and Wyndham Parkes.	**John Beynon Harris**

10 PEN-NAMES THAT HIDE THE IDENTITIES OF TWO OR MORE AUTHORS

D24

It's very common in all forms of fiction for two writers working as a team to appear under one collective pen-name. Robert Silverberg and Randall Garrett, for instance, combined on several stories as 'Robert Randall'. However it is even more common for one name to hide the identities of several writers, all working independently but under contract to one publisher. These pen names are known as 'house-names' and help insure the publisher's interest in some especially marketable commodity. Below are listed 10 of the many interesting and more important pseudonyms.

1 **Alexander Blade**
Probably the most schizoid of all pseudonyms, Blade was originally a personal pseudonym used by David Vern, with the first story *The Strange Adventure of Victor MacLeigh* appearing in the May 1941 *Amazing Stories.* The second use of the name, however, in the September 1941 issue on *Dr Loudon's Armageddon* masked the identity of Louis H. Sampliner. Between the years 1941 and 1958 nearly 60 stories and as many articles appeared bearing this by-line, but few of the real authors have been identified. Those known include Howard Browne, Millen Cooke, Randall Garrett, Chester S. Geier, Roger P. Graham, Edmond Hamilton, Heinrich Hauser, Berkeley Livingston, Herb Livingston, William P. McGivern, David Wright O'Brien, Richard S. Shaver, Robert Silverberg, Don Wilcox and Leroy Yerxa, all in the

pages of *Amazing Stories, Fantastic Adventures, Fantastic, Imagination, Imaginative Tales, Other Worlds, SF Adventures* and *Space Travel.*

2 **Gill Hunt**
Used by the London based publisher Curtis Warren on 11 novels published between 1951 and 1952. The first four, starting with *Hostile Worlds* were by Dennis Hughes who wrote the last one as well. The remainder were David Griffiths, John Jennison and E.C. Tubb, plus *Galactic Storm* by newcomer John Brunner. Brunner had disowned this novel and would never reveal his first sale. However Brunner did not realise that when the publisher released some of the books in the United States they registered them for copyright purposes in the authors' real names.

3 **Will Garth**
Used by the Standard Magazines publishing chain in the pulps *Thrilling Wonder Stories, Startling Stories, Captain Future* and *Strange Stories*. Henry Kuttner was the first to use it on *The Bloodless Peril* in the December 1937 *Thrilling Wonder* and he was followed by Otto Binder, Edmond Hamilton, Mort Weisinger, Manly Wade Wellman and possibly others. There were 16 stories in all plus the film novelisation of *Dr Cyclops* published by Phoenix Press in New York in 1941. Robert Reginald in his *Science Fiction and Fantasy Literature* credits this to Henry Kuttner whilst Peter Nicholls in his *Encyclopedia of Science Fiction* attributes it to Manly Wade Wellman. Karl Wagner does not list it in his Wellman bibliography however.

4 **Ivar Jorgensen** (also spelt Jorgenson)
There's an oft-quoted and probably apocryphal remark by Robert Silverberg that when he was young he admired the stories by Ivar Jorgensen, little knowing that he'd grow up to be Jorgensen. The name first appeared in the June 1951 *Fantastic Adventures* on the lead short novel *Whom The Gods Would Slay*. This and most later tales were the work of Paul W. Fairman but by 1957 the name was being used by Robert Silverberg alone and in his collaborations with Randall Garrett and Harlan Ellison and others almost certainly did as well. Originally belonging to the Ziff-Davis Publishing company the name later cropped up in magazines published by other firms such as *Imagination, If* and *Infinity.* The name last appeared in the magazines in 1958 in which year Silverberg used it once (as Jorgenson) on his novel *Starhaven* from Avalon Books. In 1963 Paul Fairman revived it for two novels as Jorgensen, and it last appeared on a paperback edition of *Whom the Gods Would Slay* in 1968, a reprint of the very first story.

5 **Paul Dennis Lavond**
Although this name appeared only seven times in the pulp magazines it hid the identity of four authors in a variety of collaborations. 'Lavond' had four stories in the April 1941 issues of four different magazines. *Exiles of New Planet* in *Astonishing* edited by Frederik Pohl was written by Pohl in collaboration with Cyril Kornbluth and Robert Lowndes. *Callistan Tomb* in *Science Fiction Quarterly* and *A Prince of Pluto* in *Future Fiction* both edited by Lowndes were written by Pohl and Kornbluth, whilst *The Doll Master* in *Stirring Science Stories* (edited by Donald Wollheim) was by Lowndes alone. Pohl collaborated with Kornbluth and Lowndes for one further story, and with Lowndes and Dirk Wylie for yet another story, and with Dirk Wylie alone for one final story. Lowndes apparently also had a hand in this story until Wylie's final re-write!

6 **Jeffrey Lord**
Just to show that house names are in current use the Jeffrey Lord name adorns the regular novel series about the adventures of Richard Blade which began with *The Bronze Axe* in 1969. The identities of the initial writer (or writers) have not been revealed, but it is known that most of the series since the ninth novel, *Kingdom of Royth* (1974), has been written by Roland Green, though Ray Nelson has contributed at least one book to the series.

7 **John E. Muller**
Used by the London publishing

firm John Spencer on their Badger Books supernatural and sf series. It first appeared on *Space Void* (1960) the writer of which has not been identified. Between then and *Survival Project* in 1966 it appeared on 40 novels most of which were the work of R. Lionel Fanthorpe, although John Glasby wrote three, A.A. Glynn one, and four remain unidentified. Some were later reprinted in the United States under the newly contrived house names of Mel Jay and Marston Johns.

8 **Kenneth Robeson**
Probably the best-loved and most important of all house names. It was invented by Henry Ralston of the American pulp publishing firm of Street & Smith who required a new by-line for a hero magazine he was planning. The lead novel was to be based around the adventures of the Man of Bronze, Doc Savage and Ralston hired Lester Dent to write them. The first issue of *Doc Savage* magazine appeared in March 1933 and between then and the last issue in Summer 1949, 181 adventures were related. Actually the by-line on the first issue had been Kenneth Roberts but discovering there was a real Kenneth Roberts, Ralston changed the name to Robeson with the second issue. Dent wrote all but 16 of the novels, the rest being the work of Norman Daniels, Alan Hathway and William Bogart. In 1939 Street & Smith used the Robeson by-line on a new magazine *The Avenger* only this time the novels were the work of Paul Ernst. *The Avenger* magazine only lasted 24 issues, but a few remaining stories surfaced in *Clues Detective Magazine* credited to Robeson but now the work of Emile Tepperman. In 1972 the Avenger novels were reprinted in paperback (to tie in with the successful reprinting of the *Doc Savage* novels). In addition to the Ernst novels, some new Avenger adventures were written by Ron Goulart, still as Robeson.

9 **Brett Sterling**
The adventures of Captain Future and his chums were related in *Captain Future* magazine by Edmond Hamilton and were credited to the author. However, after the United States entered World War II Hamilton thought he'd soon be called up and he notified his editor, Mort Weisinger, that he'd not be able to write any more. As it happened Hamilton was not inducted and returned to writing for *Captain Future* but by that time Weisinger had concocted the house name of Brett Sterling and commissioned Joseph Samachson to write the novels. The Brett Sterling name was soon dropped, although it did reappear in *Thrilling Wonder Stories* in 1946 to credit one story by Hamilton and once more in 1948 on a story written by Ray Bradbury.

10 **Warner Van Lorne**
One of the great mysteries of sf, this name appeared on 17 stories published between 1935 and 1939, all but one of them in *Astounding*. The first was by the editor of the magazine F. Orlin Tremaine but the author of the rest has never been identified. There was evidence to suggest that they were written by Tremaine's brother Nelson, and this may explain why stories of such poor quality continued to appear in the magazine.

20 INTERESTING DEDICATIONS

D25

Often overlooked in the pages of the book, but for me always worth a read, is the dedication. Frequently the dedication is to the author's parents, wife or children, or friends, and means little to the general reader. In some cases, however, dedications are a little story in themselves and tell much about the writer and his book. Here are some examples to give you the idea and the next time you read a book, just glance at the dedication.

1 To Kenny Gray — who'll tell me what I did wrong — and to Gloria, who knows better.
(Poul Anderson, *Guardians of Time*, 1961)

2 To Gertrude, to whom I have been, at the moment, very contentedly married for: 8 years 1 month 2 weeks 1 day 2 hours 45 minutes and a few seconds.
(Isaac Asimov, *The Stars Like Dust*, 1951. Gertrude was Asimov's first wife whom he married on 26 July 1942 — though I don't know the exact minute! They were divorced in 1973)

3 To Catherine L. Moore, First Lady of Science Fiction. I have ceased, I hope, the imitation which is said to be the sincerest form of flattery. I shall never outgrow, I hope, the desire to emulate; nor the admiration, the affection, and the inspiration which she has created in every woman who writes science fiction and fantasy — and in most of the men, too!
(Marion Zimmer Bradley, *Stormqueen!*, 1978)

4 To the still unfading memory of Leslie Ekanayake (13 July 1947-4 July 1977), only perfect friend of a lifetime, in whom were uniquely combined Loyalty, Intelligence and Compassion. When your radiant and loving spirit vanished from this world, the light went out of many lives. NIRVANA PRAPTO BHUYAT.
(Arthur C. Clarke, *The Fountains of Paradise*, 1979)

5 To Helen and Jamie in lieu of an epithalamium.
(Richard Cowper, *A Dream of Kinship*, 1981)

6 To Frederik Pohl, for insistence, persistence, assistance — and existence!
(Lester del Rey, *Nerves*, 1956)

7 For the unholy trinity of Bobs: Bloch, Heinlein and Traurig — may I meet them on the banks of the River, where we'll board the fabulous Riverboat.
(Philip Jose Farmer, *The Fabulous Riverboat*, 1971)

8 To the people whose labours go beyond ideas into the realm of 'real materials' — to the dry land ecologists, wherever they may be, in whatever time they work, this effort at prediction is dedicated in humility and admiration.
(Frank Herbert, *Dune*, 1965)

9 Every child is a born scientist. This book is dedicated to Debbie, Jane and Tina — the three young scientists who taught me to distinguish reality from illusion by asking always:
'Who says so?'
'Who's he?' and
'How does he know?'
(James Hogan, *The Genesis Machine*, 1978)

10 This book is for Bill Butler and Harrods of Knightsbridge for entirely opposite reasons.
(Michael Moorcock, *Count Brass*, 1973)

11 For Maeve, Claire, Sebastian and Fabian Peake and in love and admiration for Mervyn Peake, who died 17th November 1968, a generous man in an ungenerous world.
(Michael Moorcock, *The Time Dweller*, 1971. Moorcock's *Gloriana* is also dedicated to the memory of Mervyn Peake.

12 A dedication is only a scratch where it itches — for Anne, then, in whose bosom Rachel lies muselike, guiding my clumsy song and giggling between the lines — with blessings, Lass W.
(Walter M. Miller, Jr., *A Canticle For Leibowitz*, 1959)

13 In Memory of Scottie, Who was Nathaniel
(Clifford D. Simak, *City*, 1952. Scottie was Simak's dog.)

14 By special request this book is dedicated to everybody in the world, except Viv.
(Brian M. Stableford, *Promised Land*, 1974)

15 For Margot, who wore a diaphanous white Halston, and for Real Fantasy which, alas, is all to Rare, which is all too rare.
(Roy Torgeson, *Chrysalis 5*, 1979 — but look at the next one.)

16 Dedication 1. This is for Karen, my mother Sigvald, my father, and Tante Gudrun, my aunt.
Dedication 2. This is for all of the authors and editors who have

suffered from the mysterious curse known as typos. Caused by unseen gremlins, this bane has plagued me. Even my dedication page for *Chrysalis 5* was insidiously distorted. I will not repeat in print the way it turned out — the second line missing and the last line repeated, with a slight variation — but here is the way it *should* have read:
For Margo:
who wore a diaphanous
white Halston
and a flower in her hair
and for Real Fantasy
which, alas, is all too rare.
Notice to Gremlins: Remember that this books is a fantasy anthology and as the editor I have recourse to the Black Arts. If a single word of type is incorrectly set, I shall immmediately conjure up a spell to elimate the source of my affliction. Beware! Take care!
(Roy Torgeson, *Other Worlds 1*, 1979)

17 For the Fifteen and their mates, who are looser because they grok a lot.
(Wilson Tucker, *The Year of the Quiet Sun*, 1970)

18 To Fred Pohl who for better or worse in 1964, when he was editor of *Galaxy, Worlds of If* and *Worlds of Tomorrow* persuaded me to write science fiction again.
(A.E. van Vogt, *The Darkness on Diamonia*, 1972)

19 To all the readers and the writers of that new literature called science-fiction, who find mystery, wonder and high adventure in the expanding universe of knowledge, and who sometimes seek to observe and to forecast the vast impact of science upon the lives and minds of men.
(Jack Williamson, *The Legion of Space*, 1947)

20 To Janey and Dan Armel, with pleasant memories of crustacea craft, artillery practice, slushes, bicycles, lots of Crocketts, roads that went nowhere and never on Sunday.
(Roger Zelazny,
To Die in Italbar, 1973)

7 PECULIAR TITLES

D26

If you're like me then you'll know that there are certain titles that either make you laugh because they're so absurd or make you look twice to make sure you read aright. The following are just some of those that either amused or confused me.

1 **Gsrthnxrpqrpf** by S.J. Byrne *Other Worlds* March 1952. That's how it read on the cover. Inside however the story was headed *Qsrthnxrpqrpf**. The asterix referred to a note which said, 'An actual translation would drive you mad!' It was another of Ray Palmer's gimmick titles and was supposed to represent something said in Martian that was only understood telepathically.

2 **Dr. MacDonough's Encephalosemanticommunicator** by Leo A. Schmidt *Amazing Stories* March 1945. I hope when they invent a machine for reading minds they give it a better name. This was another Palmerism, and at 28 letters it may well be the longest 'English' word used in an sf title — though look at the next one.

3 **Kjwalll'kje'k'koothai'lll'kje'k** by Roger Zelazny from *My Name is Legion* 1976. Once you've read the story you know the title makes perfect sense to a dolphin.

4 **The Radiation of the Chinese Vegetable** by C. Sterling Gleason *Science Wonder Stories* December 1929.

5 **Great Green Things** by Thomas H. Knight *Wonder Stories* April 1931.

6 **The Mystery of the Creeping Underwear** by Tarleton Fiske *Fantastic Adventures* October 1943. Fiske was a pseudonym used by Robert Bloch who has, and let not *Psycho* dissuade you otherwise, a wicked sense of humour.

7 **The Hairy Ones Shall Dance** by Gans T. Field *Weird Tales* January-March 1938. Field is an alias of Manly Wade Wellman's and this is a good adventure story of the investigations of Judge Pursuivant...but that title always makes me laugh.

...AND 12 CONTRIVED ONES

D27

During the 1940s the pages of *Amazing Stories* and even more so *Fantastic Adventures* were littered with humorous stories about madcap inventors or layabouts and their screwball inventions or discoveries. Their titles, regardless of the author, followed the same format and were both contrived and humorous in their own right. The following are just a few to give you an idea.

1 **The Quandary of Quintus Quaggle** William P. McGivern

2 **Rewbarb's Remarkable Radio** William P. McGivern

3 **Christopher Crissom's Cravat** David Wright O'Brien

4 **Taggart's Terrible Turban** Don Wilcox

5 **Freddie Funk's Flippant Fairies** Frances Yerxa

6 **Freddie Funk's Seven League Boots** Leroy Yerxa

7 **Marlow's Malicious Mirror** John York Cabot

8 **Peter Pettigrew's Prisoner** Nelson S. Bond

9 **Sharbeau's Startling Statue** by Clee Garson

10 **The Contract of Carson Carruthers** William P. McGivern

11 **The Masterful Mind of Mortimer Meek** William P. McGivern

12 **Henry Horn's Super-Solvent** Dwight V. Swain

THE 10 MOST IMPORTANT AMERICAN SF & FANTASY MAGAZINES

D28

1 **Weird Tales** March 1923-current The first all-fantasy pulp magazine it led a precarious existence at first but has since become a legend. It ceased publication in September 1954 but has been twice revived and now continues as a paperback magazine. *Weird Tales* can claim to have 'discovered' (if one allows a certain latitude) and published most of the work (or early work in some cases) of H.P. Lovecraft, Robert E. Howard, Clark Ashton Smith, August Derleth, Edmond Hamilton, Seabury Quinn, Robert Block, Manly Wade Wellman, Henry Kuttner and Ray Bradbury.

2 **Amazing Stories** April 1926-current. The first English language sf magazine to be launched by Hugo Gernsback, as a means of teaching science through fiction. For most of its history *Amazing* has been a second- and lesser-rate magazine but it had two periods of significance. Its first three years under Gernsback showed to the world that there was a wide readership ready for sf stories, and in that period *Amazing* 'discovered' such writers as David H. Keller, Stanton Coblentz, Jack Williamson, Edward E. Smith and others. After a period of premature senility and then second childhood, *Amazing* re-matured under Cele Goldsmith in the period 1959 to 1965 when it can claim to have published most of the important early work by Ursula K. LeGuin, Thomas M. Disch, Piers Anthony and Roger Zelazny.

3 **Astounding Stories/SF** (now Analog) January 1930-current. If *Astounding*'s first three years were all the magazine was judged by then it would be eminently disposable. But in 1933 *Astounding* found a new publisher and a new editor, F. Orlin Tremaine who, in a few short months, transformed the magazine to be field leader. He published some of the best stories of the 1930s by such writers as Jack Williamson, Nathan Schachner, Donald Wandrei, Stanley G. Weinbaum, Raymond Gallun, Murray Leinster and John W. Campbell (as Don A. Stuart). Campbell took over editorship of the magazine in 1937 and raised it to even giddier heights and in its pages over the next few years modern sf was born, fathered by such writers as A.E. van Vogt, Isaac Asimov, Robert A. Heinlein, Theodore Sturgeon, L. Sprague de Camp, Lester del Rey and Clifford Simak. *Astounding* has remained the leading sf magazine ever since, although it has never equalled its Golden Age of 1940-1943.

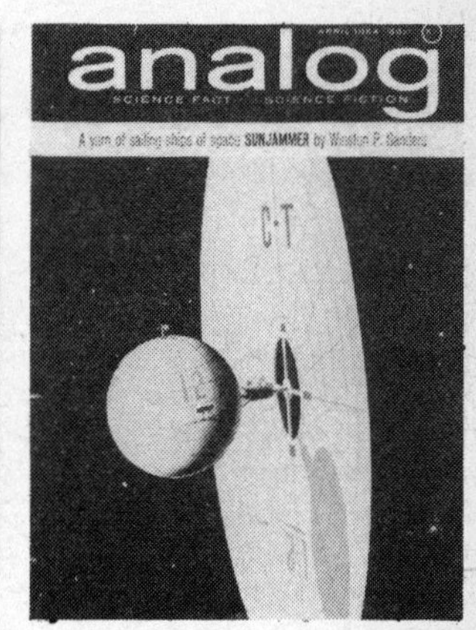

4 **Wonder Stories** June 1929-Winter 1955. Another Gernsback publication (until 1936) it started out life as *Science Wonder Stories* and later, when sold to another publisher, became *Thrilling Wonder Stories*. It can claim two heydays: the period around 1932-1935 when it was at its most 'wonderful' with writers like Edmond Hamilton, Laurence Manning, Nathan Schachner and the discovery of the decade Stanley G. Weinbaum (whose *A Martian Odyssey*

appeared in the July 1934 issue); and the period from 1945 to 1954 when under first Sam Merwin and later Sam Mines, the magazine matured to become one of the most exciting and intelligent on the stands.

5 **Startling Stories** January 1939-Fall 1955.
A companion magazine to *Thrilling Wonder* it began life during *Wonder*'s juvenile period, but like that magazine matured rapidly after the War and published some of the best sf of those years. Probably its best claim to fame was the discovery of Philip Jose Farmer whose *The Lovers* appeared in the August 1952 issue.

6 **Unknown** (later Unknown Worlds) March 1939-October 1943.
Unknown was to fantasy what *Astounding* was to sf, and since both were edited by the same man, John W. Campbell, that isn't so surprising. In a lifetime of only 39 issues *Unknown* published many unforgettable fantasies by L. Sprague de Camp, L. Ron Hubbard, Henry Kuttner, Fritz Leiber (whose Gray Mouser stories first appeared here), Frank Belknap Long and Theodore Sturgeon.

7 **Magazine of Fantasy & Science Fiction**
Fall 1949-current.
Always the most literary of sf/fantasy magazines *F & SF* has maintained a consistent quality through a series of editors from Anthony Boucher and J. Francis McComas to Robert P. Mills and Edward L. Ferman for over 30 years. A check on the Hugo and Nebula Award winners and nominees reveals that the majority of them first appeared in *F & SF*. If only one story was to be selected to demonstrate the peak of *F & SF*'s content, there could be no other choice than *Flowers For Algernon* by Daniel Keyes from the April 1959 issue.

8 **Galaxy**
October 1950-Summer 1980.
Along with *Astounding* and *F & SF*, *Galaxy* formed the Big Three of the sf magazine field during the 1950s and 60s. Under the editorship of first Horace Gold and then Frederik Pohl, it placed more

emphasis on the sociological and satirical side of sf than did *Astounding*, and thus brought to blossom the talents of Frederik Pohl, Robert Sheckley, Damon Knight and James E. Gunn, as well as showing other facets of writers like Theodore Sturgeon, Clifford D. Simak and Isaac Asimov.

9 **If** (sometimes known as Worlds of If) March 1952-December 1974.
During the 1950s *If* was a competent but unremarkable magazine; however, it was transformed during the 1960s under the editorship of Frederik Pohl, who made it into a fun magazine to appeal to all ages, and at the same time brought much verve back to the sf fields which it had lacked in recent years. In the period from 1963 to 1969 *If* brought A.E. van Vogt and E.E. Smith back to sf after many years absence, and bought much of the best new sf from Keith Laumer, Fred Saberhagen, Robert Silverberg, Harlan Ellison, Roger Zelazny, Larry Niven and Samuel Delany.

10 **Isaac Asimov's SF Magazine**
Spring 1977-current.
The most successful of the new magazines of the 1970s, *Asimov*'s is at its worst a blend of bad jokes and dreadful puns, and at its best the most entertaining magazine around. Under editor George

Scithers it can claim to have discovered, or at least nurtured the talents of Barry Longyear, Somtow Sucharitkul and John M. Ford, names that may yet mean little in Britain, but which should not be overlooked.

THE 5 MOST IMPORTANT BRITISH SF MAGAZINES

D29

Britain has no depth of quality in the sf magazine field and whilst I could list 10 magazines, only half would actually be worth the trouble tracking down. The remainder are suitable only for mad completist collectors like myself.

1 **Tales of Wonder** 1937-1942
If we ignore *Scoops*, a juvenile disaster of 1934, *Tales of Wonder* was the first British sf magazine edited by the very capable Walter Gillings. It had to rely heavily on reprints from American magazines chiefly because what talent Britain did have soon succumbed to the war effort. It's main claim to fame today is that it published the first professional pieces by Arthur C. Clarke — *Man's Empire of Tomorrow* (Winter 1938) and *We Can Rocket to the Moon — Now!* (Summer 1939).

2 **New Worlds** 1946-1979
New Worlds was the backbone of British sf during the 1950s and revolutionised the field in the 1960s, Firstly, under the control of John Carnell, it could be regarded as the British *Astounding*, and there was scarcely a British sf writer who did not appear in its pages. E.C. Tubb, James White and, in particular J.G. Ballard, all debuted here, whilst Brian Aldiss, John Brunner, Kenneth Bulmer and others made it one of their main markets. From 1964 on, edited by Michael Moorcock, it ushered in the sf 'new wave'. *New Worlds* is still officially alive, though issues have been sparse recently.

3 **Science Fantasy** Summer 1950-February 1966
A companion magazine to *New Worlds* it was edited for most of its life by Carnell. Its heyday was during the years 1958-1964 when its true character emerged. Concentrating on long lead stories

it published some of the best of John Brunner and Kenneth Bulmer, and also helped in the revival of interest in heroic fantasy, by publishing the works of Thomas Burnett Swann and Michael Moorcock (whose Elric stories first appeared here).

4 **Nebula** Autumn 1952-June 1959
Scotland's only ever sf magazine *Nebula* attracted some of the best sf from British and American writers during the 1950s. Brian Aldiss, John Brunner, E.C. Tubb

and William F. Temple were frequent contributors. Indeed *Nebula* bought the first story from Aldiss, and also bought the first sales from Barrington J. Bayley, Bob Shaw and Robert Silverberg.

5 **Science Fiction Adventures** March 1958 May 1963
Originally a British reprint edition of the American magazine of the same name, *SFA* soon took on an identity of its own, and concentrated on publishing two long stories (plus one or two shorts) per issue. John Brunner, Kenneth Bulmer, Michael Moorcock, James White were the main contributors.

12 IMPORTANT SF & FANTASY MAGAZINES FROM AROUND THE WORLD

D30

It's easy for us to take the blinkered view that sf is essentially English and American in origin and development, but there are scores of sf authors and magazines throughout the world, and the sf magazine itself did not originate in America. The following are just a few of the world's many sf magazines.

1 **Hugin** Sweden (April 1916-December 1920). The world's first sf magazine, although it was written almost entirely single-handedly by its rather eccentric editor and publisher Otto Witt.

2 **Der Orchideengarten** Germany (April 1919-May 1921). A very rare fantasy magazine that featured both new and reprinted stories from all over the globe.

3 **Jules Verne Magasinet** Sweden (October 1940-current). Originally a weekly magazine that consisted mostly of reprints *JVM* folded in 1947 but was revived in 1969 by Sam Lundwall who has since made it Sweden's leading magazine.

4 **Fiction** France (October 1953-current). Began as a French edition of *F & SF* but soon began to include new stories by French writers and established itself as the backbone of French magazine sf.

5 **Hapna** Sweden (March 1954-January 1966). The most important Scandinavian magazine of its day.

6 **Colectia Povestiri S-F** Romania (June 1955-October 1969). A weekly sf supplement to a science fiction magazine it published more issues than any other European sf magazine.

7 **SF Magazine** Japan (February 1960-current) Also originally an edition of *F & SF*.

8 **Galassia** Italy (January 1961-current). One of three magazines with the same title in Italy. Italy has published more sf magazines than any other country outside the United States.

9 **Nova** Italy (May 1967-current). Here's another example.

10 **Nueva Dimension** Spain (January 1968-current). More than once *ND* has been suppressed by the Spanish authorities but still it keeps alive the voice of sf in Spain.

11 **Galaksija** Yugoslavia (April 1972-current).

12 **Galaktika** Hungary (Fall 1972-current).

40 WORLD SF CONVENTIONS

D31

...from little acorns... The first 'Worldcon' was held in 1939 and over the following few years they were small affairs but recently have mushroomed into important, commercial events. 1953 was the first year when the Science Fiction Achievement Awards (the Hugos) were presented and they are now one of the high spots of the convention, along with the art show and the fancy dress competitions.

Year	Name	Venue	Professional Guests of Honour	Attendance
1939	**Nycon 1**	**New York**	Frank R. Paul	200
1940	**Chicon 1**	**Chicago**	Edward E. Smith	128
1941	**Denvention 1**	**Denver**	Robert A. Heinlein	90
1946	**Pacificon 1**	**Los Angeles**	A.E. van Vogt & E. Mayne Hull	130
1947	**Philcon 1**	**Philadelphia**	John W. Campbell, Jr	200
1948	**Torcon 1**	**Toronto**	Robert Bloch	200
1949	**Cinvention**	**Cincinnati**	Lloyd A. Eshbach	190
1950	**Norwescon**	**Portland**	Anthony Boucher	400
1951	**Nolacon**	**New Orleans**	Fritz Leiber	190
1952	**Chicon II**	**Chicago**	Hugo Gernsback	870
1953	**Philcon II**	**Philadelphia**	Willy Ley	750
1954	**SFCon**	**San Francisco**	John W. Campbell, Jr	700
1955	**Clevention**	**Cleveland**	Isaac Asimov	380
1956	**Newyorcon**	**New York**	Arthur C. Clarke	850
1957	**Loncon 1**	**London**	John W. Campbell, Jr	268
1958	**Solacon**	**Los Angeles**	Richard Matheson	322
1959	**Detention**	**Detroit**	Poul Anderson	371
1960	**Pittcon**	**Pittsburgh**	James Blish	568
1961	**Seacon**	**Seattle**	Robert A. Heinlein	300
1962	**Chicon III**	**Chicago**	Theodore Sturgeon	550
1963	**Discon 1**	**Washington DC**	Murray Leinster	600
1964	**Pacificon II**	**Oakland**	Edmond Hamilton & Leigh Brackett	523

1965	**Loncon II**	**London**	Brian W. Aldiss	350
1966	**Tricon**	**Cleveland**	L. Sprague de Camp	850
1967	**Nycon 3**	**New York**	Lester del Rey	1500
1968	**Baycon**	**Oakland**	Philip Jose Farmer	1430
1969	**St Louiscon**	**St Louis**	Jack Gaughan	1534
1970	**Heicon 70**	**Heidelberg**	Robert Silverberg	620
1971	**Noreascon**	**Boston**	Clifford D. Simak	1600
1972	**L.A.Con**	**Los Angeles**	Frederik Pohl	2007
1973	**Torcon 2**	**Toronto**	Robert Bloch	2900
1974	**Discon II**	**Washington DC**	Roger Zelazny	4000
1975	**Aussiecon**	**Melbourne**	Ursula K. LeGuin	2044
1976	**Mid-Americon**	**Kansas City**	Robert A. Heinlein	2614
1977	**Suncon**	**Miami Beach**	Jack Williamson	2050
1978	**Iguanacon**	**Phoenix**	Harlan Ellison	4700
1979	**Seacon 79**	**Brighton, UK**	Fritz Leiber (US) & Brian W. Aldiss (UK)	5124
1980	**Noreascon 2**	**Boston**	Kate Wilhelm & Damon Knight	5921
1981	**Denven-tion 2**	**Denver**	Clifford D. Simak C.L. Moore	3792
1982	**Chicon IV**	**Chicago**	A. Bertram Chandler & Kelly Freas	Up To You

The 1983 Worldcon will be held in Baltimore and is being called variously Constallation and Balticon. The Guest of Honour will be John Brunner.

10 SF BOOK/STORIES THAT WERE BANNED OR WITHDRAWN

D32

1 **We** by Yevgeny Zamiatin (1924). Written in 1920 the book was banned in Russia, and its first edition was an American translation published in New York in 1924. A Russian-language edition appeared in Czechoslovakia in 1927 in a magazine, and Zamiatin wisely chose to leave Russia and settle in France.

2 **Jurgen** by James Branch Cabell (1919). Although little more than a harmless fantasy, and one of a long line of novels by Cabell set in the mythical country of Poictesme, *Jurgen* was banned from publication in the spring of 1920. John S. Sumner and the New York Society for the Suppression of Vice had charged it with being 'lewd, lascivious, indecent, obscene and disgusting'. What more could Cabell wish for. Overnight he became a sensation. Two years later Judge Charles G. Nott quashed the ban, stating that he felt the book was of 'unusual literary merit'.

3 **The Cheetah Girl** by Christopher Blayre (1923). In 1921, the London firm of Philip Allan published a book called *The Purple Sapphire* credited to Christopher Blayre, but in fact the work of scientist and writer Edward Heron-Allen. The contents page listed eight stories but the last, *The Cheetah Girl*, was missing, being replaced by the statement, 'The Publishers Regret That They Are Unable To Print This MS'. No reasons were given but it was almost certainly for fear of prosecution under the obscenity laws of the 1920s. In 1971, however, bibliophile and bookdealer George Locke, had the opportunity of reading a privately

printed copy of the story, published in 1923 and limited to twenty copies. He discovered that far from being obscene, the story was unusually advanced for its day and dealt with artificial insemination and the resultant hybrid offspring, half-human, half-cheetah.

4 **Weird Tales** May-June-July 1924. After only a year *Weird Tales* was facing financial doom. Publisher Jacob Henneberger put out an anniversary issue which might well have been the last, except that it contained the story *The Loved Dead* by C.M. Eddy, Jr., one of the friends of H.P. Lovecraft who himself had a hand in revising the story. Dealing with a madman, the story included references to necrophilia which apparently caused an uproar from Citizens' Groups and Religious Societies in many towns throughout the States. Eddy claimed that although they had the issue in question withdrawn from sale, the resultant publicity was sufficient to keep the magazine alive.

5 **Paradise Crater** by Philip Wylie (1945). Written early in 1945 the story dealt with the supernatural after-effects of a nuclear explosion. Wylie included details on the manufacture of an atomic bomb and the magazine editor with due caution sent the manuscript to Washington for approval to publish. National Security promptly descended on Wylie who was placed under house arrest. Wylie's character was checked out and he was finally cleared, but the story was held over until after Hiroshima, and then published in the October 1945 *Blue Book.* There were similar incidents over other stories dealing with atomic bombs of which the most notable was *Deadline* by Cleve Cartmill in the March 1944 *Astounding*, which editor John W. Campbell had published regardless.

6 **Tarzan on Mars** by John Bloodstone. Bloodstone is the alias of Stuart J. Byrne, a popular writer of adventure sf for the pulp magazines in the 1940s and 50s, especially those edited by Raymond A. Palmer. After the death of Edgar Rice Burroughs in 1950, Palmer urged the Burroughs Estate to appoint an official successor to continue the adventures of Tarzan and John Carter. He recommended Byrne who in fact completed a novel *Tarzan on Mars* which Palmer planned to publish in *Other Worlds.* Byrne forwarded the manuscript to C.R. Rothmund the General Manager of Burroughs, Inc., who replied: '...We regret to tell you that we shall never permit it to be published'. And so it has remained. A few unauthorised Tarzan novels have been published and all subsequently 'officially' withdrawn from sale, making them highly collectible items today. These include the five novels published under the alias Barton Werper: *Tarzan and the Silver Globe* (1964), *Tarzan and the Cave City* (1964), *Tarzan and the Snake People* (1964), *Tarzan and the Abominable Snowman* (1965) and *Tarzan and the Winged Invaders* (1965) plus the anonymously published film tie-in *Tarzan and the Lost Safari* (1966).

7 **The Time Machine** by Langdon Jones (1967). This story was all set to be included in the August 1967 issue of *New Worlds* when the printer (not the publisher) decided that the story was too risky and would not print it. Ironically the story first saw print in America exactly two years later in Damon Knight's *Orbit 5* which had its own British hardback edition in 1970. It passed with scarcely a notice.

8 **New Worlds** March 1968. During the late 1960s *New Worlds* under the editorship of Michael Moorcock was trying to break down the barriers of established sf and bring the genre back into the literary mainstream. Many less liberal readers were thus not prepared to find what they thought to be a science fiction magazine

carrying 'adult' fiction, in particular Norman Spinrad's serial *Bug Jack Barron.* Amidst the shock and horror W.H. Smith decided that they would not distribute *New Worlds* on the grounds of 'obscenity and libel'. The ban was never satisfactorily lifted and to all intents it starved the magazine of circulation and contributed to its demise.

9 **Nueva Dimension** June 1970. This Spanish magazine has remarkably managed to struggle on since its first issue in January 1968; always at odds with the authorities. The June 1970 issue was seized by the State Police as representing a threat to Spanish security.

10 **More Devils Kisses** edited by Linda Lovecraft (1977). Edited pseudonymously by Michel Parry, this anthology of 'erotic tales of terror' obviously upset a number of bookstall browsers. A copy of the book fell into the hands of Scotland Yard's Obscene Publications Squad and the publisher, Corgi Books, was threatened with prosecution unless the book was withdrawn. Existing stocks were destroyed and an attempt made to recall copies already despatched. Most of the print run was eventually destroyed, but a few survive. The story which apparently upset Scotland Yard was *The Magic Show* by Chris Miller, concerning some rather unusual entertainment at a children's party. The story had previously been published, without complaint in *The National Lampoon.*

TERMS OF SF FAN-LINGO AND THEIR MEANING

D33

Science fiction fandom like any other in-group has developed its own slang, usually a short-cut language meant to aid discussion rather than act as any secret terminology. However an outsider can soon become baffled by some of the terms that fans rattle off without really thinking, so the following may help any *mundanes* or *neofen* who are considering *fanac* themselves.

actifan – **acti**ve **fan**: one who participates regularly in fandom either by writing for or producing a *fanzine* or other *fanac.*

apa – **A**mateur **P**ress **A**ssociation: in existence before *sf* fandom but rapidly adopted, it is a central organisation for the publication and circulation of a common group of *fanzines.* A fanzine produced by an apa is usually called an apazine.

BNF – **B**ig **N**ame **F**an: usually those who have been active in fandom for many years and are known to associate with the *filthy pros*, and who may even have sold professionally themselves. Such writers as Robert Silverberg, Terry Carr, Ted White, Bob Shaw, James White and Wilson (Bob) Tucker were all BNFs at one time.

corflu — **cor**recting **flu**id: the saving grace for all fanzines produced by stencils and a bad typist.

egoboo — **ego boo**st: one has a feeling of egoboo when your *fanzine* is praised in the *prozines*, or even in other fanzines.

fanac — **fan**nish **ac**tivity: actually participating actively in fandom.

fanzine — a **fan** maga**zine**: sometimes called fanmags; amateur magazines produced by *sf* fans.

femme fan — a female fan. By extension if a female fan produces a *fanzine* it is usually dubbed a femmezine.

fen — plural of fan, in the same way as men is plural of man.

fiawol — **f**andom **i**s **a w**ay **o**f **l**ife: an acronym which reveals that sf fandom is sufficiently important to dominate one's life.

fillo — **fi**ller i**llo**: a small illustration used to fill up space in a *fanzine* or *prozine*.

filthy pro — a semi-affectionate term tinged with jealousy used by fans to refer to one of their number who has sold stories to the *prozines*.

gafia — **g**etting **a**way **f**rom **i**t **a**ll: another acronym to denote an escape from *fiawol* and *fanac*, hence the verb to gafiate, or to stop ones fannish involvement.

Hugo — the Science Fiction Achievement Award presented annually at *Worldcons* and named after Hugo Gernsback, the founder of the *sf* magazine.

illo - illustration; plural illoes.

lettercol — the **letter col**umn in a magazine, also known as a *locolumn*.

letterhack — a regular writer of letters to *fanzines* or *prozines* whose letters are usually published.

loc — **l**etter **o**f **c**omment: one way to obtain a *fanzine* is to write a loc on the previous issue, hence the verb to loc, or to write a letter to a *zine* commenting on it.

locolumn — letter column, or more precisely the column for *locs*.

mundane — the world outside fandom and the people in it.

neofan — newcomer to fandom (plural neofen).

prodom — the professional counterpart to fandom.

prozine — a **pro**fessional maga**zine**, also called promags.

sercon — serious and **con**structive, an adjective that can describe either a fan or a fanzine. It means one that deals seriously with science fiction as opposed to a fanish fanzine which deals less seriously with *sf* and involves itself mostly with *fanac*.

sf — the accepted abbreviation for **s**cience **f**iction. An older variant is stef derived from Hugo Gernsback's earlier name for science fiction, viz. scientifiction. Either of these terms may be used, especially as stef is adaptable as an adjective, e.g. a book with a science fiction flavour can be described as stefnish. Under no circumstances, however, will any self-respecting fan use the term sci-fi which has come to be associated with the public image of all that is bad in science fiction. Say sci-fi to any *trufan* and watch him wince — unless he hits back first!

trufan — a tried and tested **tru**e **fan** often, but not necessarily, one of many years' standing, and who has considerable loyalty to fandom.

Worldcon — the annual World Science Fiction Convention.

zine — maga**zine**, whether *fanzine* or *prozine*.

10 COINCIDENCES AND ODDITIES

D34

1 The writer William S. Burroughs, author of *The Soft Machine, Nova Express* and other quasi-sf works is the grandson of the inventor of the Burroughs adding machine.

2 Jerry Juhl, one of the mainstay writers and puppeteers for *The Muppets* was an '*If*-first', selling a science fiction story, *The Edward Salant Letters* to Frederik Pohl. It appeared in the April 1968 *If*.

3 Morgan Robertson (1861-1915) wrote many short stories in the fields of supernatural and early science fiction but he is best remembered for his short novel *Futility* (1898). This describes, in uncanny detail, the fatal maiden voyage of a new luxury liner, claimed to be unsinkable but which struck an iceberg and sank. Robertson called it the *Titan*. Fourteen years later the *Titanic* relived those events.

4 Tennessee Williams, the noted dramatist of such works as *A Street Car Named Desire* (1947) and *Cat On A Hot Tin Roof* (1955), sold his first story to *Weird Tales. The Vengeance of Nitocris,* a tale of revenge in ancient Egypt, appeared in the issue for August 1928 under his full name of Thomas Lanier Williams.

5 Ed Earl Repp, a popular writer of sf and fantastic adventures in the 1930s was the last newspaper reporter to interview the legendary Wyatt Earp.

6 Anne McCaffrey was born in the same week that the first sf magazine *Amazing Stories,* officially appeared.

7 The most oft-used title in science fiction is *Homecoming* which has been used for at least nine stories and one novel by Ray Bradbury, Alfred Coppel, Lee Correy, Gordon R. Dickson, E.C. Tubb and others. The second most common is *Castaway,* which has been used eight times.

8 Berkeley Livingston used the title *The Gift* for two of his stories, in the August 1946 *Amazing* and the December 1947 *Fantastic Adventures.*

9 The closest coincidence of titles is when *Command Performance* was used by both Robert White in July 1954 *Amazing* and Kay Rogers in the August 1954 F & SF. Neither proved as popular as *Command Performance* by Walter M. Miller, Jr. which had appeared less than two years earlier in the November 1952 *Galaxy.* A second close coincidence was *Button, Button,* used by Isaac Asimov in the January 1953 *Startling Stories* and by Thomas Wilson in the March 1953 *Astounding.*

10 Writers often coincidentally use exactly the same idea for novels. *Shiva Descending* by Greg Benford and William Rotsler, for instance, is strikingly similar to *Lucifer's Hammer* by Larry Niven and Jerry Pournelle. Larry Niven reports that Bill Rotsler told him one night, 'No, I haven't read *Lucifer's Hammer.* I'm afraid your ideas might creep over into my own writing.' Niven's response was, 'You thought it over *that* carefully and then made the wrong decision?' Rotsler apparently 'laughed like hell. Then he read the book. Now he isn't laughing.' A similar case of involuntary duplication is *The Web Between The Worlds* by Charles Sheffield which employs the same theme of the space elevator and which appeared at the same time as Arthur C. Clarke's *The Fountains of Paradise.* Clarke actually wrote a forward to Sheffield's book highlighting the fact of coincidental generation of ideas. These occurrences should

not be confused with plagiarisms which are deliberate copies of an author's work by another without acknowledgement for profit. It is illegal to plagiarise, and it is dumb to do it in the sf field where the bibliographic knowledge of the fans will spot a plagiarism instantly. One recent plagiarism was *Star Chase* credited to 'Brian James Royal' (1979), which was the same as *Titans of the Universe* (1978) credited to 'James Harvey' and which are both plagiarisms of *Escape Across the Cosmos* by Gardner Fox published in 1964.

10 AUTHORS' WORKING DAYS

D35

1 **John Brunner** 'I once calculated I spend about as much time per year actually at my desk, writing, as a teacher spends in the classroom: i.e. about 40-42 weeks out of the year. But I don't take two-day weekends; when a book is running, I work at it at least some of every day until it's finished. If I have to break off, e.g. for a convention or to fulfil some other professional engagement, I make sure I break where I know what I'm going to say next. And research and planning *never stops.*'
(— Private correspondence, November 1981)

2 **Hal Clement** 'My working habits are most irregular; I sit down to the typewriter when the mood and the idea coincide. It must be remembered that I earn my living as a schoolteacher, and science fiction is a hobby to be indulged in when there is time; currently there is very little time. For the next year and three-quarters I am President of the New England Association of Chemistry Teachers, which also is a rather time-consuming activity; and all too often I simply sit and read.'
(— Private Correspondence, November 1981)

3 **Philip K. Dick** 'Once I start a book, I like to just go through and finish it, because there's more chance of authentic continuity that way. I could never adopt this thing you hear about writing ten pages a day, writing from nine to five. You do your ten pages, and when you've done them, you stop. If you're hot you're gonna write until you drop. If you're cold, you could sit in front of the typewriter forever. So if I'm hot, I will just write...If I could have it my way, I wouldn't sleep while I was writing a novel, I'd just sit and start at page one and write it straight through.'

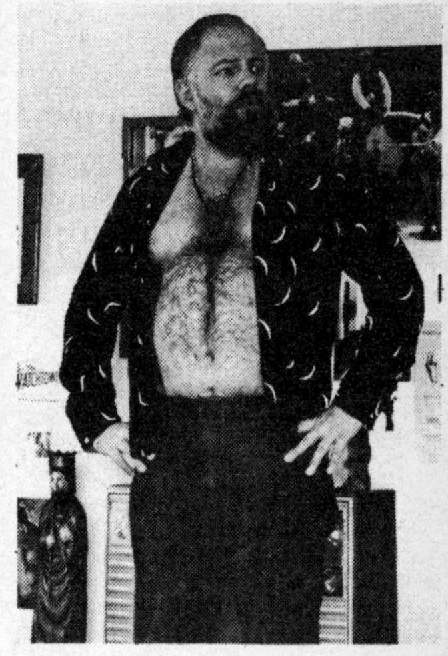

Philip K. Dick

(— part of an interview conducted by Daniel DePrez in September 1976 and published in *Science Fiction Review* 19)

4 **Lionel Fanthorpe** (As the world's most prolific sf writer Lionel's writing day must differ from those of others. At present Lionel is not actively writing; as he says '...my working day starts about 6am and finishes around midnight. I try to find time to write, run a business, run a High School in a Social Priority Area, run a judo club, lecture, broadcast, put on shows...'.) But back in the 1960s, his output was managed as follows:
'I'd scribble down enough notes to give me an outline for say two hours dictating. Then I'd rattle off the first reel of tape. This would be taken by my wife to the first typist free (we had a battery of typists available). The next reel would go out to number two and so on until all five had a reel. The first reels I often did on one side only, to get the typists something to work on. By the time I was dictating reel six, the first typist had finished, say, 20 pages or more on reel one. Reel one, plus the 20 pages, came back via Pat (my wife), who gave reel six to the typist...and so on until we're in sight of the end — 200 pages. Suppose I've got 160 pages finished and there are three reels uncollected? I then stop recording and wait for results. If I'm lucky I haven't gone over. If I'm in danger of going over, I await the last pages and write a single page galloping ending.'
(— Private Correspondence, November 1981)

5 **Philip Jose Farmer** 'My working day used to be about from eight to twelve hours, sometimes fourteen, but now it's about six and a half most of the time. I don't eat while I'm at work, or drink. I take time off for lunch, a bicycle ride, read or something; the only thing is I have a hell of a lot of correspondence, and I'm always way, way behind on that. When I'm through at the end of the day I would like to write letters, mainly because I like to get letters, but it's hard to force myself to do it.'
(— part of an interview conducted by David Kraft and Mitch Steel in June 1972 and published in *Science Fiction Review* 14)

6 **Harry Harrison** 'In the morning, anywhere between eight and ten, I go to the studio and put in a day's work. When I am working at a piece of fiction I stay with it for as many days as it takes. Early on, in honour of the Christian work ethic, I used to work the six day week and take Sunday off. I found this broke the motion of a book so I began to work straight through on the first draft. Since I average about 2,000 words a day this means at least a month of continuous writing. That's fine. It also means weeks off at a time when others are in their offices.'
(— extract from *How We Work* in *Hell's Cartographers* edited by Brian W. Aldiss and Harry Harrison, ©1975 by SF Horizons Ltd).

7 **Frederik Pohl** 'For me the procedure is simple. Once a day I sit down at my typewriter, roll a sheet of paper in and do not get up until I have produced four pages of copy. If I am going well, maybe I'll produce more; but however badly things are going, I will produce those four or die for it. It's as simple as that. Sometimes it takes forty-five minutes, sometimes twelve hours...What do I do if it's bad? I put it away and work on something else, till the ageing process has had a chance to work. Then I take it out and look at it, and most times I can see what is wrong and what I need to do to fix it.'
(— extract from *How We Work* in *Hell's Cartographers,* ©1975, as above)

8 **E.C. Tubb** (Here Ted Tub shows how he used to write back in the 1950s and how that's differed

today.)
'...The method was to sit at the machine and start writing and make the damned thing up as you went along. No rough drafts, no rewriters, no synopses. Now, as I was working during the day the actual time of real production, that is time at the machine must have been about one hour per thousand words. Maybe more, but allowing time for smoking, drinking the odd cup of tea, stretching etc., it makes a fair average. I know I used to write until it got late or I got tired or the wife finally lost her patience. I wrote a chapter each evening (3,000 words) and made up the rest on Sundays. As I grew older a higher standard was demanded. The *Cap Kennedy*'s, for example, 42,000 each, took on average about fourteen days — this as a full-time writer. The *Dumarest's* 60,000, show a steadily lengthening writing time due to format discipline. Now I write as and when the mood takes me — and the wolf is snapping at my rear.'
(— Private Correspondence, October 1981)

9 **A.E. Van Vogt** '...I never was a nine am to five pm writer. I still write from the time I wake up until the time I go to bed, except that I allow myself to be interrupted. However, I discovered a long time ago, that in order to write, you must keep at it. You can't allow yourself to take breaks. Once you start taking breaks, you lose your high energy state. It takes a considerable amount of time to bring that state up again. Writing requires an extremely high energy state. The moment you shift gears and do something else, you're immediately operating at a lower state.'
(— part of an interview conducted by Jeffrey Elliot and published in *Science Fiction Review* November 23, 1977)

10 **Jack Williamson** 'I work some five or six hours a day, sometimes more if something's going really well, these days on a word processor.'
(— Private Correspondence, November 1981)

12 SF WRITERS AND HOW THEY DISCOVERED SF

D36

1 **Brian W. Aldiss** 'The boys' magazine I took every week was *Modern Boy*, published by Amalgamated Press. I loved *Modern Boy* dearly. Sir Malcolm Campbell used to contribute to it — and Flying Officer W.E. Johns, for his Biggles stories were being published even then. What I was absolutely addicted to was Captain Justice. Justice was an elegant adventurer, much given to wearing white ducks and a naval cap and smoking a cigar. He had various bases around the world, chief of which was Titanic Tower, significantly in mid-Atlantic. From Titanic Tower, Justice sorted out the troubles of the Anglo-American world in story after story. The stories were written by 'Murray Roberts', the pen name of Tovert Murray Graydon. Justice and Co ventured into Africa to find an empire of slaves ruled by strange forces, confronted giant insects, battled with enormous robots, overcame alarming flying machines, survived a world plunged into darkness (the most enthralling of all his adventures!) and also paid regular visits to any runaway planets which happened to be passing through the solar

system at the time. So science fiction entered into and began warping my life from an early age...'
(– extract from *Magic and Bare Boards* in *Hell's Cartographers* edited by Brian W. Aldiss and Harry Harrison, ©1975 SF Horizons Ltd.)

2 **Isaac Asimov** 'Ah, yes. My father owned a candy store in my youthful days and to the candy store was attached a newsstand and a magazine rack. The magazine rack was filled with the most delectable fiction you could possibly imagine: *The Shadow, Doc Savage, Detective Stories, Argosy.* Even today the thought of it all makes me faint with desire. Yet all of it, from beginning to end, was forbidden by parental ukase.
'Came the day in 1929 when a copy of *Science Wonder Stories* appeared on the rack and attracted my attention. I sneaked a copy down when my father was taking his afternoon nap (my kindly mother was always much more permissive) and looked inside. Spaceships, monsters, ray-guns – WOW! I put it back and waited for my father to return. He did. I pointed to the magazine and said, 'Pappa, would it be all right to read a magazine about science?' My father stared at it doubtfully. His English was not yet strong, but the cover showed a futuristic airplace that looked very edifying and there was no denying the word 'science' was clearly inscribed on the cover. He said, 'All right'. And that is how I became a science fiction reader.'
(– extract from *Portrait of the Writer as a Boy* by Isaac Asimov, ©1966, Mercury Press, for *The Magazine of Fantasy and Science Fiction* October 1966)

3 **James Blish** 'The collision between the laboratory and the typewriter, now so inevitable in retrospect, was in reality curiously muffled and was a long time in producing any visible consequences. It was begun in 1931 by one of my block friends who knew of my interest in astronomy, who offered to give me a book that told all about life on other planets. This turned out to be the April 1931 issue of *Astounding Stories.* I still have a copy, although of course not *the* copy. The cover, by Wesso, shows two men in tight-fitting jodhpurs jumping with apparently suicidal intent at three much bigger crocodile-men, against a nocturnal background of cone-shaped buildings whose triangular openings glow an ominous orange. In the background, too, there appear two other crocodile-men who seem to be trying to catch the humans in the red rays of some kind of electric torch...This Wesso cover faithfully represented a scene in the lead-off story, *Monsters of Mars,* by Edmond Hamilton...'
(– extract from *The Development of a Science Fiction Writer* by James Blish for *Foundation* 2, June *1972,* © *The Science Fiction* Foundation.)

4 **Ray Bradbury** 'When I was nine, I began to collect comic strips – *Buck Rogers, Flash Gordon, Tarzan.* About that time I started to hang around circuses and carnivals. I struck up a great friendship with a man named 'Mr Electrico', who really impressed me. I think that it was his influence which really encouraged me to become a writer. After we had several long talks, I went out and bought a typewriter and started writing. I've never stopped writing since then'.
(– part of an interview conducted by Jeffrey M. Elliot and published in *The San Francisco Review of Books,* ©1977)

5 **Damon Knight** 'In the thirties I became aware that there were such things as pulp magazines. There were *Spicy Adventure* and *Spicy Mystery,* which I did not dare buy, even in the dingy little second-hand store at the bottom of a side street in town. There were air-war magazines which I did buy and

devoured. Then I saw and bought an issue of something called *Amazing Stories.* It was bigger than other pulps, about 81/2 x 11, and the cover, in sick pastels, showed two helmetted and white-suited men aiming rifles at a bunch of golliwogs. This was the August-September 1933 issue, and the cover story was *Meteor-Men of Plaa* by Henry J. Kostkos. That was the beginning.'
(– extract from *Knight Piece* by Damon Knight in *Hell's Cartographers,* ©1975 as in (1) above.)

6 **Frederik Pohl** 'At some point in that year of 1930 I came across a magazine named *Science Wonder Stories Quarterly,* with a picture of a scaly green monster on the cover. I opened it up. The irremediable virus entered my veins.'
(- extract from *As It Was in the Beginning,* Chapter 1 of *The Way The Future Was: A Memoir* by Frederik Pohl, ©1978.)

7 **Bob Shaw** '...I was an early and voracious reader who, from the age of seven, had been going through a steady one book a day from the local library...I read anything I could get hold of, but always had a strong preference for science fiction – a taste which had been nurtured by the fantastic serials which usually ran in the boys' weekly papers like *Wizard* and *Hotspur*...Nobody told me about H.G. Wells – at school we were struck with *The Cloister and the Hearth* – and the only relevant books I found in the library were *The Starmaker* and one of Burroughs' Martian series...The discovery of *Astounding,* when I was about 11, converted me from a lover of science fiction into a rabid fanatic...'
(– extract from *Escape To Infinity* by Bob Shaw in *Foundation* 10, June 1976, ©The Science Fiction Foundation.)

8 **Robert Silverberg** '...there was Jules Verne when I was nine – I must have taken the voyage with

Joan Vinge

Captain Nemo a hundred times – and H.G. Wells when I was ten, most notably *The Time Machine* (which promised to show me all the incredible eons I would never live to know) but also *The Island of Dr Moreau* and *The War of the Worlds,* the myriad short stories, and even an obscure satire called *Mr Blettsworthy on Rampole Island*...There was Twain's *Connecticut Yankee in King Arthur's Court,* which I also read repeatedly.'
(– extract from 'Sounding Brass, Tinkling Cymbal' by Robert Silverberg in *Hell's Cartographers,* ©1975 as in (1) above).

9 **John Varley** 'The first science fiction book I ever read was *Red Planet* by Heinlein, in junior high school. And I used to try to find everything the man had ever written. I was so entranced by his stories...I don't know of anybody who has a stronger story sense that Heinlein, who can tell more exciting, interesting stories set in the future, although 'set in the everyday future' is the way I think of it.'
(– part of an interview conducted by Pascal Thomas and published in *Science Fiction Times* No. 4, August 1979, ©Galileo Magazine, Inc.).

1 0 A.E. Van Vogt 'When I was fourteen, and already living in Winnipeg, I saw the November 1926 issue of *Amazing Stories* on the newsstand. I was evidently the type that was stimulated by extravagant science-fictional art. I grabbed up my copy, paid over my 25 cents — and thereafter for several years each month devoured every word printed in the magazine. I mean every.'
(— extract from *The Development of a Science Fiction Writer* by A.E. Van Vogt in *Foundation* 3, March 1973, ©The Science Fiction Foundation.)

1 1 Joan D. Vinge 'The first story that I read was Andre Norton's *Storm Over Warlock.* When I was in junior high school I found that at the corner grocery store and I read it, and I was so excited by it. I thought, gee, where has this been all my life? Just the idea of things taking place on another world and the absolute imagination of it appealed to me so much. I've never really wanted in my own writing to write anything besides science fiction.'
(— part of an interview conducted by Darrell Schweitzer and published in *Science Fiction Review* 30, March-April 1979.)

1 2 Roger Zelazny 'I first got interested in science fiction with the *Doctor Dolittle* stories in the first or second grade; I was a fantasy fan when I was very young. Then, when I was in the sixth grade, I got hold of a book — I can't think of the name of the author right now, but it was called *The Angry Planet* by John Keir Cross. I was eleven years old at the time. That was the first exposure I had to science fiction, and then I ran into a fellow who had also read it. We got to talking about it, and he said, 'Gee, there's lots of other good stuff in the school library,' so I went through the whole school science-fiction library shelves.'
(— extract from *Authorgraphs,* ©1969 Galaxy Publishing Corporation for *Worlds of If* January 1969.)

10 SF STORIES AND HOW THEY ORIGINATED

D37

1 **Isaac Asimov** *Nightfall*
'The writing of *Nightfall* was a watershed in my professional career. When I wrote it, I had just turned 21. I had been writing professionally (in the sense that I was submitting my stories to magazines and occasionally selling them) for two and a half years, but had created no tidal wave. I had published about a dozen stories and had failed to sell a dozen others.
'Then John W. Campbell, Jr., the editor of *Astounding SF*, showed me the Emerson quotation that starts 'Nightfall'. We discussed it; then I went home and, over the course of the next few weeks, wrote the story.
'Now let's get something straight. I didn't write that story any differently from the way I had written my earlier stories — or, for that matter, from the way I wrote my later stories. As far as writing is concerned, I am a complete and utter primitive. I have no formal training at all and to this very day I don't know How To Write.
'I just write any old way it comes in to my mind to write and just as fast as it comes into my mind.

'And that's the way I wrote *Nightfall*.'
(— from Asimov's own introduction to *Nightfall* as published in *Nightfall: Twenty SF Stories* ©1969 by Isaac Asimov

2 **James Blish**
Earthman, Come Home
'I came at this by an entirely roundabout route in 1948. There was a cover on an *Astounding* for that period, for a van Vogt story which I cannot identify, showing a van Vogtian superman standing in what looked like a spaceship yard filled with towering phallic shapes; this, at first glance, I took to be a city and not a spaceship yard. It occurred to me, suddenly, that if you have anti-gravity, there's no reason why there shouldn't be any limitation on the size or shape of the objects you lift. It was at that point that it also occurred to me: why should you want to do that? It was then that the concept of migrant workers came to me. Campbell contributed many, many ideas in his famous four-page letter that I hadn't thought up. The main thing that he did contribute, the central idea, was that the most valuable thing that these migrant workers could transfer in a situation involving fast inter-stellar travel was not gold, uranium, diamonds, the ability to drill for oil or whatever, but information. These are the pollinating bees of the galaxy. That was Campbell's idea, not mine, and it became the central idea of the whole series...'
(— extract from *In Conversation: James Blish talks to Brian Aldiss* in *Cypher* 10, October 1973, *James Goddard)*

3 **Philip Jose Farmer** *The World of Tiers* series.
'Well, you know, it's a funny thing, but the character Kickaha was actually created when I was going to high school. I used to write notes for fantasies and science fiction stories I was going to write, and sometimes I did write 'em, but Kickaha and the worlds projected in the first novel, *The Makers of the Universe*, was actually first conceived in embryo about 1935, when I was a junior in high school. I don't have the notes now, but I drew the Babylon, Tower of Babel type-thing, you know, the hanging Babylonian Gardens type world with the sea at the bottom of the planet, and then you could go to the edge there, and look out into empty space. And Kickaha originally was an Indian, I mean an actual Indian, that's my name for him — I put him through a few Hiawatha-type adventures and I can't remember when I actually decided to write *The Makers of the Universe*. I don't know if it was when I was reading *The Book of Wonder* again by Dunsany — I think that was it, but I wouldn't swear to it. Ah, I got the idea. Now, I'd been living in Arizona for a long time and maybe the idea of escaping from Arizona into some other world appealed to me because that's when I got the germ of the idea; being in Arizona and reading Lord Dunsay's *Book of Wonder* again at the same time. And things just developed from there, only in this case I had Kickaha be Paul Janus Finnegan, which is how I would like to be.'
(— part of an interview conducted by David Kraft and Mitch Steele in June 1972 and published in *Science Fiction Review* 14, August 1975, *©Richard E. Geis)*

4 **Harry Harrison** *By The Falls*
'*By The Falls* was a terribly emotional idea that happened in one instant. I live at the foot of a hill that just goes straight up into the air with a very severe gradient. We're at the foot of the hill where the cars roar by. A car came down one night changing gear and roaring while I was half asleep, and I went right up into the air. This terrible sensation came over me as the car missed the house and went on. At that moment I had a vision of an enormous falls. It wasn't a car but a roaring mighty falls. I was horrified, filled with emotion, and as I lay down in bed the plot came to me. The next morning I still had this emotion, and this story, is an emotional story, the first I've ever done this way. I kept the feeling I had, and went out, and wrote it in less than a day. Every time I started slacking, I closed my eyes and rebuilt that original emotion. So it was written from a very strong input at one level, and that feeling came out in the story.'
(— part of *Harry Harrison*

Frank Herbert

Interviewed by James Goddard, with help from Brian W. Aldiss and Leon Stover, in *Cypher* 9, March 1973, ©*James Goddard)*

5 **Frank Herbert** *Dune*

'Well, I had been nurturing the idea to write a treatment of the messianic impulse in human society for a long while, and my technique is to collect material. I collect file folders of material. A character idea interests me, and I put that in a folder appropriately labelled. Along the way I went to Florence, Oregon, to do an article about the U.S. Department of Agriculture's test station there, on the controls of sand dunes. The U.S. pioneered in the control of sand dunes by planting specially developed grasses and other plants to hold a dune in the wind. You see, a sand dune is just a kind of fluid, only it takes longer for it to move. It creates waves that, when you see them from the air, are analogous to waves in a sea.

'So, I did this magazine article and I started collecting material on the control of sand dunes. That lead me into ecological matters — what we were doing to the planet. One day I woke up to the fact that I had a filing drawer full and that I just couldn't do anything else but write that book. So I sat down and I plotted a much longer work than *Dune*...I took about a year and a half putting it together, writing it.'

(— part of an interview conducted by Paul Turner and published in *Vertex* October 1973, ©*Mankind Publishing Co.)*

6 **Elizabeth A. Lynn** *Chronicles of Tornor* trilogy.

'I first wrote *Dancers*, the story about the characters in that book, in 1971. I didn't see any market for it. No one was going to buy it because it was a love story between two brothers, and if they could stand homosexuality, they certainly weren't going to be able to hack the incest, or vice versa. I could understand that, in 1971. So, I put it away. When I pulled it out again I looked at it and went, 'Wait a minute. There's a story that happens before this.' And that turned out to be *Watchtower*. *Watchtower* has a funny history. There's a song called *All Along the Watchtower* by Bob Dylan, and ever since I first heard it, it seemed to me that Dylan was telling an adventure story in that song that never quite got told. *Watchtower* is that story in my mind. The final lines of *All Along the Watchtower* are: 'Two riders are approaching/The Wind began to howl.' There is a scene in *Watchtower* that is very specifically and very deliberately like that. The jester and the thief talking on the balcony became Ryke and Errel talking. Errel, of course, is the jester. The thief turned into Col, and the conversation is not exactly the same, because of course it turned into *my* story. I wanted to show an order changing, and the way I wanted to do it was to show it from the point of view of the old guard, who could see it but not necessarily understand it and who could accept it with his own values, even at the same time as he could see that those values were being threatened with destruction by what was changing. As soon as *Watchtower* had been written, it became very clear that there was a story that came after *Dancers*. And that became *The Northern Girl*. But *Dancers* was first.'

(— part of an interview conducted by debbie Notkin and published in *Janus* 15, Spring 1979, ©Janice Bogstad)

7 **Anne McCaffrey**
Dragonriders of Pern

'The true genesis of the Dragon series was a conversation I had with an underground film director, a young friend of Ed Emshwiller's,

Dick Adams. We'd seen his excellent film on the tribulations of American teachers of English in a Polish university summer course. Dick mentioned that he wanted to do a film on the 'aloneness' of man. I suggested that that had been done to death, but had he ever considered filming those times when man/woman/child are united in a common emotion?

'This must have been at the back of my mind when I started casting about my brains for a story idea. That's why the dragons are telepathic: their riders are never alone. Further, the dragon never criticizes: he adores his rider no matter what he does or is. This is the facet of the dragon stories which, I feel, has captured the attention of readers. And so much of modern literature is keyed to the statement of aloneness or sharing: the great togetherness urge.

'My idea, then, of the dragons, is scarcely original: the application is.'

(— from the entry on Anne McCaffrey *Science Fiction and Fantasy Literature, Volume 2: Contemporary Science Fiction Authors II* by R. Reginald, ©1979)

8 **Frederik Pohl**
The Space Merchants

'I was in the Army with the 456th Bomb Group near Foggia in Italy. I was kind of homesick, so I decided to write a novel about New York City, and in order to write a novel about New York City I thought it would be interesting to write about some sexy aspect of New York life. The most interesting thing I could think of to write about was the advertising industry, so I wrote a novel called *For Some We Loved*. I wrote the whole thing at Foggia or on Mt. Vesuvius a few months later, and when I got out of the Army, it occurred to me that there was one problem in having written a novel about advertising and that was that I didn't know anything about advertising. So I looked in the Sunday *Times*. There were three advertising jobs offered. I applied to them all, and one of them hired me, and I spent the next three years writing advertising copy for one person or another. During that time I had a summer place at Ashokan, N.Y., with a big fireplace, and I stayed up all of one night reading the manuscript of that novel I had written in Italy and as I read each page I threw it into the fire because it was absolutely abominable. There was nothing about it that was good. So at that point I had a great deal of information about advertising that I was making no use of, and it occurred to me to write an sf novel. So I wrote 20,000 words as the beginning of one. Then I showed it to Horace Gold who was the editor of *Galaxy* and he said, 'Finish it and I'll buy it.' And I asked Cyril Kornbluth to help me finish it and it became *The Space Merchants*.'

(— from an interview conducted by Darrell Schweitzer and published in *Science Fiction Voices* No.1, ©1979)

9 **Bob Shaw** *Light of Other Days*

'This shouldn't turn into a lecture on how to write, but that story is probably one of the most successful sf stories ever written and one of the reasons it was so successful was that I didn't rush into print as soon as I got the idea. The idea alone of a type of glass that could slow down light wasn't dramatic enough; I had to conceive in human terms what it would mean. But I couldn't get the right vehicle in the form of a plot and I kicked it around on and off for about two years before I wrote *Light of Other Days*. I find when I talk to people who have written science fiction and never sold any that they tend not to put enough time into plotting, and they tend to confuse the idea with the plot, whereas the plot is a kind of machine — a machine for screwing the last bit of dramatic juice out of the idea. You can't always construct that machine quickly and easily. You can profitably put weeks and weeks into working out the plot of a short story.

(— from an interview conducted by John Brosnan and published in *Science Fiction Monthly* Volume 2, Number 9, ©1975 by New English Library, Ltd.)

10 **Joan D. Vinge** *The Snow Queen*

'My original inspiration, Hans Christian Andersen's *The Snow Queen*, caught my fancy because most of the main active characters were female. Most fairy tales are really degenerate mythology, particularly Earth Mother/vegetation cult mythologies, yet they invariably have a patriarchal overlay of handsome princes. There are men in it, and certainly in my novel, but the women really get into the action for a change.

'Since I was also interested in goddess mythology, I read *The White Goddess* by Robert Graves. It is a fascinating study of myth origins, and it fit in perfectly, so as a result there is a wealth of symbolism and influence from the Grave's work underlying *The Snow Queen*. First and foremost, though, it really is science fiction, and I hope it reads as such for people who do not care for myths; and that it can be read on several levels by those who enjoy myth and fantasy as well.'

(— from an interview conducted by Robert Frazier and published in *Thrust — Science Fiction in Review* 16, Fall 1980, ©Douglas Fratz.)

10 MAJOR COMIC STRIP CHARACTERS

D38

1 **Buck Rogers** Based on the character Anthony Rogers created by Philip Francis Nowlan in his story *Armageddon — 2419 A.D.* *(Amazing Stories* August 1928) and its sequel *The Airlords of Han* *(Amazing* March 1929). Spotted by John F. Dille of the National Newspaper Syndicate who commissioned Nowlan to write and Dick Calkins to illustrate a picture strip — *Buck Rogers in the 25th Century* which was syndicated nationally in the American papers from 1929 to 1967.

2 **Flash Gordon** Created by artist Alex Raymond and syndicated in Sunday (and later daily) newspapers from 1934 on.

3 **Superman** Created by writer Jerome Siegel and artist Joseph Shuster, who devised the idea (based very loosely on Philip Wylie's *Gladiator)* in 1933. It took until 1938 to sell the idea and it was then an instant success. Superman appeared first in *Action Comics* in June 1938. *Superman,* the comic, did not appear until May 1939.

4 **Batman** Created by artist Bob Kane and based loosely on a character devised by Murray Leinster for the pulp magazine *Black Bat* which ran from October 1933 to April 1934. Batman emerged in his own right in *Detective Comics* in May 1939 before the *Batman* comic appeared in 1940. Curiously the character of The Black Bat was revived in *Black Book Detective* at the same time, but the development of the two superheroes was totally different.

5 **Captain Marvel** Devised by artist C.C. Beck and writer Bill Parker and launched in *Whiz Comics* in February 1940 with the *Captain Marvel* comic following in 1941. Later Otto Binder became the chief scriptwriter.

6 **Garth** Created by Steve Dowling who both wrote and illustrated the strip which first appeared in the *Daily Mirror* in July 1943.

7 **Dan Dare** Under the directive of the Reverend Marcus Morris, Dan Dare was created by artist Frank Hampson for the new educational children's comic *Eagle* launched on April 14th 1950 and running until 1967.

8 **Captain Condor** As a follow-up to the success of Dan Dare and the *Eagle,* a rival publisher launched the *Lion* comic in February 1952 with the adventures of Captain Condor devised and plotted by Frank S. Pepper.

9 **Jeff Hawke** Devised by writer Eric Souster and artist Sidney Jordan and published in the *Daily Express* from February 1954 until 1974.

10 **The Incredible Hulk** One of many new super-heroes devised by Stan Lee and created visually by Jack Kirby in 1962.